Other Books by Judas Jung:

DIRTY DEEDS DONE DIRT CHEAP: A Collection of Stories

A SILVER MOON OVER SUNSET

An Eleanor "Ellie" Vance Mystery

JUDAS JUNG

NONGE PUBLISHING

For

The Eleanor Vances of the world: the ones who not only don't look
away when things get ugly, they don't walk away from it, either.
They face the ugliness head on and get to the truth.

and

'Dawn'

Without whom Ellie would never have made it out to the world.
Thank you.

Contents

PART ONE
THE DAME AND THE DISAPPEARANCE

Dame with a Problem

The October rain came down on Los Angeles like it had a personal grudge, and I was nursing a bottle of rye that was down to its last honest swallow. The war had been over for three years, but the city kept changing—new money flowing in from defense contracts, new faces arriving every week looking for their piece of the dream.

My office occupied the third floor of a building on Spring Street that had been going to seed since Coolidge was president. The landlord kept promising to fix the radiator, and I kept pretending to believe him. The sign on my door read "Eleanor Vance, Private Investigator" in letters that had started peeling around the time Truman dropped the bomb. Folks who knew me well called me Ellie. The ones who knew me even better called me trouble.

I was studying the bottom of my glass like it held the secrets of the universe when she walked in.

Vivian Vanderbilt didn't knock. She just walked in like she owned the building, which maybe she did—I wouldn't have put it past her. Some women enter a room. Others take possession of it. She was definitely the second type.

She had the kind of looks that sold movie tickets and made sensible women check their lipstick. Her dress was black silk that cost more than my office rent, and her hat sat at just the right angle to let you know she understood exactly what she was doing to your pulse rate.

"Miss Vance?" Her voice had that husky quality that made men think about dark rooms and broken promises. "I need your help."

"Have a seat," I said, nodding to the chair across from my desk. The upholstery was trying to escape through a dozen small tears. "What's eating you? Cheating husband, lying boyfriend, or missing lapdog?"

She moved with finishing school grace, settling into the chair like she was claiming a throne. When she crossed her legs, I heard silk against silk and tried to keep my mind on business.

"My name is Vivian Vanderbilt," she said, placing a small black purse on my desk like she was claiming territory. "Perhaps you've heard of me?"

I had. Anyone who paid attention to the pictures knew Vivian Vanderbilt. She'd made three films for RKO, each one bigger than the last. The papers loved her—she photographed like a dream and spoke in sound bites that made great copy. She was Hollywood royalty, the kind of woman who made other women feel like they'd been shopping at Woolworth's their whole lives.

"I've seen your pictures," I said. "You're good at playing women men do stupid things for."

Something flickered behind her green eyes—surprise, maybe, or appreciation. "That's what I'm afraid is happening now."

I refilled my glass and offered her the bottle. She shook her head. Could be she didn't drink. Could be she didn't drink with gumshoes who worked out of basement offices. My money was on door number two.

"Tell me about it," I said.

She pulled out a silver cigarette case that cost more than my car. Fitted a smoke into a pearl holder like she'd been doing it since birth. Her hand shook just a little reaching for my lighter. Could be nerves. Could be the October chill that sometimes crept into LA when you weren't looking.

"It's Roger," she said, exhaling smoke that curled between us like a question mark. "Roger Talbot. He's... missing."

Roger Talbot. I'd heard the name around town. Independent producer trying to muscle his way into the big leagues since the war ended. Had money and wore good suits, but the real power boys kept him on the outside looking in. The kind of guy who'd sell his mother for the right introduction.

"Missing how long?" I asked.

"Eighteen days." She took another drag, and I noticed her lipstick left perfect crimson half-moons on the holder. This dame had money written all over her, from her silk stockings to that silver cigarette case. So what was she doing in my crummy office when she could afford lawyers who charged more per hour than I made in a month?

"You go to the cops?"

She laughed like someone had just told her the world was ending. "The cops couldn't care less about a missing producer. They figure he's drunk somewhere or chasing tail. Made it real clear they got better things to do."

She wasn't wrong. The LAPD had their hands full with the usual assortment of murders, robberies, and general mayhem that kept the city interesting. Missing Hollywood types were a dime a dozen. Unless you had studio muscle making phone calls, the cops had better things to worry about.

"What makes you think something happened to him?" I asked.

"Roger isn't the type to disappear." Her voice went soft around the edges, like she was trying not to cry. "He's methodical, predictable. He calls me every morning at eight-thirty. He hasn't missed a day in the six months we've been... together."

Together. Rich folks had their own way of saying things. The rest of us just called it sleeping together.

"Maybe he got tired of being predictable," I suggested. "It happens to the best of us."

Her jaw tightened. "You don't understand. Roger is working on something big—an investigation that could expose some of the most powerful men in this city. He wouldn't walk away from that. Not now." "What kind of investigation?"

She hesitated, and I saw her weigh her words like a jeweler examining stones. "I don't know the details. Roger was... secretive about what he'd found. But he was excited, more excited than I'd ever seen him. He said this would change everything."

I've heard that song before. In my experience, deals that were supposed to change everything usually changed everything, all right—just not in the way people expected.

"When did you see him last?"

"Saturday night. We had dinner at the Brown Derby, then went back to his place in the Hills. I left around midnight—I had an early call Sunday morning. When I tried to reach him Sunday evening, there was no answer. I thought maybe he was working late, but..." She shrugged, a gesture that managed to be both elegant and helpless.

"You have a key to his place?"

"No." The answer came too quick, and I filed that away for later consideration. In my experience, women who'd been "together" with a man for six months usually had keys. Unless the man was married, paranoid, or keeping secrets worth killing for.

"Any enemies you know about?"

"Roger's successful, Miss Vance. Successful men always have enemies."

That was true enough, but it wasn't an answer. I tried a different approach.

"What about family?"

"His parents died in a car accident when he was twenty. No siblings, no close relatives that I know of." "Friends?"

"Business associates, mostly. Roger wasn't the type for close friendships."

I was starting to get a picture of Roger Talbot, and it wasn't particularly flattering. A man with money but no real connections, ambition but no loyalties, secrets but no confidants. The type of man who might disappear because he'd finally run out of people willing to tolerate him.

But Vivian Vanderbilt wasn't the type of woman who'd waste her time—or her tears—on a man unless he had something worth crying over. And she was here, in my shabby office, which meant she thought I could find something the cops couldn't or wouldn't.

"What makes you think he's in trouble and not just taking a powder?" I asked.

She reached into her purse again and pulled out a folded piece of paper. When she handed it across the desk, I caught a whiff of her perfume—something French and expensive that reminded me of promises no one intended to keep.

The paper was hotel stationary from the Ambassador. The message was short and to the point: *Vivian—If something happens to me, don't trust anyone. The wolves are closer than you think.* —R "This was slipped under my door Tuesday morning," she said.

I studied the note. The handwriting was masculine, hurried but controlled. The paper was expensive, the kind of stationary you'd find at a hotel where the rooms cost more per night than I made in a week. "You sure this is his handwriting?"

"I'm sure."

"Any idea what he meant by wolves?"

"None."

I folded the note and handed it back to her. She slipped it into her purse like she was handling evidence, which maybe she was.

"My rate is twenty-five a day plus expenses," I said. "I'll need three days in advance."

She didn't flinch at the price, which told me two things: she had money to burn, and finding Roger Talbot was worth burning it. She opened her purse and counted out seventy-five dollars in crisp bills, laying them on my desk like she was dealing cards.

"I want him found, Miss Vance. Whatever it takes."

"I make no promises except to do my best," I said, pocketing the cash. "And I work alone. No studio muscle, no hired help, no interference. You hired me to find Roger, not to take direction from you."

She nodded, and I thought I saw a flicker of respect in those green eyes. Maybe I'd been wrong about her.

Maybe she was tougher than she looked.

"One more thing," she said, rising from her chair with liquid grace. "Be careful, Miss Vance. I have the feeling

Roger wasn't the only one asking too many questions."

She left me with that little bombshell and the lingering scent of her perfume. I sat in my chair, watching the rain streak down the window and thinking about missing producers and beautiful women and notes that warned about wolves.

Outside, Los Angeles churned on, indifferent to one more mystery in a city built on secrets. But I had a feeling this case was going to be different. In my experience, when dames like Vivian Vanderbilt showed up in offices like mine, somebody always ended up dead.

I just hoped it wouldn't be me.

The rain kept falling, and somewhere in the city, Roger Talbot was either having the time of his life or the last moments of it. Either way, I was going to find him.

After all, that's what they paid me for.

I finished my rye and reached for my hat. It was time to get to work.

Trail of Blood and Money

Roger Talbot's house was perched on a hillside in Laurel Canyon like it was trying to escape the city below. Spanish colonial with enough cream-colored stucco and red tile to house a small army. Money, either way you sliced it.

And if Roger was dead, it didn't matter who paid for the place.

The rain had turned the canyon road into a muddy mess. My Plymouth's tires fought for grip on every turn. I parked outside the wrought-iron gate and studied the place through my rain-spotted windshield. Three stories of stucco and tile, with enough windows to keep a glass company in business. The kind of place that cost more than most people saw in a lifetime.

Which, according to Vivian Vanderbilt, no one had been home to for five days.

The gate stood open—first red flag. Rich men in Hollywood locked their gates. Always. Unless they couldn't anymore. I walked up the flagstone path, noting the newspapers piled against the front door. Five days of newspapers piled by the door, soggy and starting to smell. Nobody home to read about their own disasters.

The front door was mahogany, solid enough to stop a truck. I tried the brass knocker first—three sharp raps that echoed inside like gunshots. No answer. The doorbell got the same response. I tried the handle, expecting resistance.

The door swung open on its own. That made two bad signs in thirty seconds.

"Mr. Talbot?" I called out. "This is Eleanor Vance. Miss Vanderbilt sent me." Dead quiet. The kind that makes your ears ring.

I stepped inside and the hair on my neck stood up. Something was wrong with this place. More than just empty.

It felt like walking into a tomb.

The entry hall had that calculated Hollywood elegance—marble floors, crystal chandelier, oil paintings worth more than most annual salaries. Someone had torn the place apart. A heavy oak table sat shoved against the wall, its impact crack spider-webbing through the plaster. The Persian rug lay bunched in a corner like something dead.

I drew my .38 from my shoulder holster. My gut was telling me to get the hell out. But gut feelings don't pay the rent.

The living room was a disaster. Expensive leather furniture overturned, bookcases dumped, liquor bottles smashed against the wall. Books scattered across the hardwood like someone had gone crazy with a baseball bat.

But it was the coffee table that made me stop cold.

The mahogany surface bore deep gouges, parallel scratches that ran from one end to the other. Four lines, evenly spaced, each about as wide as my finger. I'd seen marks like that before—on trees where bears had sharpened their claws, on fence posts where big cats had left their calling cards.

But bears didn't break into Beverly Hills mansions, and mountain lions didn't flip over furniture.

I knelt beside the table and ran my finger along one of the gouges. The wood was clean-cut, fresh. Whatever had made these marks had done it recently. I pulled out my magnifying glass—a tool that made me feel like Sherlock Holmes but had saved my bacon more than once.

The scratches were deep, precise, and sharp enough to suggest claws rather than knives. But the spacing was wrong for any animal I could think of. Too wide for a dog, too narrow for a bear. And the depth suggested something with the strength to tear through hardwood like it was paper.

"Miss Vance?"

I spun around, gun raised, heart trying to jump out of my chest. A man stood in the doorway—tall, thin, with the kind of posture that suggested either military service or very expensive tailoring. He wore a black suit that had seen better decades and a face that revealed nothing useful.

"I'm Thornton," he said, as if that explained everything. "Mr. Talbot's butler."

I kept the gun pointed at his chest. "Where the hell were you when I knocked?"

"In the kitchen, miss. Preparing tea." His voice carried a British accent thick as London fog. "I didn't hear you arrive."

"The front door was unlocked."

"Yes, miss. Mr. Talbot preferred it that way. For convenience."

That was the biggest load of bull I'd heard since Truman promised to balance the budget. Rich men didn't leave their front doors unlocked for convenience—they hired people like Thornton to lock things up tight.

"When did you last see Mr. Talbot?" I asked, but didn't lower the gun.

"Saturday evening, miss. He dismissed me at nine o'clock and said he wouldn't be needing my services until Monday morning."

"And when you came back Monday?"

"He wasn't here, miss. I assumed he'd left early for his appointments."

"What kind of appointments?"

"I couldn't say, miss. Mr. Talbot didn't share his calendar with the domestic staff."

The man was lying, and we both knew it. Butlers like Thornton knew everything—what their employers ate for breakfast, who they slept with, and what they feared in the dark hours before dawn. They had to know, or they wouldn't survive long in the service of Hollywood's elite.

"What happened to the living room?" I gestured with the .38.

"I found it this way Monday morning, miss. I've been attempting to restore order, but..." He shrugged eloquently.

"You didn't think to call the police?"

"Mr. Talbot valued his privacy, miss. He wouldn't have appreciated police attention."

"Even if he was in trouble?"

"Especially then."

I studied his face, looking for tells. Thornton had the kind of features that belonged on a poker player—smooth, controlled, unreadable. But there was something in his eyes, a flicker of fear that he couldn't quite hide.

"Who else knew about the unlocked door?" I asked.

"Very few people, miss. Mr. Talbot was quite specific about security."

"But some people knew?"

"Miss Vanderbilt, of course. And perhaps one or two others."

"What others?"

"I couldn't say, miss."

Couldn't or wouldn't—in my experience, the distinction mattered less than getting answers. I holstered the gun but kept my hand near it. Thornton relaxed slightly, which told me he'd been more worried about the weapon than he'd let on.

"Show me the rest of the house," I said.

"I'm not sure that would be appropriate, miss. Mr. Talbot valued his privacy."

"Mr. Talbot's missing, and his living room looks like a tornado hit it. I'd say privacy is a luxury he can't afford right now."

Thornton considered this with the gravity of a judge weighing evidence. Finally, he nodded.

"Very well, miss. But please understand—what you see here must remain confidential."

"I understand secrecy better than most people, Thornton. Lead the way."

He guided me through the house with the practiced efficiency of a museum curator. The dining room bore similar signs of violence—chairs overturned, a crystal chandelier hanging at a drunken angle, scratch marks on the mahogany table that matched the ones downstairs. But it was the kitchen that really caught my attention.

The room was spotless, every surface gleaming with the kind of cleanliness that suggested either obsessive attention to detail or recent scrubbing. Too clean, given the chaos in the rest of the house.

"You've been busy," I observed.

"I couldn't leave the kitchen in such a state, miss. It wouldn't be proper."

"What state was that?"

"Quite disheveled, I'm afraid. Someone had been through the cabinets rather thoroughly."

"Looking for what?"

"I couldn't say, miss."

I opened the cabinet above the sink. Dishes, glasses, the usual kitchen items. But there was a gap on one shelf, a clean rectangle in the dust that suggested something rectangular had been removed recently.

"What was kept here?" I asked.

"I believe that's where Mr. Talbot kept his special items, miss."

"What kind of special items?"

"I wouldn't know, miss. Mr. Talbot was quite particular about his private affairs."

Every answer led to another wall of polite British evasion. I was starting to understand why Vivian had hired me instead of trying to get answers herself. Thornton was the type of servant who'd die before revealing his employer's secrets—which made me wonder what secrets were worth dying for.

"Let's see the upstairs," I said.

The staircase was wide enough to drive a truck up, with a banister that probably cost more than my car. Family portraits lined the walls—stern-faced men in expensive suits, women whose beauty was preserved in oil and varnish. But none of them looked like Roger Talbot, which suggested either he was adopted or the portraits came with the house.

The master bedroom told the same story as the rooms below—expensive furniture, careful destruction, and scratch marks on every wooden surface. The bed had been torn apart, mattress pulled aside, drawers emptied onto the floor. But it was the closet that provided the most interesting details.

Half the clothes were missing. Not ransacked—removed with care. Suits, shirts, underwear, shoes. Someone had packed for a trip, but whether that someone was Roger Talbot or his kidnapper remained an open question.

"Did Mr. Talbot own luggage?" I asked.

"Several sets, miss. Quite comprehensive."

"Are they here?"

Thornton opened a door I'd taken for another closet. Inside, shelves held an impressive collection of suitcases, from small overnight bags to steamer trunks big enough to hold a body. But there were gaps—clean spaces where dust hadn't settled.

"The three-piece set is missing," Thornton said, anticipating my question. "Brown leather, very expensive. Mr.

Talbot used it for extended trips."

"When did he last travel?"

"Not for several months, miss. He'd been quite focused on his business affairs lately."

"What kind of business affairs?"

"I wouldn't presume to know the details, miss. But he'd been working quite late recently. Many telephone calls, meetings with associates."

"What associates?"

"I couldn't say, miss. Mr. Talbot conducted his business in his study. The room is quite soundproof."

That was interesting. Soundproof rooms in Hollywood usually meant one of two things: recording equipment or conversations that weren't meant to be overheard. Given the scratch marks and missing luggage, I was betting on the latter.

"Show me the study," I said.

"I'm afraid that won't be possible, miss."

"Why not?"

"Mr. Talbot kept the study locked. I don't have a key."

"But you're the butler. Don't you have keys to everything?"

"Not to the study, miss. Mr. Talbot was quite specific about that."

I studied his face again, looking for the lie. But Thornton's expression remained professionally blank—the kind of blankness that came from years of practice keeping secrets.

"We'll see about that," I said.

The study was on the second floor, down a hallway lined with more family portraits. The door was solid oak with a brass lock that looked like it meant business. I tried the handle anyway—you'd be surprised how many people forgot to engage their expensive locks.

This wasn't one of those times.

I pulled out my lock picks, a skill I'd learned during my less respectable years. Thornton watched with the kind of polite interest he might show for a dinner party trick.

"Is that strictly legal, miss?"

"Missing persons cases exist in a gray area of the law," I said, working on the pins. "Besides, if Mr. Talbot's in trouble, he'd probably want us to check his study."

"And if he's not in trouble?"

"Then he can fire me when he gets back."

The lock gave way with a satisfying click. I pushed open the door and stepped into Roger Talbot's private world.

The study was the only room in the house that hadn't been touched. Everything sat exactly where it belonged— massive oak desk, leather chairs, floor-to-ceiling bookcases filled with volumes on film production, business, and California history. A wet bar occupied one corner, glasses polished to crystal clarity. Persian rugs covered the hardwood floor in patterns that probably told stories I couldn't read.

But it was the desk that drew my attention. The surface was clear except for a leather blotter, an expensive fountain pen, and a crystal ashtray that held the remains of several cigarettes. The cigarettes were expensive— Turkish tobacco, not the kind you bought at the corner drugstore.

I opened the desk drawers one by one. The first held standard office supplies—paper clips, rubber bands, stamps. The second contained business correspondence, all of it routine. But the third drawer was locked. "Another key you don't have?" I asked Thornton.

"I'm afraid not, miss."

This lock was smaller but more complicated. It took me three minutes to crack it, with Thornton hovering behind me like a worried parent. Inside the drawer, I found what I'd been looking for.

A leather-bound notebook filled with Roger Talbot's handwriting. Names, dates, dollar amounts. Meeting times and locations. And telephone numbers with area codes I didn't recognize.

I flipped through the pages, trying to make sense of the entries. Most were cryptic—initials rather than full names, code words instead of clear descriptions. But one page made me stop cold.

At the top, in Roger's careful script: "The Pack."

Below that, a list of names I recognized. Studio heads, city council members, police commissioners. Men with enough power to make or break careers, to turn blind eyes to inconvenient crimes, to make problems disappear permanently.

And at the bottom of the list, in different ink: "They know about the silver."

I tore out the page and pocketed it. Whatever Roger Talbot had stumbled onto, it was bigger than a missing producer and more dangerous than claw marks on furniture. The wolves Vivian had mentioned weren't metaphorical.

They were real, and they were hunting.

"Miss Vance?" Thornton's voice carried a note of genuine concern. "Perhaps we should leave now. Mr. Talbot wouldn't want strangers in his private affairs."

I closed the notebook and slipped it into my jacket. "Mr. Talbot's private affairs might be the only thing that saves his life."

As we left the study, I caught Thornton watching me with something that might have been respect—or fear.

Either way, it told me I was on the right track.

Roger Talbot wasn't just missing. He was in the middle of something that involved powerful people and dangerous secrets. The kind of thing that could make a man disappear permanently.

I had a feeling this case was about to get a lot more interesting.

The Hollywood Hills Have Eyes

Consolidated Pictures covered forty acres of Culver City behind walls high and thick enough to stop a tank. The guards at the gate looked like cops between beats, and they carried themselves like they meant business.

I parked my Plymouth between a Cadillac and a Packard that made my car look like a kid's toy. The guard was young, maybe twenty-five, with a regulation haircut and a uniform that looked fresh from the cleaners.

"I'm here to see Jack Rafferty," I told him, showing my license. "Eleanor Vance, private investigator. It's about Roger Talbot."

The kid's face went through several changes—recognition, concern, and something that looked like relief. "Oh, yeah. Mr. Rafferty's been expecting someone about Mr. Talbot. Been asking around all week."

That was interesting. Studio heads didn't usually give a damn about missing producers. Unless there was serious money on the line.

"Where can I find him?"

"Building C, third floor. Just follow the yellow line painted on the sidewalk. Can't miss it."

The yellow line led me through a maze of soundstages, each one big enough to house a small town. Through open doors I saw carpenters hammering together living room sets, girls stitching period costumes, electricians rigging lights to look like stars. All fake, but the paychecks were real enough.

Building C looked like every other office building in America, except for the posters lining the walls. Movie posters lined the walls—beautiful faces selling dreams to people who couldn't afford them.

The elevator operator was a colored man about my father's age. Spotless uniform, steady hands, and eyes that had seen plenty. His manner was professional.

"Third floor," I said.

"Yes, ma'am. You here about Mr. Talbot?"

"You knew him?"

"Operated this elevator for fifteen years. I know everybody who matters in this building. Mr. Talbot was here three, four times a week the past month. Always in a hurry, always carrying that leather briefcase of his." "When did you see him last?"

"Friday afternoon. He was meeting with Mr. Rafferty. Seemed excited about something, more than usual." "Excited how?"

"Like a man who'd found oil in his backyard, if you know what I mean."

I knew what he meant. In Hollywood, there were lots of ways to strike it rich if you weren't picky about how you did it.

The elevator stopped with a gentle bump, and the operator pulled back the brass gate. "Third floor. Mr.

Rafferty's office is at the end of the hall. Tell him Eddie said hello."

"I will, Eddie. Thanks."

The hallway was carpeted in something thick enough to muffle footsteps. Oil paintings of studio founders and movie stars lined the walls, their eyes following me like I was walking through a portrait gallery in a haunted house. The whole place reeked of money and the kind of power that could destroy careers with a phone call.

Jack Rafferty's office occupied a corner of the building with windows facing both north and west. Through the glass, I could see the Hollywood Hills rising like brown shoulders above the smog. His secretary was a redhead in her thirties with the kind of figure that probably got her screen-tested before she learned to type.

"Mr. Rafferty's expecting you," she said before I could introduce myself. "Go right in."

The office was bigger than my apartment and furnished like a gentleman's club. Leather chairs, mahogany bookshelves, Persian rugs that whispered money with every footstep. The desk was large enough to land a small airplane, and behind it sat Jack Rafferty himself.

He was younger than I'd expected, maybe forty, with the kind of looks that had probably gotten him screen time before he learned the real money was behind the camera. Dark hair slicked back with pomade, brown eyes that catalogued everything, and a smile that made promises he had no intention of keeping.

"Miss Vance," he said, rising from his chair with practiced charm. "I've been hoping someone would look into poor Roger's disappearance. The man's a genius—we can't afford to lose talent like that."

He gestured to the chair across from his desk. The leather was soft enough to sink into, which made me wonder if that was intentional. Hard to negotiate from a position where you felt like you were being swallowed.

"When did you last see Mr. Talbot?" I asked, settling into the chair but keeping my posture straight.

"Friday afternoon. We had a meeting about his latest project. Very hush-hush, very exciting. The kind of picture that could change everything for this studio."

"What kind of picture?"

Rafferty's smile widened, but his eyes stayed calculating. "I'm afraid that's confidential, Miss Vance. You understand—in this business, ideas are currency. The wrong person hears the wrong thing, and suddenly your million-dollar picture is being made by the competition."

"Mr. Talbot's missing. I'd say confidentiality is a luxury he can't afford."

"Maybe you're right." Rafferty opened a silver cigarette case and offered it to me. I waved him off. He picked out a cigarette like he was choosing the right bullet and lit it with a gold lighter that could've fed a family for a month.

"Roger came to me with a story," he said, exhaling smoke toward the ceiling. "Not a script—a real story. Something he'd stumbled across in his research for another project. The kind of story that could destroy reputations, end careers, maybe even bring down some of the most powerful men in this city." "What kind of story?"

"The kind that makes people disappear when they dig too deep."

Something cold crawled up my spine. "You think someone took him because of this story?"

"Roger didn't know when to quit digging. In this town, that's a good way to end up in a shallow grave."

Rafferty leaned back in his chair and studied me through the cigarette smoke. "Tell me, Miss Vance—what do you know about the early days of Hollywood? The real story, not the fairy tale they print in the fan magazines."

"I know enough. Corrupt officials, mob money, studio heads who made their own rules."

"Kid stuff. I'm talking about the real power in this town. The families that run things, the clubs they belong to, what they do when nobody's watching."

I'd heard rumors—stories about private clubs where studio executives gathered to make deals that would never see the light of day, about ceremonies and rituals that had nothing to do with making pictures. Most people dismissed them as Hollywood mythology, like the casting couch jokes and stories about stars who weren't really dead.

"What does this have to do with Roger Talbot?"

"Roger was researching a book. Not for publication—just for his own satisfaction. He was fascinated by the occult elements in early Hollywood history. The way certain symbols kept appearing in films, certain themes that ran deeper than entertainment."

"Occult elements?"

"Miss Vance, do you know why they call it the Silver Screen?"

I'd never thought about it. "The way the light reflects off the film?"

"That's the official explanation. But silver has other properties. It's been used for centuries to ward off certain... influences. To reveal things that prefer to remain hidden."

The conversation was heading into territory that made my practical detective's mind start throwing up warning flags. But the scratches on Roger Talbot's furniture hadn't been made by anything natural, and Vivian's note had mentioned wolves.

"You're talking about werewolves," I said.

Rafferty's laugh was genuine, but not dismissive. "I'm talking about men with appetites that normal society couldn't tolerate. Men who found ways to satisfy those appetites while maintaining their positions of power. And I'm talking about a producer who may have gotten too close to secrets that some people would kill to protect."

"Are you one of those men, Mr. Rafferty?"

"I'm a businessman, Miss Vance. I make pictures that people want to see, and I make money doing it. But I'm also not naive about the forces that shaped this industry. Roger wasn't naive either—that may have been his downfall."

Rafferty stubbed out his cigarette and leaned forward, his charm replaced by something sharper. "Let me give you some advice. There are some doors in this city that are better left unopened. Some questions that shouldn't be asked. Roger Talbot opened one of those doors, and now he's gone."

"Are you telling me to drop the case?"

"I'm telling you to be careful. Very careful. Because the people who took Roger aren't just dangerous—they're connected. Police commissioners, city councilmen, federal judges. They have resources you can't imagine and reach that extends far beyond Los Angeles."

I thought about the notebook I'd taken from Talbot's study, the list of names under "The Pack." Rafferty was right about the connections. But he was also holding something back—I could see it in the way his eyes avoided mine when he talked about Roger's research.

"I need to talk to other people who worked with him," I said. "Colleagues, associates, anyone who might know what he was investigating."

"Of course." Rafferty pressed a button on his desk, and the red-headed secretary appeared in the doorway. "Carol, please arrange for Miss Vance to speak with anyone who worked with Roger Talbot. Give her whatever assistance she needs."

"Yes, Mr. Rafferty."

"And Carol—make sure security knows she's working on our behalf. We want to find Roger just as much as his fiancée does."

The secretary nodded and gestured for me to follow her. As we left Rafferty's office, I caught him watching me with the expression of a man who'd just played a card and wasn't sure if it was the right one.

Carol led me down the hall to a smaller office with windows facing the studio lot. "This is where I'll set up your interviews," she said. "I've made a list of people who worked with Mr. Talbot recently."

The list was impressive—writers, directors, cinematographers, even a few actors who'd been considered for roles in his projects. But it was the last name that caught my attention: Harold Getz, Security Chief.

"Mr. Getz has been asking questions about Mr. Talbot too," Carol explained. "He might be able to help." "What kind of questions?"

"About who Mr. Talbot had been meeting with, what projects he'd been working on. Mr. Getz takes security very seriously."

That was interesting. Studio security chiefs didn't usually get involved in missing persons cases unless there were studio interests at stake. Big interests.

"I'd like to speak with Mr. Getz first," I said.

"I'll call down to his office."

While Carol made the arrangements, I studied the view from the window. The studio lot spread out below like a miniature city, complete with streets, buildings, and crowds of people going about their business. But unlike a real city, everything here served a single purpose: creating illusions that people would pay to believe.

The question was whether Roger Talbot had gotten too close to some illusions that weren't meant for public consumption.

Harold Getz arrived fifteen minutes later. He was a big man, maybe six-four, with shoulders that suggested he'd done some serious lifting in his younger days. His hair was gray, his suit was blue, and his handshake was firm enough to crack walnuts.

"Miss Vance. Carol tells me you're looking into Roger Talbot's disappearance."

"That's right. I understand you've been asking questions too."

"It's my job to know what happens on this lot. When one of our producers goes missing, that's my concern."

We sat across from each other in the conference room Carol had arranged. Getz had the kind of presence that filled a space—not aggressive, but definitely in charge.

"What can you tell me about Mr. Talbot's recent activities?" I asked.

"He'd been spending a lot of time in Research. Looking through old files, studio records going back to the twenties. Said he was working on a historical project."

"What kind of historical project?"

"Something about the early days of the industry. The founding families, the original financial backing. Dry stuff, but Roger seemed fascinated by it."

"Did he find anything interesting?"

Getz was quiet for a moment, choosing his words with care. "Roger asked me about certain individuals who'd been involved with the studio in the early days. Investors, board members, men who'd helped establish Consolidated as a major player."

"What about them?"

"Some of those men are still alive, Miss Vance. Still influential. The kind of people who value their privacy and have the resources to protect it."

Another warning wrapped in helpful advice. It seemed like everyone in Hollywood was concerned about my safety, which made me wonder what they were really protecting.

"Do you think his research got him in trouble?"

"I think Roger Talbot was a smart man who asked the wrong questions to the wrong people. In this business, that can be a fatal mistake."

"Fatal?"

"Figure of speech, Miss Vance. But powerful men don't like having their secrets exposed. They tend to take steps to prevent embarrassment."

Getz stood up, our interview apparently over. "Let me give you the same advice I gave Roger. Some stones are better left unturned. Some history is better left buried."

"And if I don't take that advice?"

"Then I hope you're better at watching your back than Roger was."

He left me sitting in the conference room, surrounded by the ghost of another warning. Everyone seemed to know what had happened to Roger Talbot—everyone except the person trying to find him.

But I was starting to get the picture. Roger had stumbled onto something involving powerful men and old secrets. Something worth killing to protect. The question was whether I could find him before his curiosity got him permanently silenced.

Or before it got me the same treatment.

When Cops Don't Want Answers

The Los Angeles Police Department's Central Division was a squat brick building on First Street that looked like it had been designed by someone who hated beauty. The inside smelled of cigarette smoke, burnt coffee, and the particular funk that comes from housing too many people with too many problems in too small a space.

I found Detective Frank Miller at his desk on the second floor, hunched over a stack of case files that kept growing while he wasn't watching. Miller was past fifty, with gray hair that had stopped trying and a face that looked like it had been personally introduced to every type of human ugliness Los Angeles had to offer. His suit was brown, his tie was askew, and his coffee mug had a chip that probably dated to the Hoover administration. "Ellie Vance," he said without looking up from his paperwork. "I figured you'd show up sooner or later."

"Hello, Frank. Working hard or hardly working?"

"Both." He leaned back in his chair, which protested with a squeak that suggested it was older than both of us.

"I heard you're sniffing around the Roger Talbot situation."

"Word travels fast in this town."

"Faster when certain people make certain phone calls." He opened his desk drawer and pulled out a half-empty bottle of bourbon. "Coffee?"

"Little early for me, thanks."

"It's five o'clock somewhere." He poured a generous splash into his coffee mug and offered the bottle again.

When I shook my head, he returned it to the drawer with the care of a man handling precious cargo.

Miller and I went back about five years, to a divorce case that had turned ugly when the cheating husband decided to solve his problems with a .45. I'd done the legwork, Miller had done the arresting, and we'd both learned that sometimes the guilty parties save everyone trouble by confessing to more than they're asked about.

"What can you tell me about Roger Talbot?" I asked.

Miller took a sip of his enhanced coffee and grimaced. "Officially? Nothing. The man's not been missing long enough to generate paperwork, and even if he had, this wouldn't be my case."

"Unofficially?"

"Unofficially, Roger Talbot is the kind of producer who asks too many questions and doesn't know when to mind his own business. The kind of guy who might wake up one morning and decide he'd rather be somewhere else for a while."

"You think he took a powder?"

"I think Roger Talbot stepped on the wrong toes, and now he's either laying low until things cool off or laying low permanently."

Miller wasn't telling me anything I hadn't already figured out, but there was something in his voice—a note of warning that suggested he knew more than he was letting on.

"Whose toes?" I asked.

"The kind attached to feet you don't want kicking you." He finished his coffee and set the mug down with a thunk that sounded final. "Ellie, I'm going to give you some advice, and I want you to listen carefully. Drop this case."

"Why?"

"Because some people are better left unfound."

Something cold settled in my stomach. Miller wasn't the type to scare easy, and he wasn't the type to give advice unless he thought you needed it.

"What aren't you telling me, Frank?"

He was quiet for a moment, giving me the kind of look cops use when they're deciding how much truth you can handle. Finally, he sighed and reached into his jacket pocket, pulling out a small manila envelope.

"This came across my desk yesterday," he said, sliding the envelope toward me. "Unofficial-like. Somebody thought I should see it."

Inside the envelope were three photographs, black and white, grainy enough to suggest they'd been taken from a distance. But clear enough to show what they were meant to show.

The first photograph showed Roger Talbot entering what looked like a private club—stone facade, heavy wooden doors, the kind of place that didn't advertise and didn't welcome strangers. The second showed him leaving the same building, but his posture was different—hunched, hurried, like a man who'd seen something he wished he hadn't.

The third photograph made me sit up straight. It showed Roger Talbot in what appeared to be an alley behind the club, talking to two men in expensive suits. But it wasn't the men that caught my attention—it was what lay at their feet. Something that looked like it had once been a person, but wasn't anymore.

"When were these taken?" I asked.

"Three weeks ago. Two days before that body turned up in Griffith Park."

"What body?"

"Vagrant named Pete Downey. Found torn to pieces near the observatory. Papers called it a wild animal attack, but..." Miller shrugged. "Wild animals don't usually leave bodies that clean."

I studied the photographs again. In the third shot, I could just make out Roger's expression—shock, horror, and something that looked like recognition.

"Who took these pictures?"

"Source prefers to remain anonymous. But they're real, Ellie. I had them checked."

"What was Roger doing at this club?"

"That's the million-dollar question. The place is called the Crescent Club, and it's got a membership list that reads like the Los Angeles power elite. City councilmen, federal judges, studio heads, police commissioners." Police commissioners. That explained the unofficial nature of Miller's warning.

"You think Roger stumbled onto something?"

"I think Roger Talbot was doing research for that book of his, and he found out some things that certain people would prefer stayed buried." Miller leaned forward, his voice dropping to just above a whisper. "Ellie, there are clubs in this city that don't exist on paper. Gentlemen's societies that predate the movies, that predate the oil boom, that go back to when California was still part of Mexico."

"What kind of societies?"

"The kind that have rituals instead of meetings. The kind where membership comes with obligations that most people wouldn't understand." He paused, choosing his words with care. "The kind where the monthly gatherings aren't about cigars and brandy."

I thought about the scratches on Roger's furniture, the cryptic references to "The Pack" in his notebook, Vivian's warning about wolves.

"You're talking about something supernatural."

"I'm talking about men with appetites that civilized society can't accommodate. Men who've found ways to satisfy those appetites while maintaining their positions of power." Miller's voice carried the weight of a man who'd seen too much and understood more than he wanted to. "And I'm talking about what happens to people who get too close to their secrets."

"Like Roger Talbot."

"Like Roger Talbot."

Miller stood up and walked to the window, looking down at the street below. From this angle, I could see the lines around his eyes, the slump of his shoulders that suggested a man carrying burdens he couldn't share.

"There've been other disappearances," he said without turning around. "Three in the past year. All connected to people who were asking questions about certain prominent families, certain business dealings that went back to the city's founding."

"What happened to them?"

"Officially? They moved away, found better opportunities elsewhere, decided Los Angeles wasn't for them." He turned back to face me. "Unofficially? They're feeding the fish somewhere off the coast, or buried in the desert where nobody'll ever find them."

"And the police?"

"The police investigate what they're told to investigate and find what they're told to find." His voice carried a bitterness that suggested personal experience with selective justice. "When the people giving orders are the same people who might be involved, the system tends to protect itself."

I understood. Miller was a good cop, but he was also a realistic cop. He knew which battles could be won and which ones would just get you transferred to the night shift in East L.A.

"So what do you suggest I do?"

"Go back to your client and tell her Roger Talbot probably ran off with a chorus girl. Take your fee and find yourself a nice divorce case where the biggest danger is an angry spouse with a drinking problem." "And if I don't?"

Miller sat back down and met my eyes with the kind of direct stare that cops use when they're trying to communicate something they can't say out loud.

"Then I hope you've got your affairs in order. Because the people who took Roger Talbot don't leave loose ends, and private investigators who ask too many questions have a tendency to become statistics."

He handed me a business card—plain white, no company name, just a telephone number written in pencil.

"If you decide to keep digging, call this number. Tell them Frank Miller sent you. They might be able to help, or they might be able to hide you when things get too hot."

"Who are they?"

"People who know what you're up against. People who've been fighting this particular war longer than either of us has been alive."

I pocketed the card and the photographs. Miller's warning was clear enough, but it was also confirmation that I was on the right track. Roger Talbot had stumbled onto something big, something that involved the most powerful men in Los Angeles.

"One more question, Frank. How long have you known about this... organization?"

"Too long." He opened his desk drawer and pulled out the bourbon bottle again. This time he didn't bother with the coffee. "I've been a cop in this city for twenty-three years, Ellie. I've seen things that don't make it into the reports, investigated cases that disappear from the files, arrested people who never make it to trial."

"Why haven't you done something about it?"

"What exactly would I do? Walk into the captain's office and tell him the city's elite are involved in ritual murders? Present evidence against men who golf with the mayor and donate money to the police benevolent fund?" He took another drink. "Besides, who says I haven't done something about it?"

That last comment hung in the air like smoke from a dead cigarette. Miller wasn't just warning me off the case —he was telling me he'd been fighting this fight for years, probably in ways I couldn't imagine.

"The photographs," I said. "Who really took them?"

"Someone who wants these people exposed but can't do it themselves. Someone with access but not authority.

Someone who's been waiting for the right person to come along and ask the right questions."

"Someone like Roger Talbot."

"Someone like you."

I stood to leave, but Miller's voice stopped me at the door.

"Ellie? Be careful who you trust. This thing goes deeper than you can imagine, and it's got roots in places you wouldn't expect. The badge doesn't make a man honest, and money doesn't make him evil—but both can make him dangerous when he's protecting secrets that could destroy him."

I walked out of the police station with more questions than answers and a bad feeling about what I'd gotten myself into. But I also had confirmation that Roger Talbot's disappearance was part of something much bigger than a missing producer.

The photographs were proof that Roger had witnessed something horrible, something that connected him to people who made their living by violence. And Miller's warning, couched in the careful language of a cop who'd learned when to speak and when to stay silent, told me that the stakes were higher than I'd imagined.

I had a choice to make. I could take Miller's advice, drop the case, and go back to trailing cheating spouses and serving divorce papers. Or I could follow the trail that Roger Talbot had started, knowing it might lead to the same fate that had apparently befallen him.

I thought about Vivian Vanderbilt's green eyes and the fear I'd seen behind her movie-star poise. I thought about Thornton's careful evasions and the scratch marks on expensive furniture. I thought about Jack Rafferty's warnings about men who satisfied their appetites in ways civilized society couldn't tolerate.

Most of all, I thought about the card in my pocket and the phone number that might connect me to people who'd been fighting this particular battle longer than I'd been alive.

The October sky was starting to darken as I walked back to my car, and somewhere in the city, powerful men were probably deciding what to do about the private investigator who'd been asking too many questions.

Let them decide, I thought. I had some questions of my own that needed answering.

Night Visitors

The Blue Note sat on Central Avenue like something that belonged in a better neighborhood—classy, valuable, and probably paying protection money to stay that way. It was the kind of joint that came alive after dark, where the music was real, the liquor was strong, and the conversations were the sort that made cops reach for their notebooks.

I arrived at eight-thirty, when the evening crowd was just settling in but the serious drinkers hadn't hit their stride yet. The doorman was a mountain of a man named Curtis who'd played football before the war and bouncing after it. He knew me from previous cases—I'd helped his sister find her husband when he'd gone missing with the rent money and a redhead from Pasadena.

"Evening, Miss Vance. Looking for trouble or trying to avoid it?"

"Depends on how you define trouble, Curtis. I need to talk to some people about Roger Talbot."

Curtis's expression shifted, just slightly, but enough to tell me the name meant something to him. "Mr. Talbot was a regular here for a while. Haven't seen him lately, though."

"How long's a while?"

"Maybe six weeks, two months. He used to come in Friday nights, sometimes brought friends from the studio crowd."

"What kind of friends?"

Curtis glanced around, making sure no one was close enough to overhear. "The kind that talked business when they should've been listening to music. The kind that made other people nervous."

That was interesting. In jazz clubs, the music was religion and business was blasphemy. If Roger's conversations were making people uncomfortable, he was either talking too loud or talking about things that shouldn't be discussed in public.

"Can I go in?"

"Course you can. But Miss Vance? Be careful who you ask about Mr. Talbot. Some of his friends weren't the understanding type."

The club's interior was all shadow and suggestion—low lighting that made everyone look dangerous, leather banquettes that had heard too many secrets, and a stage where the best musicians in the city made their living.

The air was thick with cigarette smoke and the particular tension that comes when talented people are about to earn their money.

On stage, a trumpet player was working through a version of "Body and Soul" that would have made Coleman Hawkins weep. The rest of the quartet followed his lead, bass and drums and piano building around the melody until the whole room was listening.

I found a table near the back and ordered whiskey from a waitress with tired eyes and a smile that had seen everything twice. Her name tag said "Dolores." "You're new," she said, setting down my glass.

"Not new, just don't get out much. I'm looking for information about Roger Talbot."

The smile vanished. "Honey, this is a music club, not an information bureau."

"I'm not looking to cause trouble. I'm trying to find him. His fiancée hired me."

Dolores glanced toward the bar, where a thin man in an expensive suit was watching our conversation like it was his job. She leaned closer, lowering her voice.

"Mr. Talbot sat at table seven, over by the wall. Always brought different people, but they all had the same look.

Like they wanted something the place didn't serve."

"What kind of something?"

"Information. Connections. The sort of things men with money buy when they can't get what they want through regular channels." She straightened up as the man from the bar started walking toward us. "You want my advice? Finish your drink and leave. Some questions are better left unasked."

The man from the bar was lean and forty, built like he needed to be fast. Expensive suit, Italian shoes, and eyes like winter.

"Miss Vance," he said, settling into the chair across from me without being invited. "I hear you've been asking about Roger Talbot."

"Word travels fast."

"In my line of work, it pays to stay informed. Vincent Torrino. I work for Mr. Grasso."

Mickey "The Fang" Grasso. Even I'd heard of him—one of the West Coast's most successful entrepreneurs, if you counted gambling, loan sharking, and various forms of persuasion as entrepreneurship. The kind of man who solved problems with methods that didn't appear in business school textbooks.

"What kind of business interests?"

"Movie business, my boss's business—more overlap than people think. Money, favors, keeping people quiet."

Torrino signaled the waitress, who appeared with a bottle of expensive scotch and two glasses. He poured for both of us, though I hadn't asked for a refill.

"Mr. Talbot was a client," he continued. "A valued client who understood the importance of discretion in certain business arrangements."

"What kind of arrangements?"

"The kind where a producer needs financing for projects that traditional banks won't touch. Independent pictures, controversial subjects, stories that might make some people uncomfortable."

Sounded innocent enough, but Torrino's tone said different. When mobsters talked about discretion, somebody usually ended up dead.

"When did you last see Mr. Talbot?"

"Three weeks ago. He came in here quite agitated, said he needed to change the terms of his arrangement with
Mr. Grasso."

"Change them how?"

"He wanted out. Said he'd gotten in over his head and needed to end his business relationship with us." Torrino sipped his scotch and studied me over the rim of his glass. "That's not how it works, lady. You get in bed with us, you don't just walk away."

"Are you saying your employer had Roger Talbot killed?"

"Mr. Grasso didn't like Roger changing his mind. But you don't kill paying customers. Dead men don't pay, and they don't bring in new business."

That made sense from a business perspective, but it didn't explain Roger's disappearance or the photographs Miller had shown me.

"What was Roger involved in that made him want out?"

Torrino was quiet for a moment, and I could see him weighing his options. Finally, he leaned forward, lowering his voice so that even the people at nearby tables couldn't hear.

"Mr. Talbot thought he was financing movies. What he was actually financing was much more interesting." "Such as?"

"Private gatherings. Exclusive events for very selective clientele. The kind of entertainment that certain gentlemen require but can't obtain through conventional means."

The pieces were starting to fit together—Roger's research into occult elements in Hollywood history, the photographs of him at the Crescent Club, the references to men with appetites that civilized society couldn't tolerate.

"What kind of entertainment?"

"Stuff that happens after dark. Private stuff. The kind where everybody keeps their mouth shut or else."

"You're talking about the Crescent Club."

Torrino's face stayed blank, but his hand drifted toward his jacket. I knew that move.

"I'm talking about business arrangements that Mr. Talbot found distasteful once he understood their true nature.

He wanted to withdraw his financial support and return to legitimate movie production."

"And Mr. Grasso's other clients didn't appreciate that decision."

"Mr. Grasso's other clients value their privacy above all else. They don't like complications, and they especially don't like people who might compromise their arrangements."

"So they made Roger disappear."

"So they encouraged him to reconsider his position. What happened after that..." Torrino shrugged eloquently.

I was getting the picture. Roger had stumbled into something that went far beyond movie financing. He'd become part of a network that provided services to men with very specific and very dangerous tastes. When he'd tried to extract himself, he'd learned that some business relationships don't have exit clauses.

"Where is he now?"

"That's the question, isn't it? Mr. Grasso would very much like to know the answer. Mr. Talbot owes considerable money, and his disappearance has left certain arrangements in an awkward position." "What kind of arrangements?"

"The kind that require ongoing financial support. The kind where missing payments cause problems for everyone involved."

Torrino drained his scotch and stood up, smoothing his jacket like he'd done this before.

"Miss Vance, let me give you some friendly advice. Mr. Talbot got involved with people who don't forgive and don't forget. If he's smart, he's somewhere far away and staying very quiet. If he's not smart..." Another eloquent shrug.

"And if I keep looking for him?"

"Then you better watch your back."

Torrino walked away, leaving me alone with my whiskey and a growing understanding of just how deep Roger Talbot had gotten himself into trouble. But I also had confirmation that he was involved with the same people Miller had warned me about—the Crescent Club members who required entertainment that civilized society couldn't provide.

I was about to leave when Dolores appeared at my table again, this time carrying a folded piece of paper.

"This was left for you," she said, glancing nervously toward the bar where Torrino had been standing.

I unfolded the paper. Written in pencil, in block letters that suggested someone trying to disguise their handwriting: "If you want to know what happened to the producer, be at Griffith Observatory tomorrow night at ten. Come alone."

"Who left this?"

"Nobody I recognized. Small guy, maybe fifty, wearing a hat pulled down low. Paid his tab in cash and left through the back door."

I pocketed the note and finished my drink. The trumpet player had moved on to "Strange Fruit," and the room seemed to fill with shadows that hadn't been there before.

As I walked toward the exit, I noticed that several of the other patrons were watching me with the kind of attention that suggested word of my questions had spread through the club faster than I'd expected. In Los Angeles, information was currency, and I'd apparently been spending freely.

Curtis was still at the door, but the friendly act was over.

"Find what you were looking for, Miss Vance?"

"Some of it. Curtis, you know anything about Roger Talbot's business arrangements?"

"I know he started coming in here about six months ago with men who made regular customers nervous. I know those men stopped coming around about a month ago, but Mr. Talbot kept showing up, acting like a man with something heavy on his mind."

"Heavy how?"

"Like a man who'd made a deal with the devil and was starting to understand what he'd signed."

That seemed to be the consensus—Roger Talbot had gotten involved with something that had started as business and turned into something much darker. The question was whether he'd managed to escape or whether his attempt to get out had gotten him killed.

I walked back to my car, aware that I was being watched from the shadows across the street. Torrino's warning had been polite but clear—some people valued their privacy enough to kill for it, and Roger Talbot had threatened that privacy.

The note in my pocket might get me answers. Or it might get me killed. Either way, I'd be at Griffith Observatory tomorrow night.

But I'd come too far to quit now. Roger needed help, and Vivian needed answers. Besides, this thing was bigger than one missing producer. It was bigger than Hollywood.

The October night was getting colder, and somewhere in the city, powerful men were probably deciding what to do about the private investigator who wouldn't take friendly advice.

Let them decide. Tomorrow night, I'd find out what they'd been so eager to hide.

The Crescent Club

Following someone in LA takes a good car, patience, and the ability to blend into traffic that barely moves. I had the first two. The third was a matter of staying far enough back that my Plymouth looked like just another pair of headlights in Vivian Vanderbilt's mirrors.

She lived in a Spanish-style house in the Hills that cost more than I'd make in ten years. Circular driveway, perfect palm trees, and a view of the whole city spread out like a promise.

I'd been parked across the street for two hours, drinking coffee from a thermos and smoking cigarettes I didn't really want, when she finally emerged. Even at nine in the morning, she looked like a movie poster. Red dress, hat tilted just so, sunglasses that cost more than my car payment.

Her car was a cream-colored Cadillac convertible with enough chrome to signal Mars. She drove like she owned the road, which she probably did. I gave her a half-block head start and pulled into traffic behind a delivery truck that provided perfect cover.

We headed south on Laurel Canyon, then east toward Hollywood proper. Traffic was thick enough to give me cover three cars back. Vivian drove like someone who'd never worried about money—for gas or anything else.

She parked outside Musso & Frank's, where studio executives made their deals and played at being gentlemen. I found a spot half a block away and settled in to wait.

Through the restaurant's windows, I could see her being seated at a corner table that offered privacy and a good view of the dining

room. She ordered coffee and checked her watch with the precision
of someone expecting company.

Jack Rafferty arrived fifteen minutes later.

He moved through the restaurant like he owned it, nodding to
other patrons, shaking hands with the maître d', playing the part of
the successful studio head making his rounds. But when he sat down
across from Vivian, the performance dropped away, and I could see
tension in the set of his shoulders.

I couldn't hear their talk, but I could read the body language. This
wasn't social. This was business, the kind that made both of them
jumpy.

Vivian leaned forward, talking fast, hands moving like she was
trying to convince him of something. Rafferty just listened, his face
getting darker by the minute. Whatever she was telling him, he
didn't like it.

They talked for maybe twenty minutes. No food was ordered, just
coffee that sat cooling while they worked through whatever problem
had brought them together. When Rafferty finally spoke, it was with
the kind of emphatic gestures that suggested he was either giving
orders or delivering ultimatums.

Vivian sat back in her chair, and even from across the street, I could
see her posture change. Whatever Rafferty had said, it hadn't been
what she wanted to hear.

They left separately—Rafferty first, striding out of the restaurant
with the aggressive confidence of a man who'd just settled a difficult
negotiation in his favor. Vivian waited ten minutes, then paid the
check and walked to her car with the careful grace of someone trying
not to show she was shaken.

I had a choice to make. Follow Rafferty and try to figure out what
he was planning, or stick with Vivian and see where she went next.
In my experience, the person who looks worried usually knows more
than the person who looks confident.

I followed the Cadillac.

She drove aimlessly for a while, taking the long way through
neighborhoods that didn't lead anywhere in particular. The kind
of driving people do when they need time to think, when the
destination matters less than the journey. Finally, she pulled into the

parking lot of a small café in West Hollywood, the kind of place that served decent coffee and minded its own business.

I watched from my car as she sat at a window table, smoking cigarettes and staring at nothing in particular. Every few minutes she'd check her watch, but she wasn't waiting for anyone—she was buying time, trying to work through whatever problem Rafferty had presented her with.

After an hour, she drove home. I waited until she was inside before making my decision.

It was time to have another conversation with Miss Vivian Vanderbilt.

I gave her thirty minutes to get settled, then walked up the flagstone path to her front door. The house looked even more expensive up close—hand-painted tiles, wrought-iron details that probably came from Spain, and a garden that someone was paying serious money to maintain.

She answered the door still wearing the red dress but looking like she'd aged ten years since morning. Her makeup was perfect, her hair was flawless, but her eyes held the kind of fatigue that sleep wouldn't cure.

"Miss Vance." She didn't sound surprised to see me. "I suppose you'd better come in."

The interior was all white marble and dark wood, the kind of décor that cost serious money without shouting about it. Oil paintings, Persian rugs, furniture that belonged in galleries. But it felt cold, like a museum after hours.

She led me to a living room with windows looking out over the city. In daylight, LA looked almost innocent— palm trees and red tile roofs stretching to the horizon.

"Drink?" she asked, walking to a bar cart that probably cost more than my car.

"Little early for me."

"It's five o'clock somewhere." She poured herself three fingers of scotch and took a sip that suggested this wasn't her first glass of the day. "I assume you have questions."

"A few. Starting with your meeting with Jack Rafferty this morning."

She sat with the light behind her so I couldn't see her face clearly. In my line of work, that's usually a bad sign.

"You've been following me."

"You hired me to find Roger Talbot. In my experience, clients don't always tell the whole truth."

"What makes you think I'm lying?"

"Secret meetings with studio heads while Roger's missing. Not acting surprised when I said Roger was in trouble. Drinking scotch before lunch."

She laughed like she'd just heard her own death sentence. "You don't miss much."

"Goes with the job. What did Rafferty want?"

Vivian finished her scotch and walked back to the bar cart. This time she poured four fingers and didn't bother with ice.

"Jack is concerned about certain business arrangements that Roger was involved in. He wanted to know if

Roger had shared any details with me before he disappeared."

"What kind of details?"

"Names. Locations. Financial records. The kind of information that gets people killed." "And had he?"

"That's what I told Jack I was trying to find out. That's why I hired you."

Something in her tone suggested there was more to the story, but I decided to try a different approach.

"How long have you known Jack Rafferty?"

"We've known each other for years. He helped me get my first contract with RKO."

"Business relationship or personal?"

"Both, at various times."

"Were you sleeping with him?"

Her glass stopped halfway to her lips. "I don't see how that's relevant."

"It's relevant because people who used to sleep together sometimes have complicated relationships.

Complicated enough that one might lie to a private investigator to protect the other."

She set down her glass and turned to face me directly. Without the backlighting, I could see her expression clearly—and what I saw was fear.

"Miss Vance, let me ask you a question. What do you know about the early history of Hollywood?"

"I know enough. Oil money, railroad money, men who came west to make fortunes and didn't much care how they made them."

"What about the families who controlled those fortunes? The men who decided which pictures got made and which ones disappeared? The people who built this town according to their own particular... interests?"

I thought about Miller's photographs, about Roger's notebook with its references to "The Pack," about the scratches on expensive furniture.

"Are we talking about the Crescent Club?"

Her face went pale. "Where did you hear that name?"

"I hear a lot of names in my line of work. Most of them don't make movie stars look like they've seen a ghost."

Vivian walked to the window and stared out at the city below. When she spoke again, her voice was barely above a whisper.

"The Crescent Club isn't just a gentlemen's society, Miss Vance. It's an organization that's controlled Hollywood since before there was a Hollywood. The founding families, the original investors, the men who built the studios and created the system."

"What kind of organization?"

"The kind that holds ceremonies instead of meetings. Where membership means doing things most people couldn't stomach."

"You're talking about something supernatural."

"I'm talking about men who discovered certain... capabilities... and found ways to use those capabilities to build an empire. Men whose appetites go beyond money and power."

It was starting to make sense. The claw marks, the wolf references, the entertainment that couldn't be bought with regular money.

"You're talking about werewolves."

"I'm talking about men who can become something else when the sun goes down. Men who've used that ability to intimidate rivals, eliminate threats, and satisfy hungers that normal society couldn't tolerate."

"And Roger found out about this."

"Roger was researching a book about Hollywood's occult history. He thought it was all folklore and mythology.

But the deeper he dug, the more he realized that some of the old stories were true."

"What happened when he realized the truth?"

"He tried to expose them. He gathered evidence, took photographs, documented their meetings and their... activities."

"The photographs Detective Miller showed me."

Her eyes widened. "How did you—never mind. Yes, Roger had been watching them for weeks, trying to build a case that would expose the truth about how this town really operates."

"And they found out."

"They found out, and they made him an offer. Join them, become part of their organization, or disappear permanently."

"What did he choose?"

"He chose a third option. He ran."

Vivian turned away from the window and met my eyes directly. "Miss Vance, Roger Talbot isn't missing. He's hiding. And if you keep looking for him, you're going to lead them right to him."

The truth hit me like cold water. I hadn't been hired to find Roger Talbot—I'd been hired to stop looking for him. Vivian's real job wasn't to locate her missing fiancé, it was to make sure the investigation went nowhere.

"You're working with them," I said.

"I'm working for them. There's a difference." She finished her scotch and set the glass down with shaking hands. "They told me to hire a private investigator, someone who would ask the obvious questions, follow the obvious leads, and eventually conclude that Roger had run off with another woman or gotten himself killed by gambling debts."

"But instead you hired someone competent."

"Instead I hired someone who's gotten closer to the truth than they expected. Someone who's asking the right questions and finding the right answers."

"And now they want me stopped."

"They want you stopped, and they want Roger found. Jack's meeting this morning was to inform me that my usefulness has ended. They're going to handle the situation themselves."

"What does that mean?"

"It means Roger has maybe twenty-four hours before they find him and eliminate the problem permanently. And it means you have maybe less than that before they decide you know too much to live."

The fear in her voice was real, and suddenly I understood why she'd been drinking scotch at ten in the morning. She'd been trying to protect Roger by misdirecting the investigation, but she'd underestimated both my abilities and the consequences of failure.

"Where is he?"

"I don't know. He contacts me through intermediaries, but I don't know his location. It's safer that way—for both of us."

"How do I reach him?"

"You don't. You run, Miss Vance. You take whatever money you have and you leave Los Angeles tonight. You go somewhere far away and you never come back."

"And leave Roger to die?"

"Roger made his choice when he decided to expose them. Don't make his mistake."

I stood up, my mind already working through the possibilities. Roger was alive but in hiding. The Crescent Club had decided to handle the situation directly. Vivian had been trying to protect him by sabotaging the investigation, but that protection was about to end.

"One more question," I said. "The note I received last night, arranging a meeting at Griffith Observatory—was that from Roger?"

"I don't know. But if it was, don't go. It's too dangerous."

"And if it wasn't?"

"Then it's a trap, and you'll be walking into an ambush that will solve their problems permanently."

I walked toward the door, but her voice stopped me.

"Miss Vance? Whatever you decide to do, be very careful who you trust. This thing has roots everywhere—in the studios, in the police department, in city hall. People you think are allies might be working for them. People you think are enemies might be your only hope."

"Including you?"

"Especially me."

I left her sitting in her expensive living room, surrounded by beautiful things that couldn't protect her from the mess she'd helped create. The October sun was getting lower, and in a few hours, I'd have to decide whether to keep the appointment at Griffith Observatory.

Roger Talbot was alive but running out of time. Vivian had been playing a dangerous game to protect him, and now that game was almost over.

I had some thinking to do.

Dead Man's Warning

Breaking into Consolidated Pictures at ten o'clock at night was either smart or stupid. I'd find out soon enough.

The security guard made his rounds every two hours. Plenty of time to slip through the fence and get to Building C. Old Pete's flashlight was about as bright as a dying match, which helped.

Roger Talbot's office was on the second floor, down the hall from Jack Rafferty's corner suite. Solid oak door with faded gold letters: "R. TALBOT - INDEPENDENT PRODUCTIONS." Good lock, but nothing I couldn't handle.

It took me three minutes to get inside and another thirty seconds to realize I wasn't the first person to search Roger's office.

Someone had torn through the place like they were looking for buried treasure. Desk drawers hung open, their contents scattered across the floor. File cabinets gaped open, manila folders scattered everywhere. Books had been pulled from shelves and discarded. Even the couch cushions had been flipped, revealing stains that told stories I didn't want to hear.

I closed the door behind me and turned on my flashlight, keeping the beam low and away from the windows. Whatever the previous searchers had been looking for, they'd been desperate enough to tear the place apart and confident enough not to worry about covering their tracks.

Expensive mahogany desk, now treated like firewood. Every drawer had been emptied, every secret compartment probed. Business letters scattered across the floor—contracts, invoices, the usual paperwork that kept Hollywood running.

But it was the filing cabinets that told the real story.

Someone had gone through them looking for something specific. The remaining folders held routine business records—payroll for crews, permits for location shooting, insurance policies that covered everything from equipment damage to star tantrums. What was missing were the files that would have contained the interesting information—financial records, correspondence with investors, and anything that might document Roger's more unusual business arrangements.

I was examining the debris around the filing cabinets when my flashlight beam caught something the searchers had missed. Wedged behind the bottom drawer of the leftmost cabinet, almost invisible unless you were looking for it, was a small manila envelope that had somehow escaped notice.

Inside the envelope were photocopies of financial ledgers, and one look told me why Roger had hidden them.

The entries were in Roger's handwriting, but they documented transactions that had nothing to do with movie production. Monthly payments to something called "Crescent Holdings." Regular transfers to accounts labeled only with initials—"M.G." for what I suspected was Mickey Grasso, "V.T." for Vincent Torrino, and others I didn't recognize. But it was the notation column that made the picture clear.

Next to each payment, Roger had written cryptic descriptions: "November gathering - six participants."

"December ritual - bloodline verification." "January ceremony - new member initiation."

This wasn't movie financing. This was documentation of Roger's involvement in whatever the Crescent Club was doing with their monthly meetings. And if Vivian was right about the supernatural nature of those gatherings, Roger had been keeping careful records of activities that most people wouldn't believe and powerful people would kill to keep secret.

I was photographing the ledger pages with the small camera I kept for evidence gathering when I heard footsteps in the hallway.

Heavy footsteps. Moving with purpose rather than the casual patrol pattern of a security guard making his rounds.

I switched off my flashlight and moved away from the windows, keeping low and trying to remember the layout of the office well enough to navigate in the dark. The footsteps stopped outside Roger's door, and I heard the quiet sound of someone testing the handle.

The lock I'd picked was good enough to keep out casual intruders, but it wouldn't fool anyone who knew what to look for. And the person outside Roger's door definitely knew what to look for.

I heard the soft scrape of metal on metal—someone working on the lock with professional tools. They were being quiet about it, which meant they didn't want to attract attention any more than I did. That was either very good news or very bad news, depending on whether they were friend or foe.

The lock gave way with a barely audible click, and the door swung open with the kind of oiled silence that suggested whoever was out there had done this before. A lot.

I crouched behind Roger's overturned desk and tried to make myself invisible. Footsteps crossed the office with the confidence of someone who belonged there. A flashlight beam swept the room, brighter than mine, checking corners and examining the mess.

"Damn." The voice was male, middle-aged, with an accent I couldn't place. "Someone beat us here."

"Find anything useful?" This voice was younger, with the kind of nervous energy that suggested this wasn't his first break-in but probably wasn't his hundredth either.

"Hard to tell. They were thorough, whoever they were."

The flashlight beam passed over my hiding spot, and I pressed myself closer to the floor, trying to become one with the Persian rug that had probably cost more than most people's cars. The beam moved on, and I heard the sound of papers being shuffled.

"Check the safe," the older voice said.

"Already did. Empty. Professional job—they knew the combination or had someone who did."

That was interesting. Roger's safe had been opened by someone with inside knowledge, which narrowed down the list of potential searchers considerably. Either someone had tortured the combination out of Roger, or someone with legitimate access had decided to clean house.

"What about the filing cabinets?"

"Cleaned out. Financial records, correspondence, anything that might document his business arrangements."

"They miss anything?"

"Maybe. Check behind the—"

The younger man's words were cut off by the sound of footsteps in the hallway. Different footsteps—the heavy, irregular pattern of someone who wasn't trying to be quiet.

"Security guard," the older voice whispered.

I heard rapid movement as my uninvited companions prepared to leave the same way they'd come in. But the security guard's footsteps were getting closer, and there wasn't time for a graceful exit.

The office went dead quiet. My heart was hammering like a drum. Through the crack under the door, I could see the guard's flashlight beam sweeping back and forth across the hallway floor.

The flashlight beam stopped moving. That wasn't good.

"Hello?" The guard's voice carried the authority of someone who'd found something that shouldn't be there.

"Building's supposed to be locked up for the night."

I heard the door handle turn, and the office was suddenly filled with light from a flashlight that could have guided ships to safety. The guard stepped inside, moving with the careful caution of someone who'd learned that late-night disturbances in Hollywood studios could be anything from star-struck kids to well-armed burglars. "Jesus Christ," he muttered, taking in the destruction. "What the hell happened here?"

Big guy, over six feet, built like he'd worked with his hands. Clean uniform, polished badge, and a gun that looked well-maintained.

He moved through the office methodically, checking corners and examining the wreckage with professional interest. When his flashlight beam found me crouched behind the desk, I thought my heart was going to stop entirely.

"Well, well," he said, keeping the light trained on my face. "What have we got here?"

I stood up slow, hands where he could see them. "Evening. This looks worse than it is."

"I'll bet it does. Turn around, hands on the wall."

I did as instructed, feeling the familiar indignity of being searched by someone who knew what they were doing. He found my .38, my lock picks, and the camera with the photographed ledger pages.

"Private investigator, huh?" He'd found my license in my jacket pocket. "Eleanor Vance. What's your business here, Miss Vance?"

"I'm working a missing persons case. Roger Talbot."

"Mr. Talbot's been missing for a week. What makes you think you'd find him in his office?"

"Looking for anything that might tell me where he went. Business papers, letters, whatever."

He looked at me like he'd heard this song before. "So you figured breaking in was the smart play?"

"Figured it beat waiting for a warrant that'd never come."

He was quiet for a moment, considering his options. Finally, he holstered his gun and handed back my license.

"Bill Kowalski. Been working security here fifteen years. I knew Roger."

That was unexpected. "Knew him how?"

"Good guy. Got in with the wrong crowd. Smart enough to realize it, not smart enough to know how to get out."

Kowalski walked to the window and looked out at the studio lot, his back to me. "You want to know what happened to Roger Talbot? He found out something he shouldn't have found out, and now he's either dead or wishing he was."

"What did he find out?"

"That some of the men who run this town aren't really men at all. That the deals that built Hollywood were made with things that hunt in the dark and feed on fear."

Kowalski turned back to face me, and in the dim light I could see something in his eyes that looked like recognition.

"You're the private investigator who's been asking questions about the Crescent Club." "Word travels fast."

"It travels faster when the people being asked about have ways of making sure they stay informed." He gestured toward the destroyed office. "This wasn't random vandalism, Miss Vance. This was a professional operation designed to remove any evidence of Roger's involvement with certain organizations."

"Organizations like the Crescent Club?"

"Organizations that have been operating in this city since before it was a city. Organizations that don't like publicity and don't tolerate interference."

Kowalski walked to the filing cabinet and ran his hand along the back of the bottom drawer, just as I had done.

But unlike me, he found what he was looking for.

"Roger was a careful man," he said, producing a small silver box that had been taped to the inside back panel of the drawer. "He knew the risks of getting involved with these people, and he took precautions."

The box was about the size of a cigarette case, made of tarnished silver with strange markings etched into the surface. Kowalski opened it carefully, revealing a single item nestled in black velvet.

A dried flower. Purple petals, spiky leaves, stem carefully preserved. It looked harmless enough, but something about it bothered me.

"Wolfsbane," Kowalski said. "Also called monkshood or devil's helmet, depending on who you ask. Very rare in

California, very expensive to obtain, and very dangerous to the kind of people Roger was dealing with." "You're talking about werewolves."

"I'm talking about men who can change their shape when the moon is right and use that ability to do things that normal men can't do. Things that have helped them build fortunes and eliminate problems for over a century."

Kowalski closed the box and handed it to me. "Roger left this here as insurance. If something happened to him, whoever found it would know what they were dealing with."

"Why are you helping me?"

"Because Roger Talbot was a good man who tried to do the right thing. Because this city has been controlled by monsters for too long.

And because somebody needs to know the truth, even if they can't do anything about it." Kowalski walked toward the door, then stopped and looked back at me.

"Miss Vance? That meeting at Griffith Observatory tomorrow night—don't go. It's not Roger who wants to see you. It's them, and they're tired of playing games."

"How do you know about the meeting?"

"Same way I knew you'd be here tonight. Same way they know everything that happens in this city." He paused at the door. "Some battles can't be won, Miss Vance. Sometimes the best you can do is survive long enough to warn the next person."

He left me alone in Roger's wrecked office, holding a silver box that contained protection against things that weren't supposed to exist. Outside the window, Los Angeles stretched in all directions—a city built on secrets darker than most people suspected.

I pocketed the silver box and gathered the photocopied ledger pages. Roger Talbot had been keeping records of his involvement with the Crescent Club, documenting transactions and meetings that proved the organization was more than it appeared.

The wolfsbane was supposed to offer protection. Given what I'd learned over the past few days, I had a feeling it would take more than dried flowers to keep me safe.

But it was something. And in a case where nothing made sense and everyone was lying, something beat nothing.

Even if that something meant the monsters were real, and they'd been running Hollywood from the beginning.

Wolves in Three-Piece Suits

I should have known better than to park in the same spot twice.

It was past midnight when I left Consolidated Pictures, the silver box and photocopied ledgers tucked safely in my jacket. The studio lot was quiet except for the distant hum of traffic on Pico Boulevard and the occasional sound of night creatures going about their business in the shadows between buildings.

My Plymouth waited where I'd left it, three blocks away in an alley behind a diner that had been closed since the war ended. The kind of place where working people used to grab coffee and eggs before their shifts, back when there were shifts to be worked and money to pay for them.

I was fishing for my car keys when I heard the footsteps.

Two sets, moving with the deliberate pace of men who had business to conduct and weren't worried about an audience.

"Miss Vance." The voice came from behind me, smooth as silk and twice as expensive. "Mr. Grasso would like a word."

I turned slowly, keeping my hands visible and away from my .38. Two men stood between me and the mouth of the alley—both wearing dark overcoats that probably cost more than most annual salaries, both carrying themselves like professionals who handled problems for a living.

The one who'd spoken was tall and thin, with sharp features that belonged on an undertaker. His hair was slicked back with pomade, and his smile suggested he enjoyed his work more than most people would find comfortable. The other was shorter but built solid, with hands that looked like they could crack walnuts and a face that showed the wear that comes from settling disputes physically.

"Gentlemen," I said, trying to keep my voice steady. "Little late for a business meeting, isn't it?"

"Mr. Grasso keeps irregular hours," the thin one said. "Professional necessity. I'm Sal Benedetto, and my colleague here is Tony Marconi. We handle delicate matters for Mr. Grasso."

I'd heard of Sal Benedetto. Word was he'd started as a numbers runner in Chicago before moving west to handle Mickey Grasso's more sophisticated operations. The type who could discuss philosophy while breaking your fingers, making both seem equally reasonable.

Tony Marconi was new to me, but his reputation was written all over his scarred knuckles and the careful way he moved his left shoulder. A fighter, probably ex-boxer, definitely the type who did his talking with his hands.

"What does Mr. Grasso want?" I asked.

"He wants to know why a private investigator is asking questions about his business associates," Sal said, lighting a cigarette with a gold lighter that caught what little light filtered into the alley. "He wants to know why those questions are making certain people nervous."

"And he wants to know if you're smart enough to stop asking them," Tony added. His voice was rougher than Sal's, with the kind of Brooklyn accent that suggested he hadn't been in Los Angeles long enough to lose his East Coast edges.

I glanced toward the mouth of the alley, calculating distances and odds. Sal was blocking the direct route to the street, positioned with the kind of casual precision that suggested this wasn't his first midnight conversation. Tony had moved to cover the far side of the alley, cutting off any retreat deeper into the shadows. Professional work, the kind that came from years of practice.

"I'm working a missing persons case," I said. "Roger Talbot. His fiancée hired me to find him."

"Mr. Talbot made some poor business decisions," Sal said, exhaling smoke that curled between us like a question mark. "He chose to terminate his relationship with Mr. Grasso in a manner that left certain obligations unfulfilled."

"What kind of obligations?"

"The kind that don't disappear just because a man decides he no longer wants to honor them." Sal's smile widened, but his eyes stayed cold. "Mr. Grasso is a reasonable businessman, Miss Vance. He understands that people sometimes make mistakes. But he also expects those mistakes to be corrected."

"And if they can't be corrected?"

"Then alternative arrangements must be made."

Tony had been quiet during this exchange, but I could see him shifting his weight, loosening up like a boxer before the first round. Whatever alternative arrangements Sal was discussing, Tony would probably be implementing them.

"Here's the situation," Sal continued. "Mr. Talbot owes Mr. Grasso a considerable amount of money. That debt doesn't vanish just because Mr. Talbot has chosen to make himself scarce. Someone needs to be held responsible for the financial shortfall."

"Let me guess—me."

"You're investigating Mr. Talbot's affairs. That makes you privy to information about his business dealings, his assets, his various sources of income. Mr. Grasso believes you might be able to help locate resources that could be applied toward settling the outstanding debt."

"And if I can't?"

"Then you become part of the problem instead of part of the solution." Sal dropped his cigarette and ground it under his heel with the kind of deliberate motion that suggested he was preparing to move on to the next phase of our conversation.

I'd been in tight spots before—occupational hazard of being a private investigator in a city where everyone had secrets and some of them had guns. But this was different. Sal and Tony weren't just muscle hired to rough me up and send a message. They were professionals who'd been sent to solve a problem permanently.

"Mr. Grasso seems to think I know more than I do," I said, trying to buy time while I worked through my limited options. "Roger Talbot kept his business affairs private. I've been trying to piece together what happened to him, but I don't have access to his financial records or his assets."

"That's disappointing to hear," Sal said. "Mr. Grasso was hoping you might be more cooperative."

Tony cracked his knuckles with the sound of dry wood breaking. "Maybe she needs some encouragement to remember better."

The alley was maybe thirty feet long, with brick walls on both sides that rose high enough to block out most of the light from the street. A few garbage cans, some wooden crates, a fire escape that was too far away to do me any good. Not much room to maneuver, and nowhere to run.

But I had two advantages: I knew they wanted information from me, which meant they couldn't just kill me outright, and I had my .38 in a shoulder holster that they probably hadn't thought to check for yet.

"Tell you what," I said, starting to reach slowly toward my jacket. "Let me show you what I've found so far.

Maybe it'll help settle Mr. Talbot's debt."

"Slowly," Sal warned, but he was curious enough to let me continue.

I pulled out the photocopied ledger pages, holding them where both men could see. "Roger kept detailed financial records. Names, dates, amounts—everything Mr. Grasso would need to track down his money."

Sal stepped closer, interested despite himself. Tony moved with him, their professional formation breaking down as they focused on the papers in my hand.

That's when I went for my gun.

The .38 cleared leather faster than I'd ever drawn it before, trained on Sal's chest before he could react. But Tony was quicker than I'd expected—his hand was already moving toward his own weapon, and I had maybe two seconds before this turned into a shooting match I probably wouldn't win.

"Easy," I said, keeping the gun trained on Sal while watching Tony in my peripheral vision. "Nobody needs to get hurt here."

Sal raised his hands slowly, but his expression suggested he was more annoyed than scared. "Miss Vance, you're making this more complicated than it needs to be."

"Complicated is my specialty." I backed toward the mouth of the alley, trying to keep both men in sight. "Tony, let's see your hands where I can see them."

Tony's hand froze halfway to his jacket. "You're making a big mistake, lady."

"Wouldn't be my first. But it might be my last if I don't make it."

I was maybe ten feet from the street when Tony made his move. He dove left, rolling behind a pile of garbage cans while pulling a gun that looked like it could stop a truck. Sal went right, using the brick wall for cover while reaching for his own weapon.

I put two shots into the garbage cans where Tony had disappeared, then spun toward Sal's position. His gun was already out and tracking toward me, muzzle flash lighting up the alley like deadly fireworks.

The bullet chipped brick next to my head, close enough that dust got in my eyes. I returned fire, aiming center mass but hitting wall as Sal ducked back.

Tony popped up from behind the garbage cans, his gun seeking me in the dim light. I put another round in his direction, then ran for the street like hell was chasing me.

Which, given the circumstances, it probably was.

I made it to the mouth of the alley before Tony's next shot, the bullet sparking off the pavement behind me. My Plymouth was parked across the street, keys in my pocket, engine cold and probably not eager to cooperate.

More shots echoed behind me as I sprinted across the empty street, keeping low and weaving like I'd learned during the war. Glass exploded in a storefront window to my left—someone was shooting to kill now, the conversation phase of our relationship officially over.

I reached my car and dove behind it just as another bullet punched through the rear window, safety glass cascading over the seat like expensive confetti. The keys were in my hand, the driver's door was yanked open, and I was behind the wheel before my brain caught up with my body.

The engine turned over on the second try—one of the few times my beat-up Plymouth had ever cooperated when I needed it most.

I floored the accelerator and peeled out of the parking space, tires screaming against wet pavement as more shots rang out behind me.

In the rearview mirror, I could see Sal and Tony standing in the mouth of the alley, watching my retreat with professional disappointment. They made no attempt to pursue—they'd delivered their message, and whether I'd understood it was my problem now.

I drove randomly through the city for an hour, taking turns at random and doubling back through neighborhoods I didn't recognize, making sure I wasn't being followed. My hands were shaking, my heart was trying to climb out of my chest, and there was a ringing in my ears that had nothing to do with the Plymouth's engine.

But I was alive, and I still had the ledger pages and the silver box. More importantly, I now knew for certain that Mickey Grasso was connected to Roger Talbot's disappearance, and that connection was worth killing to protect.

I finally stopped at an all-night diner in Burbank, parking under a streetlight where I could see any approaching cars from inside. The waitress was a tired-looking woman in her fifties who poured coffee without being asked and didn't comment on the fact that I looked like hell.

"Rough night?" she asked, setting down a cup that was strong enough to wake the dead.

"Getting rougher by the hour."

I sat in a corner booth with my back to the wall and thought about what I'd learned. Roger Talbot had borrowed money from Mickey Grasso to finance his involvement with the Crescent Club. When he'd tried to get out, he'd defaulted on the loan and disappeared, leaving Grasso with a financial loss and me with a target on my back.

The question was whether Roger was hiding from Grasso's people, from the Crescent Club, or from both. And whether he was still alive to care about the distinction.

The coffee was helping my hands stop shaking, but it wasn't doing much for the certainty that this case was going to get me killed if I didn't find a way to end it soon. Sal and Tony had been polite about it, but their message was clear: drop the investigation or become another Los Angeles statistic.

I should've listened. Should've taken their money and found myself some nice cheating husband to follow around. Maybe dodge a few bottles, duck some thrown dishes. Easy work.

But the wolfsbane was still in my pocket. And I kept hearing Bill's voice: "Some fights you can't win, but somebody's gotta throw the first punch."

Roger was out there somewhere—dead or hiding—and I was all he had left.

I left a dollar on the table—good tip, friendly customer. The kind a waitress remembers if cops come asking.

The night air bit through my coat. Somewhere across town, powerful men were deciding how to handle the dame who'd just cost them two soldiers.

I'd come too far to quit now. Roger needed help, and something rotten was eating this city from the inside. Maybe I couldn't stop it, but I could bloody its nose.

Tomorrow night: Griffith Observatory, maybe a trap, maybe answers. Tonight: find a bed where their boys couldn't find me. In this city, both were long shots.

The October wind cut through downtown. In some expensive office, men in thousand-dollar suits were planning my funeral.

Let them plan. Tomorrow night, we'd see who was tougher—me or their secrets.

The Observatory Trap

Smart thing was to find a hotel and disappear till morning. Instead, I drove back to the office at three A.M.

Sometimes you make the dumb choice because it's the only one that feels right.

The building looked dead as always. But stepping out of the Plymouth, my skin crawled. Wrong kind of quiet— like the whole street was waiting for something bad to happen.

I climbed the stairs to the third floor with my .38 in my hand, stepping carefully on the treads that didn't creak. The hallway was dark except for the dim glow from the exit sign at the far end, casting everything in a red light that made shadows look like blood.

Door was closed, lock looked fine. But something felt off about it. Professional job—somebody who knew locks and didn't want to leave calling cards.

I listened at the door for thirty seconds, hearing nothing but the building's natural sounds—pipes settling, wood expanding, the distant rumble of the heating system that barely worked on the best of days. If someone was waiting inside, they were being very quiet about it.

The lock opened easily to my picks, and I pushed the door open just wide enough to slip inside. The office was dark, but enough light filtered in from the street to show me what I needed to see.

Someone had torn the place apart.

My desk had been pulled from the wall, drawers yanked out and contents scattered. The filing cabinet lay on its side, manila folders spread everywhere. Books had been pulled from shelves, pages riffled through and discarded. Even the couch had been moved, cushions slashed open.

Whoever trashed the place knew what they wanted. No anger in it, just business.

I closed the door behind me and turned on my desk lamp, keeping the beam low and away from the windows. In the yellow light, the destruction looked even more complete. Papers everywhere, furniture overturned, my few possessions examined and dismissed.

Whoever had done this had been looking for something small enough to hide but valuable enough to justify the risk of breaking into a private investigator's office. Something like photocopied ledger pages documenting financial transactions with occult organizations.

I checked the obvious hiding places first—the false bottom in my desk drawer, the space behind the radiator, the loose floorboard under the filing cabinet. All of them had been found and searched. The ledger pages were gone, along with the notes I'd made about the case and the photographs Detective Miller had shown me.

But it was what else was missing that made my blood run cold.

The silver box with the wolfsbane was gone.

I tore through the office again, checking every corner and crevice where something that size might be hidden.

Under the overturned couch, behind the books, in the pockets of the coat I kept hanging on the door. Nothing.

Someone had broken into my office specifically to take the one item that was supposed to protect me against supernatural threats. That suggested either remarkable coincidence or inside knowledge of what I'd found at the studio.

I was examining the slashed couch cushions when I heard footsteps in the hallway. Not the casual steps of a tenant heading home late, but the deliberate pace of someone who knew exactly where they were going.

I switched off the lamp and moved to the window, keeping low and to the side where I could see the street without being seen. A black sedan was parked across from my building, engine running, exhaust visible in the cold night air. Too expensive for this neighborhood, too clean for this time of night.

The footsteps stopped outside my door.

I drew my .38 and positioned myself behind the overturned desk, trying to become invisible in the shadows. The door handle turned slowly, testing whether it was locked.

"Miss Vance?" The voice was cultured, educated, with the kind of accent that suggested expensive schools and old money. "I know you're in there. Your car is parked outside, and the night watchman saw you enter the building."

I didn't answer. In my experience, when well-dressed strangers visited private investigators at three in the morning, the conversation rarely ended with everyone shaking hands and going home satisfied.

"My name is Edward Whitmore," the voice continued. "I represent certain interests that have been affected by your investigation into Mr. Talbot's disappearance."

Edward Whitmore. The name was familiar, though I couldn't place it immediately. Someone important enough that his name occasionally appeared in the society pages, connected to organizations and charities that attracted old money and older secrets.

"I'd like to propose a mutually beneficial arrangement," he said. "May I come in?"

"Door's unlocked," I said, keeping my gun trained on the entrance.

Whitmore looked like money—tall, silver-haired, maybe sixty. Cashmere coat, leather shoes that cost more than my car. The kind of bearing that came from never hearing the word 'no.'

His eyes were wrong—pale as winter ice. Looking into them made my stomach drop.

"Evening, Miss Vance. Sorry about the hour, but this couldn't wait." He stepped into the office with the confidence of a man entering his own home.

"What circumstances?"

"Your continued investigation into matters that don't concern you." He gestured at the destroyed office. "As you can see, other parties share my interest in discouraging your involvement."

"Other parties?"

"Grasso's boys were here first—Sal and Tony, right after your alley chat. They're good at muscle work, lousy at thinking. Grabbed your papers but missed what counted." Whitmore's smile was polite but cold.

"The silver box."

"Indeed. Wolfsbane is quite rare in California, Miss Vance. Even more rare is someone who understands its proper application." He removed his gloves with careful precision, revealing hands that were pale and elegant.

"Fortunately, I was able to retrieve the item before Mr. Grasso's men realized its significance."

Whitmore reached into his coat and withdrew the silver box, holding it where I could see it but not reach it. The strange markings on the surface seemed to shift in the lamplight, forming patterns that hurt to look at directly.

"This belongs to you now," he said. "A token of good faith, and a reminder that some protections are more valuable than others."

"What do you want?"

"I want you to stop looking for Roger Talbot."

"People keep telling me that. Makes me wonder what I might find if I keep looking."

"You might find that some secrets are kept secret for very good reasons." Whitmore set the silver box on my overturned desk, but didn't move away from it. "Roger Talbot was a foolish man who interfered with arrangements that have existed for over a century. His curiosity has already cost him dearly." "Is he dead?"

"Roger's alive, technically. But his mind..." Whitmore shrugged. "Let's say we're very good at breaking people."

The temperature in the office seemed to drop ten degrees. "What did you do to him?"

"We showed him the truth about the forces that built this city. Some people can accept that truth and find their place within the existing order. Others..." Whitmore shrugged eloquently. "Others require more intensive education."

I kept my gun trained on his chest, but something told me bullets wouldn't help against whatever Edward

Whitmore really was. "And if I don't stop looking?"

"Then you'll join Mr. Talbot in his educational program. The Crescent Club has facilities that are quite private, quite secure, and quite effective at helping people understand their proper role in the natural order." "The natural order?"

"Los Angeles was built by men who understood that civilization is just a thin layer over much older truths. We are predators by nature, and the strongest rise to the top." His pale eyes caught the streetlight, reflecting it back like an animal's. "Some of us have embraced that nature more completely than others."

"You're talking about werewolves."

"I'm talking about evolution, Miss Vance. About adaptation. About men who discovered abilities that allowed them to dominate their competitors and build empires that have lasted for generations." Whitmore moved closer to my desk, and I could smell something sharp and wild, like pine trees and running water. "We are what humans could become if they stopped pretending that civilization has tamed their animal instincts."

"And Roger Talbot threatened that."

"Roger Talbot attempted to document our activities and expose our membership to the general public. He believed that ordinary people had a right to know how their betters operated." Whitmore's smile was sharp enough to cut glass. "We corrected his misunderstanding."

I thought about the photographs Miller had shown me, about Roger's careful financial records, about the wolfsbane that was supposed to protect against creatures that shouldn't exist in a rational world.

"Where is he now?"

"Safely contained, Miss Vance. Being educated about the realities of power in Los Angeles." Whitmore reached for the silver box. "The question is whether you require similar education, or whether you're wise enough to accept a generous offer to withdraw from this case."

"What kind of offer?"

"Ten thousand dollars. Cash. Untraceable. Enough to relocate to another city and establish a new practice, far from the complexities of Los Angeles politics."

Ten thousand dollars was more money than I'd ever seen in one place. Enough to start over anywhere in the country, enough to buy a house with a yard and neighbors who didn't disappear in the middle of the night.

"And all I have to do is stop looking for Roger Talbot."

"You stop looking, you forget what you've learned, and you never speak of the Crescent Club to anyone. In return, you receive financial security and the opportunity to live a long, peaceful life somewhere else." "And if I refuse?"

"Then you join Mr. Talbot in discovering just how much education a human mind can absorb before it breaks entirely."

Whitmore picked up the silver box and held it out to me. "The wolfsbane will provide some protection, Miss Vance, but it's not a permanent solution. There are limits to what dried flowers can accomplish against creatures who have been perfecting their predatory skills for decades."

I reached out and took the box, feeling the cold silver against my palm. The weight of it seemed heavier than it should be, as if it contained more than just a pressed flower.

"I need time to think about your offer," I said.

"Of course. But don't take too long. The next full moon is in three days, and that's when the Crescent Club traditionally handles its most... intensive educational programs." Whitmore moved toward the door with fluid grace. "I'll expect your answer by tomorrow evening."

"How will you know my decision?"

"Miss Vance, we've been monitoring your activities since the day Vivian Vanderbilt walked into your office. We know where you go, who you talk to, what you discover. We know about your meeting with Detective Miller, your conversation with Vincent Torrino, your break-in at the studio." His pale eyes fixed on mine. "We know about the meeting arranged for tomorrow night at Griffith Observatory."

"That meeting—"

"Is not what you think it is. Roger Talbot did not arrange that meeting, Miss Vance. We did. To see how much you'd learned, and how much danger you represented to our interests."

The cold in my chest spread through my whole body. "It's a trap."

"It's an opportunity. A chance for you to demonstrate wisdom by accepting our generous offer, or to prove that you require the same educational program that Mr. Talbot is currently enjoying."

Whitmore paused at the door and looked back at me. "Think it over, Miss Vance. Come the full moon—that's three days—we're settling the Roger situation for good. Don't make us include you in that settlement."

He left me in my wrecked office, holding a silver box and a choice. Ten grand to disappear, or join Roger in whatever hell they'd cooked up for him. Outside, the sedan pulled away, engine purring like a well-fed cat.

Ten thousand dollars and a new life in another city, or Roger Talbot's fate at the hands of monsters who had been perfecting their cruelty for over a century.

I looked at the silver box in my hands and thought about Bill Kowalski's words: some battles couldn't be won, but somebody had to fight them.

Tomorrow night at the Observatory, I'd learn if I had what it took to fight monsters. Or if I'd end up like Roger —alive but wishing I wasn't.

Silver and Wolfsbane

The telephone rang at six-thirty in the morning, dragging me out of the first real sleep I'd had in three days. I'd spent the night in a Glendale flophouse, paying cash for a room that reeked of Lysol and broken dreams.

"Vance," I mumbled into the receiver, my voice thick with exhaustion.

"Ellie, it's Frank Miller. You need to get down here."

Miller didn't rattle easy, but he sounded shaken. Like somebody who'd just had his world turned inside out.

"Where's here?"

"Griffith Park. Near the observatory. We've got a body, and it's..." He paused, choosing his words with care. "It's not like anything I've seen in twenty-three years of police work."

Griffith Park. The same place where I was supposed to meet Roger Talbot's contact tonight, assuming the meeting wasn't the trap Edward Whitmore claimed it was. The coincidence twisted my stomach.

"What happened and what's the name of the victim?"

"Studio security guard named Walt Henley. Worked the night shift at Consolidated Pictures. Someone called in a report about screaming around three this morning, but by the time the patrol car got here, all they found was..." Miller's voice trailed off. "Just get down here, Ellie. And bring a strong stomach."

I dressed quickly and drove across the city as the sun painted the sky the color of dried blood. Morning L.A. looked clean and soft compared to the night city. But you could still feel the shadows underneath, waiting for dark.

Griffith Park spread across the hills like a green wound in the concrete. Usually full of families and kids playing ball. This morning it was swarming with cops, their red and blue lights making the trees look sick.

I found Miller standing beside a cluster of uniformed cops, all of whom looked like they'd rather be anywhere else. He was smoking a cigarette with the desperate focus of a man trying to wash a bad taste from his mouth.

"Jesus, Frank," I said, taking in his appearance. "You look like hell."

"Feel worse." He took a long drag and exhaled slowly. "Body's over there, behind those trees. Fair warning— this is going to stay with you for a while."

He led me down a path that wound through a grove of eucalyptus trees, their leaves rustling with a sound like whispered secrets. The morning air was cool and clean, filled with grass and flowers and growing things. But underneath was something else—the metallic smell of blood and the sour stench of death.

Walt Henley's body lay in a small clearing about fifty yards from the main path. What was left of it.

I'd seen plenty of death. Army nurse in the war, patching up GIs. Suicides in hotel rooms back home. But this was different. This was something that shouldn't exist.

The body had been torn apart with savage efficiency. Arms separated from torso, legs twisted at impossible angles, chest cavity opened like someone had been looking for something specific inside. But it wasn't the dismemberment that made my hands shake—it was the precision of it.

"Jesus Christ," I whispered.

"Coroner's preliminary assessment is wild animal attack," Miller said, his voice flat and professional. "Mountain lion, maybe a bear that wandered down from the mountains. That's what'll go in the papers." "But you don't believe it."

"Look at the wounds, Ellie. Look at them carefully."

I forced myself to examine the body more closely, fighting the urge to turn away and lose what little breakfast I'd managed to keep down. The wounds were too clean, too precise. Whatever did this had claws like razors and knew how to use them. Not random killing—this was planned.

"The cuts are too clean," I said. "And too precise."

"That's what I thought. Look at this." Miller pointed to the ground around the body. "See the footprints?"

I knelt down and studied the earth, still soft from the previous night's dew. Between the cops' boot prints were others—almost human, but wrong. Too long, too narrow. And those weren't toenails at the tips.

"Human feet," I said. "But not quite."

"Human feet that changed into something else," Miller said.

I stood up, brushing dirt from my knees and trying to keep my voice steady. "You're talking about a werewolf."

"I'm talking about evidence that don't make sense. Walt clocked out of Consolidated at midnight, came straight here. Car's parked by the observatory—he was meeting somebody."

"Any idea who?"

"That's what I was hoping you could tell me. Word is you've been asking questions about supernatural activities in this city. About organizations that might have... unusual members."

I thought about Edward Whitmore's pale eyes and sharp smile, about the silver box in my jacket pocket that contained my only protection against creatures that hunted in the darkness.

"Walt Henley worked at Consolidated Pictures?"

"Night security. Fifteen years on the job, clean record, no enemies that anyone can identify. The kind of guy who minded his own business and went home to his wife and kids every morning."

"Unless he saw something he wasn't supposed to see."

Miller nodded grimly. "That's my thinking. Walt was working the night shift when you broke into the studio.

Maybe he saw more than just one private investigator looking for answers."

"Maybe he saw who else was interested in Roger Talbot's office."

"Maybe he saw enough to become a problem."

I walked around the body, studying the scene from different angles. The attack had been vicious but not random —everything about it suggested planning, purpose, and abilities that normal humans didn't possess.

"Frank, what do you know about the Crescent Club?"

"Officially? It's a private gentlemen's society for business and civic leaders. Members include some of the most powerful men in Los Angeles—studio heads, city councilmen, federal judges." "Unofficially?"

Miller was quiet for a moment, studying the body at our feet. "Unofficially? Word is they do more than play cards and smoke cigars. Rumors about rituals, about appetites most people wouldn't understand." "What kind of appetites?"

"The kind that might explain how Walt Henley ended up torn apart in a public park." Miller dropped his cigarette and ground it under his heel. "Ellie, I'm going to ask you something, and I want a straight answer. How deep are you into this case?"

"Deep enough that people are trying to kill me to shut me up."

"And are you planning to let them?"

I thought about Edward Whitmore's offer—ten thousand dollars and a new life somewhere far from Los Angeles. About Roger Talbot, who was supposedly alive but broken, being educated about the realities of power by creatures that fed on fear and violence.

About Walt Henley, who'd probably been killed simply because he'd been in the wrong place at the wrong time, trying to do his job and provide for his family.

"No," I said. "I'm not going to let them."

Miller studied my face with the careful attention of a cop reading a suspect. "Then you need to know what you're up against. This isn't just about organized crime or political corruption. This is about things that hunt human beings for sport and have the power to cover up their activities."

"How long have you known?"

"About the supernatural angle? Since I found that vagrant's body three weeks ago—the one the papers said was killed by wild animals. Same wounds, same precision, same impossible footprints." Miller lit another cigarette. "About the Crescent Club's involvement? Since yesterday, when I started connecting names from Roger Talbot's research to the membership list of a gentlemen's society that meets during the full moon."

"Why haven't you done something about it?"

"What exactly would I do? Walk into the captain's office and tell him the city's elite are werewolves? Present evidence against men who play golf with the mayor and donate money to the police benevolent fund?"

I understood. Miller was a good cop in a bad spot. Even if he could prove what we both suspected, who'd believe him? And who'd risk going after the city's most powerful men?

"So what do we do?"

"We?" Miller gave me a look that was equal parts concern and respect. "Ellie, this isn't a 'we' situation. This is a

'you decide how much you're willing to risk to save a man who might already be beyond saving' situation." "Roger's still alive."

"According to who? Edward Whitmore? The same man who's probably responsible for Walt Henley's death?"

Miller had a point. I had only Whitmore's word that Roger was alive, and that word came from someone who'd just threatened to drive me insane if I didn't take his money and disappear.

But I also had the wolfsbane, and Bill Kowalski's conviction that somebody had to fight battles that couldn't be won. And I had Walt Henley's body as proof that the stakes were higher than I'd imagined.

"The meeting tonight at the observatory," I said. "It's a trap."

"Obviously. Question is, are you walking into it anyway?"

I looked at Walt Henley's remains, at the evidence of violence that went beyond human capability, at the footprints that told the story of something changing from man to monster while it killed. "Yeah," I said. "I think I am."

"Then you're either very brave or very stupid."

"Probably both."

Miller walked back toward the cluster of police cars, leaving me alone with the body and the morning light filtering through the eucalyptus trees. Walt Henley had been a security guard doing his job, a husband and father who'd gotten caught up in something that shouldn't exist in a rational world.

Now he was dead, torn apart by creatures that had been hiding in plain sight for decades, using their supernatural abilities to build fortunes and eliminate threats.

I thought about Roger Talbot, who'd tried to expose the truth and ended up broken by it. About Vivian Vanderbilt, caught between loyalty and survival. About the choice Edward Whitmore had offered me—ten thousand dollars or joining Roger in his educational program.

Smart thing was to take Whitmore's money and disappear before the next full moon. But Walt Henley was dead for being in the wrong place. He deserved better than being written off as an animal attack.

I reached into my jacket and felt the silver box with its pressed wolfsbane flower. Protection against creatures that hunted in the dark, according to Bill Kowalski. Insurance against monsters that had been perfecting their predatory skills for decades, according to Edward Whitmore.

Tonight at the Observatory, I'd learn what the wolfsbane was really worth. One P.I. with a gun and some dried flowers against monsters who'd been running this city for decades.

Long odds but Walt deserved better than being chalked up to wild animals.

PART TWO

THE SCENT OF BLOOD

Five Killer Footprints

No cops at Griffith Park when I returned later, but Walt Henley's outline was still there—white chalk against dark earth, already fading. The October wind through the eucalyptus trees carried their sharp medicinal smell and something else underneath—metallic, like old blood. Made my throat tighten.

Something had been bothering me about the crime scene since Miller walked me through it at dawn. The cops had been looking for evidence of a human killer using human weapons. I needed to look for something else entirely—claw marks in tree bark, footprints that didn't belong in any police manual, signs of predators that wouldn't show up in their reports.

Walt had died thirty feet off the main trail. Far enough that nobody would hear him scream. Close enough that somebody would find the body by morning.

Hit me all at once—this wasn't random. Walt had been killed in this exact spot on purpose, by something smart enough to know the body would be discovered at first light.

I dropped to one knee beside the chalk outline and studied the ground with battlefield eyes. The earth here held impressions like wet cement—every footprint, every drop of blood, every place where something heavy had pressed down hard. Miller had walked me through the obvious evidence yesterday: human shoe-prints that gradually became clawed pads as the killer transformed mid-attack.

But there was more.

Blood trail leading away from where Walt died. Small drops, not the obvious mess from the killing. Something had been bleeding when it walked away.

I followed the blood trail through the manzanita bushes, pushing aside branches heavy with morning dew. The drops were spaced about three feet apart, consistent with someone walking at a normal pace rather than running.

Someone confident they wouldn't be pursued.

The trail led downhill toward the park's eastern boundary, where Griffith Park butted up against the expensive neighborhoods of Los Feliz. After about fifty yards, the blood drops stopped at a small clearing surrounded by coastal live oaks.

And there, pressed into the mud beside a fallen log, was what Miller's boys had missed entirely.

One footprint. Clear as a photograph, preserved in the soft earth like evidence waiting for someone smart enough to look.

Not human. Not animal either. Something in between—too long, too narrow, with claws that bit deep into the mud.

But it was the other marks that made my blood turn to ice water.

Four more prints around the first one. Smaller, more human. Like they'd stood watching while their leader changed back.

I stared at those prints for a long time, feeling the October morning turn colder around me. This wasn't just one creature acting alone. Walt Henley had been killed by a pack.

The Crescent Club.

I thought about Edward Whitmore's pale blue eyes and cultured voice, about his casual threat to drive me insane if I didn't take his money and disappear. About Jack Rafferty's charming smile and his warnings about "powerful men with old secrets." About the photographs Detective Miller had shown me of Roger Talbot witnessing what looked like ritual murder.

They'd killed Walt Henley not because he was a threat, but because he was a message. A demonstration of what happened to people who got too close to their secrets. And they'd done it together, as a group, because that's what packs did.

I pulled out my notebook and sketched the arrangement of footprints, noting the measurements and positions as precisely as I could. This was evidence that could prove the supernatural connection—if I could find someone willing to believe it, and if I lived long enough to present it.

The sound of footsteps on the main trail made me look up sharply. A park ranger was walking toward my position, his uniform crisp and his expression carefully neutral. But something in the way he moved, the toostraight posture and the way his eyes never quite met mine, sent alarm bells ringing in my head.

"Morning, miss," he called out as he approached. "I'm going to have to ask you to move along. This area's been closed to the public pending investigation."

"What investigation?" I asked, closing my notebook and slipping it back into my jacket. "I thought the police finished up here yesterday."

"New developments," he said, still not meeting my eyes. "City wants a more thorough examination of the scene."

Something wrong with his face—too pale, like Whitmore's. Kept his hands behind his back, like he was hiding something. Like claws.

"I understand," I said, backing toward the trail. "Wouldn't want to interfere with official business."

The ranger nodded but didn't move to follow me. He stayed in the clearing, watching me retreat with eyes that reflected the morning light in a way that human eyes shouldn't.

Walked back to the trail, trying not to run. Heart pounding, expecting to hear footsteps—or something worse crashing through the brush behind me.

It wasn't until I reached my Plymouth and locked the doors that I allowed myself to breathe normally again. The ranger was still somewhere in the woods behind me, probably destroying the evidence I'd just discovered. But I had my sketches, and I had the knowledge that Walt Henley's murder was more orchestrated than anyone had realized.

The Crescent Club wasn't just covering up their secret. They were actively hunting anyone who threatened to expose them. Which meant Roger Talbot, if he was still alive, was living on borrowed time.

And so was I.

I started the Plymouth and pulled away from the curb, checking my rearview mirror for any sign of pursuit. The park ranger was nowhere to be seen, but I had the distinct feeling I was being watched from somewhere in the trees.

Two days until the full moon. Two days until whatever Edward Whitmore had planned reached its climax. I thought about his ultimatum—ten thousand dollars to disappear, or joining Roger in his "educational program." The smart money was still on taking the cash and running.

But Walt Henley's chalk outline was burned into my memory, along with the image of those five footprints arranged in their predatory circle. The Crescent Club had been hunting L.A. for decades. Built their fortunes on blood while the city looked the other way. Nobody expects monsters in thousand-dollar suits.

Someone had to stop them.

Driving through morning traffic, thinking about silver bullets and wolfsbane. About Walt dying for being in the wrong place. About Roger, broken for trying to tell the truth.

The Observatory meeting was still a trap. But Walt hadn't been random—he'd been a message. And I was listening.

The question was whether one private investigator with a .38 revolver and some dried flowers could do anything about creatures that had been perfecting their hunting skills since before Los Angeles was a city.

I pulled into a gas station on Vermont Avenue and used the pay phone to call Detective Miller.

"Miller."

"It's Ellie. I need you to meet me somewhere we can talk without being overheard."

"What did you find?"

"Evidence that Walt Henley wasn't killed by one creature. He was killed by a pack. And they're covering their tracks."

Silence on the other end of the line. Then: "How sure are you?"

"Sure enough to know that tonight's meeting at the Observatory isn't just a trap for me. It's the opening move in something bigger."

"Where do you want to meet?"

"Clifton's Cafeteria on Broadway. One hour."

"I'll be there."

I hung up the phone and walked back to the Plymouth, feeling the weight of the silver box in my jacket pocket.

Whatever the Crescent Club had planned for tonight, they were going to discover that some prey fought back.

Even when the odds were impossible.

Especially then.

Coffee and Corruption

Clifton's Cafeteria on Broadway was the kind of place where conversations got lost in the clatter of dishes and the steady hum of people minding their own business. Steam rose from serving trays behind the counter, mixing the smells of roast beef and coffee with cigarette smoke and the particular staleness that came from too many people sharing too little air.

I found Miller in a corner booth, coffee growing cold in front of him, studying a manila folder like his life depended on it. His jacket hung loose on his shoulders, and I noticed the slight bulge under his left arm where he'd started carrying his service revolver even off duty.

"You look like hell," he said as I slid into the seat across from him.

"Feel worse. What's in the folder?"

Miller glanced around the dining room, checking for ears that might be listening too close. A businessman in a rumpled suit was reading his newspaper three tables over. Two secretaries shared a late lunch near the window, discussing their weekend plans in voices that carried just enough to confirm they were talking about movies and men, not monsters. Satisfied we were anonymous among the lunch crowd, he opened the folder and spread out photographs.

"Missing persons reports. Forty-seven cases over the past five years. All unsolved. All following the same pattern."

I studied the photos. Men and women, various ages, but they shared something—a particular look of intelligence, ambition. People who asked questions and expected answers. A real estate developer who'd been investigating irregularities in Hollywood Hills property sales. A newspaper reporter who'd been working on a series about municipal corruption. A secretary from the mayor's office who'd apparently been asking too many questions about certain budget allocations.

"What pattern?"

"They all had contact with members of exclusive social clubs in the month before they disappeared. Private parties, business meetings, charity functions." Miller's finger traced connections between photos. "And they all vanished during lunar cycles."

"Full moons?"

"New moons, full moons, sometimes the quarters. But always during significant lunar phases." He pulled out a calendar marked with red X's. "Forty-seven disappearances. All timed to celestial events. Look at this one—"

He pointed to a photograph of a young woman with intelligent eyes and a determined expression. "Patricia Hensley, age 28, secretary at Paramount Pictures. Disappeared two months ago after attending what her roommate described as 'a very exclusive party in the Hills.' Her body was found three days later in Runyon

Canyon, torn apart by what the coroner officially ruled were 'wild animals.'"

"Like Walt."

"Exactly like Walt. Except Patricia's roommate mentioned something interesting. She said Patricia had been excited about meeting 'important people in the film industry' and that she'd been specifically invited because she was 'exactly what they were looking for.'"

I felt cold fingers walking up my spine. "They're selecting specific types."

"That's what I'm thinking. Look at the others—" Miller spread out more photographs. "All young, all attractive, all involved in industries where they might have access to information or influence. And all invited to exclusive social events before they disappeared."

I studied the faces, noting the similarities. These weren't random street crimes or crimes of opportunity. These people had been hunted as deliberately as deer during hunting season.

"Show me the lunar calendar again."

Miller unfolded the chart, and the pattern became clear immediately. The disappearances clustered around astronomical events—not just full moons, but new moons, eclipses, and what looked like seasonal celebrations. "It's ceremonial," I realized. "They're not just feeding. They're conducting some kind of ritual calendar."

I showed him my notebook sketch of the five footprints arranged around the central lycanthrope track. "It's not random hunting, Frank. It's organized predation."

Miller went very still looking at my drawing. "How many prints did you say?"

"Five total. One central print from the killer, four human witnesses arranged in a circle."

"Christ." He pulled out a photograph I hadn't seen before. "This was taken three months ago at Jack Rafferty's estate. Private party, very exclusive guest list."

The photo showed five men in expensive evening wear standing around a small stage. Even in the grainy blackand–white image, I could recognize the formation—a circle, with one figure at the center holding what looked like a ceremonial knife. "Same arrangement."

"Same pack structure. Alpha in the center, subordinates holding the perimeter." Miller's voice dropped lower.

"Ellie, these aren't just killers. They're conducting rituals."

"What kind of rituals?"

"The kind that require witnesses. The kind where everyone has to participate so nobody can walk away clean." He gathered the photographs. "Walt Henley wasn't killed because he was a threat. He was killed because they needed a sacrifice, and he happened to be available."

The implications hit like cold water. "Meaning they'll need another sacrifice soon."

"Tomorrow night. Full moon peak, lunar maximum." Miller checked his watch. "Which gives us about thirty hours to figure out how to stop them."

"Any ideas?"

"One. But you're not going to like it." He pulled out a business card with elegant script lettering.

"Vivian Vanderbilt - Private Social Consultant." Fancy words for what Miller was telling me.

"Social consultant?"

"Euphemism. She arranges introductions between wealthy men and women who provide... companionship... at exclusive gatherings." Miller's expression was grim. "She's been supplying girls to Crescent Club parties for the past two years."

My stomach clenched. "She's working with them."

"More than working with them. She's part of their operation. The parties where people disappear? Vivian Vanderbilt arranges the guest lists."

I thought about her perfect performance in my office, the tears that had seemed so genuine, the desperate story about Roger Talbot's disappearance. All of it carefully constructed to get me involved in whatever game they were playing.

"She hired me to fail."

"She hired you to walk into a trap." Miller leaned forward. "But three days ago, she stopped answering her phone. Whatever spooked her, it was big."

"What?"

"Maybe she found out what really happens to the people who disappear from those parties. Maybe she realized she wasn't just arranging social encounters—she was selecting victims."

I stared at the business card, thinking about Vivian's performance and wondering how much of it had been genuine fear versus calculated manipulation. But if Miller was right, if she'd recently discovered the truth about her role...

"She might cooperate."

"She might. If she's more afraid of them than she is of us." Miller stood and tossed coins on the table for the coffee. "But Ellie, if you're thinking of confronting her, be careful. People who work for monsters don't stay clean very long. Even if she wants to help now, she's got blood on her hands."

"Where are you going?"

"To follow up on some of these missing persons cases. See if I can find patterns that might tell us where they plan to strike next." He paused. "And to visit a priest I know who might have some unconventional ideas about dealing with supernatural threats."

"A priest?"

"My father mentioned him once. Said there were clergy who understood that evil sometimes wore faces other than human ones." Miller's expression was hard. "If we're going to war with monsters, we might need some divine assistance."

We parted company on the sidewalk outside Clifton's, Miller heading downtown toward the cathedral district, me walking toward my Plymouth with Vivian's business card burning in my pocket like evidence of my own stupidity.

The afternoon sun was already beginning its descent toward the western horizon, casting long shadows between the buildings on Broadway. Office workers were starting their early exodus from downtown, filling the sidewalks with the purposeful movement of people who had homes to go to and families who expected them for dinner. Normal people living normal lives, unaware that their city was controlled by creatures who saw humans as a renewable resource to be managed and harvested.

I sat in the Plymouth for several minutes, studying Vivian's business card and thinking about everything Miller had revealed. "Forty-seven missing persons over five years. They're not just hunting for food—they're hunting for what people know."

The smart move would be to stay away from Beachwood Drive, to avoid confronting a woman who might be more dangerous than she appeared. But Miller was right about one thing—if Vivian had recently discovered the truth about her role in the Crescent Club's activities, she might be the only person who could provide inside intelligence about their operations.

And if she'd been selecting victims for supernatural predators, she might know who was marked for tomorrow night's ritual. She might know enough to help us prevent it, or at least to understand what we were really fighting against.

I started the Plymouth and headed for the Hills, wondering if I was driving toward answers or straight into another trap. The radio played soft jazz as I navigated through traffic that was already starting to thicken with the evening commute, but the music couldn't drown out the echo of Miller's words about ritual patterns and ceremonial selections.

Downtown turned into neighborhoods, then the winding roads up to where the rich folks lived, high enough to pretend the rest of us didn't exist. Beachwood Drive curved through stands of eucalyptus and oak, past houses that grew larger and more isolated as the road climbed higher. I'd been in these neighborhoods before, on cases involving adultery and embezzlement and the kinds of sophisticated crimes that required expensive lawyers and quiet settlements. But those had been human problems with human solutions.

This was different.

Hard to escape when the things hunting you could afford better neighborhoods than their prey.

Vivian Vanderbilt's house number matched the address on her business card, and I slowed the Plymouth as I approached the property. Spanish Colonial architecture, red tile roof, white stucco walls that probably cost more than most people made in five years. The kind of place that whispered money from every carefully manicured detail.

But something was wrong with the picture.

The front gates hung open, which might have been normal during daylight hours. But there were no cars in the circular driveway, no sign of servants or gardeners or the kind of staff that houses like this usually required. The windows were dark despite the approaching evening, and the silence felt too complete, too deep—like a sound-stage between takes.

I parked on the street and walked through the open gates, noting details with the automatic caution that came from years of walking into situations where appearances could be deadly deceptions. The front door was unlocked, which either meant Vivian was expecting visitors or she'd stopped caring about security.

Both possibilities worried me.

The inside matched the outside—furniture that looked like it belonged in a museum, paintings worth more than my Plymouth, money that didn't need to shout because it knew you were listening. But it was the silence that made my skin crawl. Houses this size should have some kind of background noise—servants moving around, telephone conversations, radios playing in distant rooms.

Instead, there was nothing but the sound of my footsteps on marble floors and the whisper of air moving through rooms that felt abandoned.

I found her in what looked like the main sitting room, curled in a cream armchair that cost more than I made in six months. Blue silk robe, crystal glass, gin fumes that hit me from ten feet away. Her face looked like she'd aged ten years since walking into my office, and her hands shook as she lifted the glass to her lips.

Her eyes told the story—the hollow look people get when they find out the people they trusted have been lying all along. I'd seen that look before, in veterans who'd survived battles that officially never happened and witnesses who'd seen crimes that couldn't be prosecuted.

"Hello, Ellie." Voice steady, hands shaking. "Figured you'd show."

The greeting confirmed what Miller had suspected—this wasn't a surprise visit. She'd been waiting for me, probably since the moment she'd stopped taking calls from her Crescent Club contacts. Waiting for the confrontation that would determine whether she lived as a collaborator or died as a liability.

Empty gin bottles crowded the side table. Newspapers spread across the coffee table, headlines about missing people and bodies nobody could explain. And everywhere, the sense of a woman who'd run out of places to hide and was making her stand in the one place that had seemed safe.

Time to find out if Vivian Vanderbilt wanted to help stop the monsters, or if she was one of them.

The Starlet's Secret War

Vivian's house looked even worse in daylight—too quiet, too empty, like everyone had cleared out in a hurry.

The Spanish Colonial mansion still cost more than I'd make in ten lifetimes, but something was off.

I checked the property from my Plymouth. No gardeners. No help. Nobody moving behind those wrought-iron gates hanging open like an invitation.

The front door was unlocked.

She sat curled in a cream armchair that cost more than I made in six months. Blue silk robe, crystal glass, gin fumes at ten AM. Her face looked like she'd aged ten years since walking into my office. "Hello, Ellie. Figured you'd show up sooner or later."

"Did you."

"Ever since Walt died. Poor bastard never knew what hit him."

I didn't sit down. "Wrong place, wrong time?"

Bitter laugh. "Nothing's wrong place, wrong time anymore. Everything's right where it should be."

"Including hiring me."

"Especially that."

So I'd been right. Didn't make hearing it any easier.

"They told me to hire you."

"They told me Roger was safe. That you'd just ask a few questions and drop it. That nobody else would get hurt."

"Who's 'they,' Vivian?"

"You know who. Whitmore. Rafferty. The others you've probably met by now."

"The Crescent Club."

She flinched like I'd slapped her. "Don't. Not here."

"They listening?"

"Always listening." She took a long pull of gin. "Every deal in this town goes through them. They own the banks, the studios, the cops. And they think we're cattle."

I sat across from her. Close enough to see the fear, far enough to move fast. "Tell me about Roger."

"Roger was clean when I met him. Honest producer, trying to make pictures without studio money." She studied her gin. "Then the invitations started."

"What kind?"

"Parties for the right people. The kind that make careers in this town. Roger thought he was networking." "But it wasn't."

"They don't just hunt people, Ellie. They recruit them. Find guys with ambition, reel them in slow. Some go along with it once they know. Others end up dead."

"End up like Roger."

"Roger started asking questions six months ago. About things he'd seen at parties. Things that didn't make sense if everyone was human."

She was quiet for a long moment. When she spoke, her voice sounded empty.

"Roger saw Rafferty kill a man at a party. With his bare hands. The other guests just watched. Some helped clean up after."

"A murder."

"A feeding." Matter-of-fact. "They brought that man there to kill him. Roger realized he'd been watching executions dressed up as parties."

The room felt colder despite morning sun through the windows. I thought about the crime scene photos Miller had shown me, about Roger's terrified face watching something impossible.

"Why not go to police?"

Vivian's laugh was bitter. "Half the commissioners belong to them. The other half know better than to ask about midnight parties in the Hills."

"So he tried to get out."

"Tried to expose them." She finished her gin in one swallow. "Started documenting everything—names, dates, money connections. Thought if he could prove what they were, somebody would listen." "They found out."

"They always find out." Her hands shook harder. "They've controlled this city for decades, Ellie. Maybe longer.

They know when someone starts asking dangerous questions."

"Is Roger dead?"

The question hung between us. Vivian stared at her empty glass, that movie-star composure finally cracking.

"Don't know." Voice broke. "They took him three weeks ago. Said he was being educated about betrayal. Said he'd come back when he learned to keep quiet."

"You don't believe that."

Tears started down her cheeks, ruining makeup that cost more than most people made in a month. "They don't return people, Ellie. They eliminate problems. Roger was a problem."

"Then why hire me?"

"Because they told me to." She wiped her eyes with the back of her hand. "They wanted somebody investigating, but somebody they could control. Someone who'd ask the right questions and find the wrong answers."

I stood and walked to the window. Manicured gardens, expensive cars. Beautiful, perfect, normal. The kind of neighborhood where monsters wore three-piece suits and went to charity functions.

"Until I found the right answers."

"Until you found Walt's body and realized what you were really dealing with." Something like respect mixed with terror in her look. "They underestimated you. Thought you'd take their money and disappear when things got complicated."

I pulled out my notebook and showed her the footprint sketch. "Five of them killed Walt. A pack."

She went white looking at the drawing. "The inner circle. Whitmore, Rafferty, plus the three founding members."

"Founding members?"

"Built Hollywood from orange groves. Running this city sixty years." "Names?"

Vivian's hands trembled pouring another gin. "Marcus Grayson. Theodore Ashworth. Harrison Blackwood. Came to Los Angeles in 1891, started buying property all over the valley. By 1903, they controlled enough to establish the club."

"Still alive?"

"Lycanthropy extends natural lifespan. They're each over eighty, look fifty. Move like men half their age." She pointed to a society page photo on the side table. "That's from last month's charity gala."

I picked up the photo. Three distinguished older men in tuxedos, standing with Hollywood royalty at some glittering function. They looked prosperous, respected, human.

"Sixty years of killing people."

"Longer. Native tribes have stories about shapeshifters in the mountains, creatures that hunted during certain lunar cycles. When these families arrived, they brought their own supernatural problems."

Vivian stood and walked to an ornate desk against the far wall. She pulled out a manila folder thick with documents and photos.

"Roger wasn't just documenting recent stuff. He was researching the club's entire history, trying to prove they were behind decades of disappearances."

She handed me the folder. Inside were newspaper clippings from the 1890s, police reports, even what looked like mission records from the Spanish colonial period. All documenting attacks blamed on wild animals, mysterious disappearances, unexplained violence following lunar patterns.

"Roger spent months in archives, libraries, newspaper morgues. Built a case going back fifty years." Vivian's voice got stronger, like sharing the burden helped her think clearly. "Found connections between the founding members and every major development in LA history."

I flipped through the documents. This wasn't random killing—this was organized predation spanning generations.

"They've been shaping the city's growth to serve their needs. Every major business deal, every political appointment, every piece of infrastructure—all designed to give them better hunting grounds and more control."

"Why they couldn't let Roger expose them. Wasn't just about protecting current activities. It was about protecting sixty years of city planning."

Vivian nodded, tears still flowing but voice steadier. "When Roger realized the scope of what they'd built, he knew he couldn't walk away. Too many people had died. Too many more would die if somebody didn't stop them."

"So he tried to be that somebody."

"And look where it got him." She gestured around the expensive room. "Three weeks ago, they came here. Told me Roger had been taken into protective custody while they decided his fate. Said I could help decide what happened to him by cooperating with their investigation management."

"Investigation management?"

"Hire a PI who'd ask predictable questions and reach acceptable conclusions. Someone they could monitor and control." Vivian met my eyes. "Someone they could eliminate quietly when the investigation reached its endpoint."

I closed the folder and studied her face. "But you're telling me anyway."

"Because Walt's dead, and it's my fault. Because I helped them set you up, and now you're going to die like Roger did."

"Maybe."

"There's no maybe, Ellie. These aren't men playing at monsters. These are monsters pretending to be men.

They've been hunting in this city since before it had a name."

I picked up the society photo again and studied the three founding members. Distinguished, respectable, the kind of men whose words carried weight in boardrooms and backrooms.

"Tell me about their gathering places."

"The club meets monthly at different locations. Private estates, exclusive restaurants, sometimes rented halls." Vivian sat back down hard. "But their main base is Marcus Grayson's estate in the Hollywood Hills. Isolated, heavily secured, perfect for activities they can't do in public."

"What activities?"

"Recruitment ceremonies. Punishment sessions for pack discipline. And..." She stopped.

"And what?"

"Processing." Barely audible. "When they decide someone knows too much to live but might have useful information first. They don't just kill threats. They break them down piece by piece, extract everything they need, then dispose of the remains."

Gin and morning light couldn't warm the chill in my bones. "That what they're doing to Roger?"

"I think so. Edward Whitmore specializes in psychological conditioning. Breaking resistance, extracting information, ensuring compliance." Vivian's voice went mechanical, like emotional distance was the only way she could discuss it. "Roger's been in his hands three weeks. Whitmore's very good at his job."

"How do you know all this?"

"They told me." She looked up with those hollow eyes. "They wanted me to understand what would happen if I didn't cooperate. Described Roger's situation in detail, made sure I knew they could do the same to me."

"But you're risking it anyway."

"Because you're going to die, and Roger's going to die, and they'll keep killing people another sixty years if somebody doesn't fight back." Vivian stood with new determination. "I can't save Roger. But maybe I can help you save the next person they target."

I studied her face. The fear was still there, but underneath was anger. And underneath that was steel that Hollywood stardom probably required.

"What are you proposing?"

"I know their schedules. Meeting locations. Security arrangements." She walked back to the desk and pulled out another folder. "Roger wasn't the only one documenting their activities. I've been watching them for months, trying to find some way to get him back."

"What did you find?"

"Their weaknesses. Times and places where they're vulnerable. When they meet in small groups instead of the full pack. When their security's focused elsewhere." She handed me the folder. "Everything I've learned about their operations."

Inside were detailed notes on Crescent Club activities, maps of properties, even what looked like guard schedules and patrol patterns. This wasn't documentation of a helpless victim—this was intelligence gathering by someone planning an assault.

"Vivian, this is military-grade reconnaissance."

"Roger wasn't the only one who learned things during the war. I spent three years entertaining troops, visiting bases, watching how things worked." Pride in her voice now instead of fear. "I learned how to watch, how to notice patterns. Roger taught me how to document what I saw."

"Why didn't you act on this?"

"Because I'm one person with a .32 and no experience killing supernatural predators. I needed help, but didn't know who to trust." She met my eyes. "Until yesterday, when I realized you'd survived encounters that should have killed you." "I got lucky."

"Luck doesn't account for Walt's crime scene. You found evidence police missed. You identified pack hunting. You recognized supernatural predation." Vivian's voice was stronger, more focused. "That's not luck. That's skills applied to an impossible situation."

I looked through her intelligence files. Weeks of careful observation and documentation. Guard rotations, meeting schedules, property layouts, even psychological profiles of individual members.

"This is good work, Vivian. Really good."

"It's a start. But it needs someone who knows how to use it." She pulled out a city map marked with red pins.

"These are confirmed club properties. These are suspected ones. And these..." She pointed to pins in the

Hollywood Hills. "These are where they conduct their most sensitive activities."

"Including where they're holding Roger?"

"I think so. Grayson's estate has basement facilities that don't appear on public records. Underground levels that could hold prisoners without neighbors hearing anything."

I studied the map, noting the isolation of the Hills properties and defensive advantages they provided. "What about their full moon activities?"

"Tomorrow night. They always gather for the lunar peak, but the location rotates. This month..." She checked a handwritten calendar. "This month it's supposed to be Jack Rafferty's estate in Laurel Canyon." "Supposed to be?"

"They may have changed locations after realizing you've been investigating. But I have contacts in the catering industry who handle their events. If they've moved the gathering, I can find out where."

The scope of her preparation was impressive. This wasn't amateur hour—Vivian had been conducting a detailed intelligence operation.

"You've been planning to go after them yourself."

"Planning to try. But I know the odds." She looked at the gun cabinet across the room. "Roger left me some guns, showed me how to use them. But silver bullets are expensive, and I don't have connections for specialized ammunition."

"I might know someone who does."

"The bookstore owner? Alistair Finch?" At my surprised look, she smiled grimly. "I told you I've been watching them. That includes their enemies. Finch's father investigated the club decades ago, got killed for it. Finch has been continuing that investigation ever since."

"You've been surveilling everyone involved."

"Everyone I could identify. You, Finch, Detective Miller, even Mickey Grasso's operations. I needed to understand all the moving pieces before deciding how to act."

Morning sun had climbed higher, throwing different shadows through the windows. Vivian's living room felt like a command center now instead of a place where a broken woman waited to die.

"What do you know about Miller?"

"Honest cop in a corrupted system. His father was a beat cop in the twenties who suspected supernatural activities but never had proof. Miller inherited both the suspicion and some kind of insurance policy." She pulled out a surveillance photo of Miller entering a downtown jewelry shop. "He's been visiting Goldstein & Sons regularly, always carrying small packages."

"Silver."

"That's my guess. Building an arsenal slowly, same as his father probably did." Vivian's intelligence network was more detailed than

I'd imagined. "He's also been visiting the public library, researching the same historical documents Roger was studying."

"So we have allies."

"We have people fighting the same enemy, but not coordinating their efforts. That's why they're picking us off individually instead of facing united opposition."

I closed the intelligence files and studied Vivian's face. The gin-soaked despair from earlier had been replaced by tactical focus. This was what she'd been hiding beneath the grieving starlet performance.

"What are you proposing?"

"Coordination. Pool our resources, share intelligence, plan operations together instead of stumbling around separately." She walked to the window and looked out at her manicured gardens. "They've spent sixty years building their power base. We have maybe forty-eight hours before they eliminate all the loose ends permanently."

"Why forty-eight hours?"

"Because tomorrow night's full moon gathering isn't just their monthly meeting. According to Roger's research, it's when they initiate new members and eliminate threats permanently. They've been planning something special for months."

Hit me all at once. "A mass elimination."

"Everyone who knows too much. Everyone who's asked dangerous questions. Everyone who's survived encounters they shouldn't have." Vivian turned from the window. "Roger will be there. You'll be there, one way or another. Probably Miller and Finch too."

"As victims or observers?"

"As examples. Public demonstrations of what happens to people who challenge their authority."

I thought about Whitmore's ultimatum, about his certainty I'd attend the Observatory meeting despite knowing it was a trap. Not because I was stupid, but because they'd make sure I had no choice.

"How do we coordinate?"

"Start by not splitting up. They're stronger when we're isolated, weaker when we work together." Vivian moved to the gun cabinet and pulled out a key. "Roger left me more than just guns."

Inside the cabinet were two rifles, a shotgun, several handguns, and boxes of ammunition. But also something else—silver jewelry, coins, even what looked like silver bars.

"Roger was preparing for war?"

"Roger was preparing to do whatever it took to stop them. He liquidated most of his assets and converted them to silver, thinking he might need specialized weapons." She hefted one of the silver bars. "There's enough raw material here to cast forty or fifty bullets."

"You've been sitting on an armory."

"Been waiting for someone who knew how to use it. Someone with experience fighting impossible odds and winning."

I picked up one of the handguns—a .45 automatic in good condition. Military issue, probably war surplus.

"Roger's gun?"

"Roger's backup gun. He carried a .38 for daily use, kept this for serious trouble." Vivian's smile was sad but determined. "He always said if monsters were real, you needed to be ready for monsters."

The weight of the .45 felt familiar in my hands. Good balance, well-maintained, the kind of weapon that could stop a charging bull or a supernatural predator.

"So what's our next move?"

"Visit your bookstore expert together. Pool our intelligence with his research, then coordinate with Detective Miller." Vivian was already moving toward the stairs. "Give me ten minutes to change into something more practical than a silk robe."

"Vivian."

She paused on the staircase. "Yes?"

"Why didn't you tell me all this when you first hired me?"

Her expression was complex—part guilt, part calculation, part genuine regret. "Because I wasn't sure you could handle the truth. And because I wasn't sure I could trust you not to make things worse."

"And now?"

"Now I'm sure we're all going to die if we don't work together. And I'm sure you're the kind of person who fights instead of runs, even when the odds are impossible."

She disappeared upstairs, leaving me alone with enough firepower to outfit a small army and intelligence files that could bring down a supernatural conspiracy spanning decades.

I walked back to the window and looked out at Los Angeles spread across the basin below. Millions of people going about their morning routines, unaware that their city's fate was being decided by a PI, a broken starlet, and maybe a few other people crazy enough to fight monsters.

The smart money was still on taking Whitmore's cash and catching the first train out of California.

But Vivian was right about one thing—I was the kind of person who fought instead of ran, even when the odds were impossible.

Time to show the Crescent Club what happened when they underestimated people with nothing left to lose and everything necessary to win.

When Vivian came back downstairs, she was wearing dark slacks, a practical jacket, and the kind of determined expression that had probably gotten her through three years of war work.

"Ready?"

She picked up Roger's .45 and checked the action. Smooth, reliable, loaded with regular ammunition but ready for silver when the time came. The weight of it seemed to steady her hands.

"Let's go educate some monsters about the price of underestimating their prey."

We walked out into Los Angeles morning sun, partners in a war that had been going on for sixty years and was finally about to reach its conclusion.

One way or another.

Silver Bullets and Hard Choices

Finch's Rare Books sat on Spring Street like a fortress built from old paper and stubborn knowledge, its windows so dusty you couldn't tell if anybody was home. The kind of place you had to know existed to find it.

Vivian parked her Packard behind my Plymouth. "You sure about this guy?"

"He's the only expert we've got." I adjusted my .38 Special in its holster. "Besides, you wanted coordination. This is how we pool resources."

Door chimes announced us into a maze of shelves packed with books older than California statehood. The air smelled of leather bindings, old paper, and something else—herbs that belonged in somebody's garden, not a bookstore.

"Miss Vance." Alistair Finch emerged from behind a stack of books that might have contained the secrets of the universe. Thin, scholarly, wire-rim glasses that had seen decades of close reading. "Figured you'd be back."

"Mr. Finch, this is Vivian Vanderbilt. She hired me to find Roger Talbot."

Finch studied Vivian with the careful attention of a man who'd learned to read trouble. "The woman who's been watching my place for the past month."

Vivian didn't flinch. "Among other places. I needed to know who Roger's enemies were before I decided who his friends might be."

"And?"

"Your father died trying to protect this city from the same things that took Roger. You've been continuing his work." She pulled out one of her intelligence folders. "I know about the founding members. Their feeding schedule, their properties. What I need to know is how to kill them."

Finch adjusted his glasses and looked between us. "You're planning to fight them."

"We're planning to end them." I set Vivian's weapons inventory on his counter. "Two rifles, shotgun, six handguns, forty pounds of pure silver. Plus whatever specialized ammunition you can provide."

"This isn't some romantic adventure, Miss Vance. These creatures have been perfecting predation longer than Los Angeles has been a city." Finch moved to a cabinet that didn't belong in any normal bookstore. "But if you're set on this course, there are rules."

He opened the cabinet to reveal the kind of collection that belonged in somebody's private war against supernatural creatures—silver bullets, wooden stakes, glass vials filled with dried herbs, and books bound in materials I didn't want to think about.

"First rule: silver's got to be pure. Ninety-nine percent minimum. Anything less might wound them, won't kill them. They heal from regular injuries in minutes, but silver stops that cold."

Vivian leaned forward. "How much per kill?"

"One bullet, placed right. Heart or brain. Anything else just makes them mad." Finch pulled out a tray of bullets that gleamed like mirrors. "I keep a supply for emergencies, but forty pounds of raw silver could arm a small war."

I picked up one of the bullets. Heavier than lead, perfectly balanced. "How long you been preparing?"

"Forty years. Since they killed my father." Quiet determination in his voice. "Benjamin Finch was investigating disappearances in Griffith Park when the Crescent Club decided he knew too much. Made it look like a wild animal attack, but he'd taught me to recognize pack killing." "What else?" Vivian asked.

"Tomorrow night's your best shot. Full moon makes them strongest, but also dumbest. The transformation goes involuntary, uncontrolled. They lose human smarts, fight like animals instead of generals."

Finch moved to another section of his arsenal and pulled out glass vials filled with what looked like dried weeds.

"Wolfsbane causes disorientation, temporary paralysis. Won't kill them, buys you escape time. Mountain ash works similar. Running water screws up their tracking—streams, rivers, even big pipes with water flowing." "Pack behavior?" I asked.

"Hierarchical. Marcus Grayson's the alpha, top dog. Kill him, others lose coordination temporarily. But they'll fight harder to protect him, so he'll be the most heavily guarded."

Vivian spread her property maps on Finch's counter. "My surveillance shows they're gathering tomorrow night at Jack Rafferty's estate in Laurel Canyon. Isolated, hard to reach, perfect for business they can't do in public."

Finch studied the maps with professional interest. "How many?"

"Forty, maybe fifty. Full membership plus help and guards." Vivian pointed to guard positions she'd documented. "Not all of them are werewolves. Some are human collaborators—easier to kill but more expendable to the pack leaders."

"Fifty against two?" Finch shook his head. "This is suicide, even with proper weapons."

"Three," I corrected. "You're coming with us."

"Miss Vance, I'm a sixty-year-old bookstore owner. I do research, not gunfights."

Vivian pulled out another folder, showed him crime scene photos. "Walt Henley. Sal Benedetto. A dozen others this past year. How many more die while you do research?"

Finch examined the photographs with the careful attention of a man who'd seen similar work before. "They're escalating. Moving from isolated kills to public displays."

"Because they're getting ready to stop hiding," I said. "Roger's research shows they've been building toward something for months. Tomorrow night isn't just their monthly feeding. It's when they eliminate all remaining threats and take control permanently."

"Mass elimination of witnesses and enemies." Finch set down the photos. "They've done this before, other cities. When they decide an area's become too dangerous for covert operations." "Other cities?" Vivian asked.

"San Francisco, 1906. Most people remember the earthquake and fire. They don't remember the unexplained deaths in the weeks before, when certain business leaders and politicians disappeared." Finch moved to his father's research files. "Chicago, 1919. Detroit, 1925. Same pattern—build control gradually, then eliminate threats in one coordinated action."

"How do we break it?"

"Attack first. During the full moon, when they're least rational and most vulnerable." Finch opened a medical diagram that looked like it belonged in a textbook for hunting supernatural predators. "Silver disrupts their transformation. A wounded werewolf trapped between human and wolf form is in agony and can't fight effectively."

I studied the diagrams. "Where do we aim?"

"Center mass first—disrupts the transformation. Then head or heart for the kill. Don't waste shots on arms and legs unless you're trying to disable for escape."

Vivian was taking notes like she was planning a military campaign. "Coordinated pack attacks?"

"They hunt like wolves—flanking moves, coordinated strikes, one drives prey toward others. But unlike wolves, they keep human intelligence and can use tools and weapons." Finch pulled out tactical diagrams his father had created. "Benjamin documented their hunting patterns over months of observation."

"How do we counter that?"

"High ground, make them come at you from where you can see them coming." Finch studied Vivian's maps.

"Rafferty's place is in a canyon. Two roads in, nowhere else to go. Set up right, you could pick them off." "Unless they come cross-country," Vivian pointed out.

"Then you need early warning. Tripwires, noise makers, anything that alerts you to movement in the brush." Finch was warming to the tactical discussion, his bookish manner shifting toward something more practical.

"My father designed several detection methods."

Back of the store looked like a gunsmith's shop crossed with a chemist's lab. Bullet molds, silver bars, bottles of chemicals I couldn't name. And stuff that definitely wasn't standard—contraptions with wires and dials that hummed when he turned them on.

"You've been preparing for war," I said.

"I've been preparing to finish what my father started." Finch picked up a device that looked like a modified radio. "This thing can tell when they're changing. Works about half a mile out. Won't give you much time, but it's better than walking in blind."

Vivian examined the equipment with professional interest. "How accurate?"

"Works most of the time. Sometimes picks up thunderstorms or big metal things, but nothing sounds like them changing."

"We'll take it." She turned to me. "Along with everything else he's got."

I looked around the workshop, calculating resources. "How much ammunition can you cast from forty pounds of silver?"

"Two hundred rounds, various calibers. Enough for a sustained battle if your shooting's accurate." Finch was already moving toward the casting equipment. "But it takes time. Eight hours minimum for proper cooling and finishing."

"We've got time. The gathering isn't until tomorrow night."

"Then we start now." Finch fired up the furnace. "Miss Vanderbilt, your silver's going to become the means of this city's liberation."

Vivian smiled grimly. "Roger would've liked that."

We spent the afternoon melting silver and casting bullets. Hot work, but precise. Every bullet perfect, because we wouldn't get a second chance.

As evening approached and the last batch of bullets cooled in their molds, Finch pulled out his father's final research notes.

"Full moon makes them crazy. More animal, less human. They'll charge straight at you instead of thinking it through."

"That helps us," Vivian said.

"Also makes them stupid dangerous. Smart werewolf runs when he's beat. Crazy werewolf keeps coming till you put him down."

I checked the action on one of the newly loaded weapons. Silver bullets in every chamber, backup ammunition distributed among all of us. "Then we better not miss."

Finch handed me a leather bag packed with supplies. "Wolfsbane, mountain ash, the detector. Everything my father thought might help."

"My father knew everything about these things. Thirty years of research. But he went after them alone, and they killed him for it."

"We're not alone."

"No. And that might be enough to tip the balance." Finch looked out his window at Los Angeles evening, lights beginning to twinkle across the basin. "They've run this city for sixty years, but they've never had anybody shoot back with the right ammunition."

Vivian shouldered her rifle and checked the silver bullet count one final time. "Time to show them what organized opposition looks like."

We left as the sun was setting, three people with a bag full of silver bullets and the guts to use them. Tomorrow night, the Crescent Club was planning a party. We were planning to crash it.

How to Kill a Monster

The next morning found us back at Finch's store, but this time it felt different. Less like desperate consultation, more like a war council. The silver bullets we'd cast the night before lay arranged on his counter in neat rows— two hundred rounds of death waiting to be loaded.

Vivian showed up carrying coffee and pastries from down the street, looking more like a military officer than a grieving starlet. "Got word from my catering contact. Rafferty's estate is confirmed for tomorrow night, eight PM."

She set down her intelligence folders next to the ammunition. "But there's trouble. They've increased security— hired shooters from Mickey Grasso's crew."

I picked up one of the silver bullets, feeling its weight. "Human collaborators."

"Expendable ones," Finch corrected, emerging from his workshop with coffee that smelled like it could raise the dead. "They'll put the humans on the perimeter, keep the werewolves safe inside."

"Smart move," Vivian said, spreading out updated property maps. "Human guards can use regular weapons, night vision, radio communications. The werewolves stay clean, keep their hands off the dirty work if anything goes sideways."

Finch poured coffee into three chipped mugs and settled behind his counter. "Which brings us to what we're facing tomorrow night."

He pulled out his father's most detailed research—journals bound in cracked leather, filled with observations that had gotten Benjamin Finch killed.

"The transformation takes about ninety seconds. Heart rate spikes, body temperature jumps fifteen degrees, muscle mass increases forty percent. Looks painful as hell." "Can they control it?" Vivian asked.

"Experienced ones can transform at will, but it costs them. They prefer to save voluntary changes for hunting, intimidation, or when human strength isn't enough."

I leaned forward. "What about tomorrow night?"

"Full moon makes it involuntary and complete. No choice, no holding back." Finch opened to a section filled with his father's urgent handwriting. "This is from his final months, when he knew they were onto him. Pack behavior, hierarchy, who runs the show."

The careful script described a world that followed predator rules:

Pack structure mirrors wolf behavior, not human society. Marcus Grayson commands absolute authority as alpha. Theodore Ashworth and Harrison Blackwood serve as lieutenants, commanding newer recruits like Rafferty and Whitmore. Leadership challenges get settled through combat, usually during full moon gatherings when transformation is involuntary.

"They fight each other?" Vivian asked.

"Regularly. Maintains pack order, determines who leads next." Finch pointed to another entry. "My father witnessed three dominance battles during his infiltration. Two resulted in serious injuries, one in death." "They kill their own people?"

"When they need to. These things are predators, Miss Vanderbilt. They work together because it's smart, not because they care about each other."

Made sense now. "Roger's alive proof they screw up. Can't have that getting around."

"Exactly. Let him survive, and it suggests weakness in their selection process. Other potential recruits might think they can betray the organization without consequences."

Finch closed that journal and selected another volume, this one bound in snakeskin. "The lunar cycle affects them profoundly, though not like the movies suggest. They can transform anytime, but the full moon makes it involuntary and more complete."

"More complete how?"

"During voluntary transformation, they retain most human intelligence. Can make tactical decisions, communicate with pack members, even speak somewhat. But during the full moon, animal consciousness dominates completely." He showed us sketches comparing the two states—drawings that captured something essential about controlled versus uncontrolled lycanthropy. "Full moon strips away human strategic thinking.

They become pure predators, operating on instinct and pack dynamics."

Vivian studied the drawings with professional interest. "So tomorrow night they'll be stronger but dumber?"

"Stronger, faster, more aggressive, but operating on pure predator instinct instead of human strategy. More dangerous in terms of raw physical capability, but less sophisticated in hunting methods." "Gives us advantages and disadvantages," I said.

"Right. They'll be at peak physical condition but minimum tactical thinking. If you can survive the initial assault, you might outmaneuver them using superior strategy."

Outside, Los Angeles was waking up—people heading to work, living normal lives. They had no idea three people in a dusty bookstore were planning to save their asses.

"Tell me about their physical capabilities," Vivian said, taking notes like she was preparing a military briefing.

Finch moved to another cabinet and pulled out what looked like a medical textbook, but one devoted to subjects no medical school would teach.

"Full transformation, they're about three times stronger than a man. Jump fifteen feet straight up, twenty across. Bite hard enough to snap bones like dry twigs." "Speed?" I asked.

"Forty miles per hour in short bursts, twenty-five sustained over distance. In human form, they're still significantly faster and stronger than normal people, just not to supernatural degrees." He flipped to a section on sensory capabilities that read like military intelligence.

"Enhanced hearing can detect heartbeats at fifty yards, footsteps at twice that distance. Night vision is excellent but not perfect—they need some ambient light. Most importantly, their sense of smell can track individual scents over considerable distances and time periods." "How long?" Vivian asked.

"Days, if conditions are right. They can follow a trail that's forty-eight hours old, distinguish between individual humans by scent alone, even track someone through crowded urban environments by filtering out background odors."

The tactical implications were sobering. "So once they have our scent..."

"They can find you anywhere in Los Angeles, given time and motivation." Finch closed the book and looked at both of us seriously. "Which is why tomorrow night has to end decisively. Wound them without killing them, escape without eliminating the threat permanently, they will hunt you until one side is dead." "What about their healing?" Vivian asked.

"Accelerated but not miraculous. Minor wounds heal in hours, major injuries in days. However, they can die from blood loss, organ damage, or catastrophic trauma same as humans—just takes more damage to achieve lethality."

Finch pulled out another locked cabinet and revealed samples of different metals, each labeled with precise percentages and test results.

"Silver disrupts lycanthrope cellular regeneration. Pure silver contact causes immediate, intense pain. Prolonged exposure kills tissue. Enough in their bloodstream shuts down their enhanced healing entirely."

He handed me a silver blade that caught the morning light. "Purity matters. Sterling silver hurts them but won't finish the job. You need the pure stuff—99.9 percent—to put them down for good."

The bullets we'd cast gleamed on the counter. "These came from melted silver dollars, refined to remove impurities. Each one carries enough pure silver to kill if it hits vital organs." "How many vital areas?" Vivian asked.

"Same as humans in transformed state. Heart, brain, major arteries. Difference is their enhanced healing means you need to cause catastrophic damage quickly—they can survive wounds that would kill normal people if given time to regenerate."

Finch returned the knife to its case and locked the cabinet. "There are other weaknesses, though less reliable than silver."

"Such as?"

"Running water disrupts their scent tracking and causes disorientation. Not fatal, but can buy escape time if you're being pursued." He pulled out vials of dried herbs. "Wolfsbane causes temporary paralysis and severe pain. Mountain ash has similar effects. Not lethal, but useful for creating opportunities." "What about pack coordination?" I asked.

"This is where their intelligence becomes crucial. In human form, they coordinate like military units—radio communications, tactical planning, coordinated attacks. During full moon transformation, they lose the technology but retain pack hunting instincts."

Finch opened his father's tactical observations, pages covered with diagrams showing werewolf hunting patterns.

"Hunt in groups of three to five. One chases you toward the others waiting to cut you off. They don't need to talk—they just know."

"How do we counter that?" Vivian asked.

"High ground, make them come at you from where you can see them coming." Finch studied Vivian's maps.

"Rafferty's place is in a canyon. Two roads in, nowhere else to go. Set up right, you could pick them off." "Unless they come at us from multiple directions simultaneously," I pointed out.

"Which is why you need early warning systems and fallback positions." Finch moved to his detection equipment. "The electromagnetic detector will give you about sixty seconds warning when they begin mass transformation. Not much time, but enough to prepare for contact."

"What's our ammunition situation?" Vivian asked, examining the rows of silver bullets.

"Two hundred rounds across various calibers. Your rifles pack enough punch to drop one if you hit right. Ellie's .38 won't reach as far, but it's easier to move with."

I checked my weapon, ensuring the cylinder was loaded with silver rounds. "How many shots do we realistically get before they close distance?"

"Depends on range and terrain. At one hundred yards with good visibility, maybe ten to fifteen shots per rifle before they reach your position. At fifty yards, perhaps five or six. Closer than that, you're fighting hand-tohand."

"Hand-to-hand against creatures three times stronger than normal humans," Vivian said grimly.

"Which is why accuracy matters more than rate of fire. Every shot has to count." Finch handed us additional equipment—silver-tipped blades, wolfsbane powder, even what looked like silver wire. "Close-quarters weapons for emergency use."

The reality of what we were planning began to sink in. Three people armed with experimental weapons against forty supernatural predators in their natural environment during their period of maximum strength.

"You realize this is probably suicide," Vivian said.

"Probably," I agreed. "But the alternative is letting them eliminate everyone who knows the truth, then continue hunting in this city for another sixty years."

"More than that," Finch added. "My father's research suggests they're approaching critical mass. Within five years, they'll have enough numbers and resources to abandon secrecy entirely."

"Meaning what?"

"Open hunting. No more hiding. Rule by fear instead of backroom deals. Los Angeles would be the first, but not the last."

The scope of the threat extended far beyond Roger Talbot's disappearance or even our personal survival. This was about preventing a fundamental change in how human civilization operated.

"There's something else about tomorrow night," Finch said. "Full moon affects them psychologically as well as physically. They become more aggressive, less cautious, driven by hunting instincts rather than strategic thinking."

"That helps us," Vivian said.

"Also makes them crazy dangerous. Smart one runs when he's losing. Crazy one keeps coming till somebody's dead."

I checked the silver bullets in my .38 one more time. Six rounds, each one the difference between survival and death. "Then we better make sure they're the ones who die."

"Miss Vance," Finch handed me a leather bandolier filled with additional silver ammunition. "My father knew everything about these things. Thirty years of research. But he went after them alone, and they killed him for it." "We're not alone."

"No. And that might be enough." He looked out his window at Los Angeles spread across the basin, millions of people going about their daily lives. "They've run this city for sixty years, but they've never had anybody shoot back with the right ammunition."

Vivian shouldered her rifle and checked the scope alignment. "Time to find out if organized opposition is enough."

"One more thing," Finch said as we prepared to leave. "If something goes wrong tomorrow night, if the situation becomes untenable, remember that your primary objective isn't killing all of them. It's surviving long enough to expose them publicly."

"How?"

"Photographs, evidence, documentation that can't be dismissed or covered up. If you can't destroy them militarily, destroy them politically by forcing them into the open."

Vivian patted her camera bag. "Already planned for."

We left Finch's store armed with two hundred silver bullets, detailed intelligence on werewolf capabilities and weaknesses, and a plan that balanced desperate necessity with calculated risk. Tomorrow night, the Crescent Club would gather for what they expected to be a celebration of their final victory over Los Angeles.

Instead, they were going to find out what happened when prey fought back with the right ammunition and nothing left to lose.

Tomorrow night, we'd see who was really at the top of the food chain.

Blood in the Streets

The call came at six in the morning, jerking me out of a dream where things that used to be human were chasing me through the Hollywood Hills.

"We got another one," Miller's voice carried the weight of a man who'd seen too much death in too short a time.

"Griffith Park, near the observatory road. You need to get down here."

I was dressed and driving before I was fully awake, my .38 Special loaded with silver rounds. The morning air was cool and sharp, carrying eucalyptus and something else—something that made my skin crawl.

By the time I reached the crime scene, the area was wrapped in yellow tape and crawling with cops, photographers, and coroner's assistants who looked like they'd rather be anywhere else. Miller was standing near a cluster of oak trees, smoking what looked like his third cigarette judging by the butts at his feet.

"What've we got?" I asked, showing my license to the uniform guarding the perimeter.

"Sal Benedetto," Miller said. "One of Mickey Grasso's boys. The one who tried to muscle you outside your office."

Hit me like cold water. Sal Benedetto—the thick-necked enforcer who'd made it clear that Mickey Grasso wanted me to drop the Vanderbilt case. The guy who'd threatened to break my fingers if I kept asking inconvenient questions.

"When?"

"Jogger found the body at five-thirty this morning. Coroner says time of death between midnight and two AM."

Miller crushed his cigarette under his heel. "Ellie, this one's bad. Worse than Walt."

I followed him through the trees toward a clearing that looked like a nightmare. What had once been Sal Benedetto was now spread across fifty yards of parkland like somebody's sick idea of confetti.

"How long did this take?" I asked Peterson, the LAPD photographer who'd been documenting crime scenes for fifteen years.

"Based on blood spatter and the way things are... distributed, at least twenty minutes." Peterson wiped sweat from his forehead despite the cool air. "They weren't just killing him. They were having fun."

Different from Walt's murder entirely. Walt had been killed quick, efficient—single predator making a clean kill.

This was something else. This was a pack showing what happened to people who became problems.

Miller led me to an oak tree near the edge of the killing ground and pointed to something carved into the bark.

Four parallel claw marks gouged deep, same as Walt's scene.

But underneath the claw marks was something new: letters scratched in with what looked like human fingernails. E.V.

My initials.

"They left you a message," Miller said, lighting another cigarette with hands that weren't quite steady. "Question is, what you going to do about it?"

I stared at those letters, carved by something that wanted me to know exactly who'd killed Sal Benedetto. The Crescent Club wasn't just cleaning house—they were rubbing my nose in it.

"Timeline doesn't work, Frank. Last night I was at Finch's place until eight, learning about bloodlines and silver bullets. By midnight I was home loading my .38."

"So?"

"While I was getting ready to fight monsters, the monsters were hunting the guys who'd tried to muscle me for them." I walked around the crime scene, studying the evidence. "Sal worked for Mickey Grasso. Grasso's been bankrolling the Club for years. Why kill one of his boys?"

Miller lit fresh tobacco and studied the scene with twenty years of cop instincts. "Maybe Sal knew too much.

Saw something he shouldn't. Or maybe they're cleaning house before the main event."

Made sense. Sal had braced me on Grasso's orders, and Grasso took orders from the Club. Sal knew about my investigation, knew about the pressure to make me disappear. He'd become a problem.

"Where's Tony Marconi?"

"Good question. Been trying to find him since we identified Benedetto. Hasn't been seen since yesterday afternoon."

I had a feeling Tony Marconi's absence wasn't voluntary. If the Crescent Club was eliminating loose ends, they wouldn't leave Sal's partner alive to discuss their methods.

"What about Mickey Grasso?"

"Holed up in his compound in Beverly Hills with a dozen bodyguards. Scared out of his mind, according to my contacts. Word is some of his business associates were having personnel problems."

Miller walked over to examine something the coroner's assistant was photographing—a section of ground where the grass had been torn up.

"Ellie, look at this."

The torn earth showed the same footprint progression I'd seen at Walt's crime scene: human shoe impressions that gradually became clawed pads as the killer transformed during the attack. But there were more prints this time, at least five different attackers.

The entire Crescent Club inner circle had participated in Sal Benedetto's murder.

"They're not even trying to hide it anymore," I said.

"Why should they? There's not a judge in Los Angeles who would issue warrants against Marcus Grayson or Theodore Ashworth based on footprint evidence. And even if there was, what prosecutor would take the case?"

Miller was right. The Crescent Club had spent sixty years building influence throughout the city's power structure. They owned judges, prosecutors, police commissioners. They could kill with impunity because the system was designed to protect them.

"There's something else," Miller continued. "The attack pattern here's different from Walt's murder."

"Different how?"

"Walt was killed quick, efficient. Single attacker, minimal struggle, clean termination. This—" He gestured at the blood-soaked clearing. "Pack kill. They wanted to make an example." Made sense with what Finch had told us about how they work.

"They wanted Sal to suffer. Wanted him to know exactly why he was dying."

"And they wanted anyone who found the body to understand what happens to people who work against them." Miller pointed to something I'd missed—a piece of paper pinned to the oak tree with what looked like a six-inch claw.

I unfolded it carefully. It was a surveillance photograph of me walking out of Finch's bookstore, Vivian beside me, our arms full of weapons and ammunition. The photo was stamped with yesterday's date.

"They've been watching us since we visited Finch," I said.

"Watching and planning. This whole thing was orchestrated to send a message." Miller studied the photograph. "They know about your alliance with Miss Vanderbilt. They know about the silver bullets. They know you're preparing for war."

If they'd been watching since yesterday, they knew everything. The weapons, the plans, where we were going tomorrow night.

"We've been outmaneuvered from the beginning."

"Maybe. Or maybe they're getting sloppy because they think they've already won." Miller pocketed the photograph. "Either way, we need to warn Miss Vanderbilt. If they're eliminating loose ends, she's next on the list."

I was already moving toward my Plymouth when Miller called out.

"Ellie, there's one more thing."

He led me to where the coroner was preparing to remove what remained of Sal Benedetto. In the dead man's jacket pocket was something that made my blood freeze—a business card for my investigator's license, covered in blood but still legible.

"They planted it." Miller lit a cigarette. "Means they didn't just kill Sal on impulse. They've been planning this."

"Which means?"

"Tomorrow night's gathering isn't just their monthly feeding. It's the end of a long-term plan to eliminate every threat to their operation." Miller looked around the crime scene, taking in the calculated brutality. "Sal was just the appetizer."

I thought about Vivian, probably still asleep in her Beachwood Drive mansion, unaware that creatures running Los Angeles since before she was born had marked her for death. I thought about Finch, surrounded by his books and his father's research, believing that knowledge and silver bullets would be enough to win a war against apex predators.

And I thought about Roger Talbot, wherever they were keeping him, knowing that his attempt to expose the truth had set all of this in motion.

"Frank, I need to ask you something, and I need you to tell me the truth."

"Shoot."

"Do you really believe we can win this?"

Miller was quiet for a long moment, studying the carnage around us. When he spoke, his voice carried the weight of a man who'd spent twenty years watching the system fail the people it was supposed to protect.

"Seventeen people have died on my watch in the past month because monsters decided to stop pretending to be human. Walt, Sal, probably Tony Marconi, and a dozen others whose deaths got written off as gang violence or wild animal attacks."

He crushed his cigarette and looked me in the eye.

"I've been a cop twenty years, Ellie. Seen corruption, brutality, stupidity, cowardice. But I've never seen anything like this—an entire power structure designed to enable supernatural predators to hunt human beings for sport."

"That's not an answer."

"Because if we don't, they keep hunting. They keep killing. And Los Angeles stays theirs." Miller's jaw tightened. "I'm not okay with that. Are you?"

I looked around the crime scene one more time, taking in the evidence of what happened when ordinary people tried to work within a system controlled by monsters. Sal Benedetto hadn't been a good man, but he'd died screaming because he'd been caught in the machinery of something larger and more vicious than human corruption.

"No. I'm not willing to accept that."

"Then we better get moving. If they know about your weapons cache and your alliance with Miss Vanderbilt, they'll be making their move soon."

We left Griffith Park as the morning sun climbed higher over Los Angeles, two people who'd seen too much death and were preparing to see more. Behind us, crime scene techs continued documenting evidence that would never be used in any courtroom, building a case that no prosecutor would ever file.

They'd been hunting us for sixty years. Now we were hunting them.

I drove straight to Vivian's house, my Plymouth pushing through morning traffic that seemed oblivious to the carnage in the hills above them. People heading to work, kids walking to school, ordinary citizens living ordinary lives while supernatural predators decided which of them would die next.

Vivian answered the door in a silk robe, looking like she'd slept about as well as I had.

"You look like hell," she said.

"Sal's dead. They took their time with him. Left my initials carved in a tree and a photo of us from yesterday."

Her composure cracked. "They know about the weapons."

"They know about everything. The silver bullets, our alliance, probably our plan for tomorrow night." I followed her into the living room where Roger's arsenal was still spread across her coffee table. "We've been playing their game by their rules since the beginning."

Vivian poured gin despite the early hour, her hands shaking slightly. "So what do we do?" "We change the rules."

She looked up at me with eyes that had seen too much grief and were preparing to see more. "How?"

"By accepting we're probably not walking away from this." I picked up a silver bullet. "They want us dead tomorrow night? Fine. But we're taking some of them with us."

"As what?"

"As the people who burn their whole operation to the ground, even if we die doing it."

Vivian lifted her glass. "Roger would've wanted this."

We spent the morning changing the plan. No more sneaking around. Hit them hard, make sure people see what they really are. If we couldn't survive the confrontation, we'd at least ensure that the Crescent Club's existence became undeniable.

By noon, the plan had changed. We weren't sneaking in any-more—we were kicking the door down. They'd been running Los Angeles for sixty years. Time somebody punched back.

Full Moon Rising

The day of the full moon started wrong and got worse.

By noon, Los Angeles felt like a powder keg looking for a match. Three shootings before breakfast, two bank robberies by lunch, and a street fight outside Grauman's that took six cops to break up. The emergency frequencies crackled with reports of domestic disturbances, bar fights, and what the dispatchers called "unusual aggressive behavior" throughout the basin.

"It's them," Vivian said, standing at her window with coffee that had gone cold hours ago. "The full moon affects more than werewolves. Makes everyone more aggressive, more violent. They've been feeding off this city's energy for nearly sixty years."

I was cleaning my .38 Special for the third time that morning, checking each silver bullet. Nervous energy needing somewhere to go.

"How do you know?"

"Roger's research. He documented the correlation between lunar cycles and crime statistics going back to 1903." She pulled out one of his files, pages covered with charts and graphs. "Every full moon, violent crime spikes thirty percent. Emergency room admissions double. The whole city goes a little crazy." "And tonight?"

"Tonight's different. This isn't just any full moon—it's the harvest moon, when the lunar influence is strongest.

Roger's notes suggest they've been planning this particular gathering for months."

The files painted a picture of systematic manipulation spanning decades. The Crescent Club hadn't just been hunting randomly—they'd been cultivating Los Angeles like a farmer tends crops, shaping the city's growth to maximize feeding opportunities while maintaining cover for their kills.

"They're not just predators," I said, studying Roger's documentation. "They're ranchers. We're the cattle."

"Which is why tonight has to end them permanently." Vivian moved away from the window and began checking her rifle for the tenth time. "If we don't stop them now, they'll have enough power to abandon secrecy entirely."

Finch arrived at two PM carrying a leather satchel that clinked with metal. "Additional supplies," he said.

"Wolfsbane, mountain ash, silver wire. Also this."

He pulled out a device that looked like a military radio crossed with a direction finder. "Electromagnetic field detector, modified to register werewolf transformation signatures. Range about half a mile."

"Will it work?" Vivian asked.

"My father's notes suggest it should. Transformation generates a distinctive electromagnetic pulse—something about rapid cellular restructuring." Finch adjusted dials on the device. "Won't tell us exactly where they are, but it'll warn us when the changing begins."

We spent the afternoon going over our revised plan, accepting that stealth was finished. The surveillance photo from Sal's murder meant they knew we were coming. Our only advantage was that they expected victims, not soldiers.

"The gathering starts at sundown," Vivian said, spreading her property maps across the coffee table. "But the real ceremony won't begin until the moon's fully risen. That gives us maybe two hours to get into position."

"What about the human guards?" Finch asked.

"They'll be on the perimeter, probably armed with regular weapons. Once the transformation begins, they'll either run or try to help their supernatural employers." I marked guard positions on Vivian's map. "Either way, they're not our main problem."

"Our main problem," Vivian said quietly, "is that there are forty of them and three of us."

"Two hundred silver bullets," Finch corrected. "If our shooting's accurate, that's enough ammunition to kill every werewolf in California."

I checked my .38 one more time, feeling the weight of the silver rounds. Six shots before I'd need to reload. In a firefight against supernatural predators with enhanced speed and strength, six shots might not be enough time to breathe, much less win.

"What happens if one of us doesn't make it?" Vivian asked.

Nobody had wanted to say it, but there it was.

"If I go down," I said, "you take the evidence to every newspaper in Los Angeles. Photos, documents, Roger's research. Force them to publish the truth."

"If I don't survive," Finch added, "my bookstore contains forty years of research on werewolf activities. It's all documented, catalogued, ready for the right person to continue the work."

Vivian was quiet for a long moment, staring at the intelligence files that had consumed her life for the past month. "If something happens to me, make sure Roger knows I tried to save him. That's all I want—for him to know I didn't abandon him."

As the sun began its descent toward the Pacific, we loaded our weapons and prepared for what might be the last night of our lives. The city's aggressive energy was building to a crescendo—sirens wailing in the distance, radio reports of violence escalating throughout the basin.

At six PM, we left Vivian's house and headed for the Hills. Three people with a bag full of silver bullets and the guts to use them.

The moon was already up, fat and silver in the eastern sky, climbing higher.

Rafferty's place spread across ten acres of Hollywood Hills—Spanish Colonial mansion, gardens big enough to hide an army. Money and power in every carefully trimmed hedge.

I parked my Plymouth behind eucalyptus trees two hundred yards from the main gate, close enough to observe but far enough to avoid immediate detection. Vivian had positioned herself on higher ground with her rifle and field glasses, while Finch waited in his Ford at the canyon mouth with the radio equipment and our escape route.

Finch's detector sat quiet on the seat next to me. When they started changing, it would tell us.

I checked my watch: seven-fifteen. Fifteen minutes until the first guests were scheduled to arrive.

The radio crackled. Vivian's voice: "I'm in position. Got eyes on the whole place."

I keyed the microphone. "Any movement?"

"Kitchen staff moving around inside. Caterers setting up in the garden. Looks like a legitimate party so far." Her voice carried tension despite the professional tone. "How's your position?"

Through my field glasses, I could see torches, tables, a string quartet setting up. Looked like a society party.

Which is exactly what they wanted it to look like.

"Good concealment, clear sight lines to the main garden. Finch, you copy?"

Finch's voice came through with static interference. "Canyon mouth is secure. Escape route confirmed.

Electromagnetic detector shows baseline readings citywide." The first guests started arriving at seven-thirty.

Black Cadillacs and silver Packards wound up the canyon road in a steady stream, their headlights cutting through the gathering dusk. I recognized some of the license plates from Vivian's surveillance notes—studio executives, bank presidents, city council members. The cream of Los Angeles society arriving for what the invitation probably called a charity function or business dinner.

Each arrival followed the same pattern: expensive cars, well-dressed occupants, brief conversations with what looked like valet parking. But something felt wrong about the rhythm of it. Too choreographed. Too precise.

"I'm in position. Count twenty vehicles so far. Passengers moving toward the garden in groups of three to five.

Very organized for a social gathering."

I adjusted my field glasses and focused on the arriving guests. Evening wear that probably cost more than I made in six months. Jewelry that caught the torchlight like captured stars. The kind of people whose names appeared in newspaper society columns.

But their movements were wrong.

Even from two hundred yards out, something looked wrong. They moved too careful, too alert. Not like people at a party. Like hunters checking territory.

"Notice anything unusual about their behavior?"

"Copy that. They're not mingling like normal party guests. Groups of three to five, spread out across the garden, each group watching a different direction. Like soldiers playing dress-up."

By eight PM, at least forty vehicles were parked in the circular drive. The garden was filled with guests in expensive evening wear, champagne glasses catching torchlight, the kind of sophisticated gathering that graced society pages.

But instead of the random social mixing you'd expect at any normal party, the crowd had arranged itself in precise patterns. Groups of three to five people positioned at regular intervals throughout the garden, each commanding clear sight lines to the surrounding area.

It looked like a military formation disguised as a cocktail party.

Marcus Grayson emerged from the mansion at eight-fifteen, wearing a white dinner jacket that made him look distinguished and civilized. But his bearing was that of a commanding officer reviewing troops before battle.

When he raised his hand, the murmur of conversation stopped immediately.

Every head snapped toward him at once. Like they'd been waiting for orders.

"My friends," his voice carried clearly across the canyon despite its conversational tone, "tonight we celebrate not just the lunar cycle, but our dominion over this city and everyone in it."

I adjusted the field glasses and focused on his face. Even at two hundred yards, I could see the change in his expression. The cultured businessman was gone, replaced by something ancient and predatory.

"For nearly sixty years we have built Los Angeles according to our vision, shaped its development to serve our needs, eliminated those who threatened to expose our methods. Tonight marks the beginning of the final phase."

Other figures moved to stand beside him—Theodore Ashworth with his silver hair gleaming in the torchlight, Harrison Blackwood moving with the fluid grace of a much younger man. The founding members of the Crescent Club, apex predators who'd been hunting in this city since before it had a name.

"Are you getting this?"

"Copy. I can hear him clearly from up here. Ellie, there are more people arriving. Service vehicles approaching from the back road."

I swung my field glasses toward the rear of the property and saw what she meant. Three black panel trucks winding up a service road that didn't appear on any of our maps. No lights, moving carefully through the darkness.

"Finch, you monitoring radio traffic?"

"Police frequencies show increased activity citywide, but nothing focused on this area. Whatever those trucks contain, it's not triggering official response."

The trucks disappeared behind the mansion, but I could see figures moving in the shadows near what looked like service entrances. Too dark and too distant to make out details, but their movements had the same controlled precision as the party guests.

"We no longer need to hide," Grayson continued, his voice carrying new authority. "We no longer need to pretend. Los Angeles belongs to us, and it's time everyone understood that truth."

A murmur of excitement rippled through the crowd. Forty of the city's most powerful figures nodding in agreement, raising their glasses in a toast to abandoning the pretense of humanity.

At eight-twenty, the moon cleared the mountains.

It hung in the eastern sky like a silver searchlight, bright enough to throw shadows across the garden. Beautiful and terrible, ancient and immediate. The kind of moon that had inspired fear since humans first looked up at night.

The change in the gathering was immediate.

Conversations stopped. Heads turned upward with synchronized precision. Even from my hiding spot, I could feel something building in the air—an electromagnetic tension that made my skin crawl and my teeth ache.

The detector beside me began clicking softly, its needles starting to dance.

The Beast Revealed

The clicking from the electromagnetic detector grew faster, needles jumping as something fundamental began to change in the air itself. Even from two hundred yards away, I could feel the buildup—like moments before a thunderstorm when the atmosphere gets charged. "You feeling this?"

"Copy. Something's happening up here. The air tastes different. Metallic." Vivian's voice carried new tension.

"My hair's standing on end like I'm next to a power line."

Through my field glasses, I watched the party guests react to the rising moon. What had started as synchronized attention was becoming something else. Their postures were changing—spines straightening, shoulders broadening, heads tilting at angles that looked wrong for human necks.

The detector's clicking accelerated, needles now dancing wildly across their gauges.

"Eleanor Vance!" Grayson's voice cut through the night air like a blade. "I know you're out there, watching us. Why don't you join the party?"

Blood turned to ice water. He was looking directly at my hiding spot, his eyes reflecting the moonlight like mirrors. At two hundred yards, in near darkness, with me concealed behind eucalyptus trees.

No human could have spotted me.

"You've been quite the hunter, hunting for us," he continued, his voice carrying impossible distances without amplification. "Asking questions, gathering intelligence, preparing for war. But you've been playing by human rules, and we stopped being human long before your grandparents were born."

I keyed the radio with shaking fingers. "He knows I'm here."

"We see it," Vivian replied. "They're all turning toward your position. Get ready to move."

The electromagnetic detector was clicking faster now, needles jumping into the red zone. Around the garden, something was beginning that defied everything I thought I knew about the natural world.

It started subtle—guests adjusting their evening wear as if their clothes had become uncomfortable. Women reaching up to touch their faces as if checking makeup that suddenly didn't fit right. Men rolling their shoulders as if their dinner jackets had shrunk.

Within seconds, the changes were accelerating.

A woman near the fountain gasped and doubled over, her champagne glass shattering on the flagstone. Her companions didn't rush to help—they stepped back, giving her space as if this was expected, routine.

Her spine was extending.

Through the field glasses, I could see her elegant black dress stretching and tearing as her torso lengthened. Her face was changing shape, features becoming more angular, more predatory. When she straightened up, she stood eight inches taller than she had moments before.

She wasn't the only one.

Throughout the garden, forty of Los Angeles' most powerful figures were undergoing the same impossible transformation. Evening gowns and dinner jackets splitting at the seams as bodies expanded. Elegant hairstyles becoming wild manes. Manicured fingernails extending into claws.

"Jesus Christ," Finch's voice crackled through the radio static. "The readings are off the charts. Like a power station exploding."

"You see, Miss Vance," Grayson's voice was deeper now, rougher, carrying an undertone that belonged to something no longer human. "We've been expecting you. The surveillance photos, the murdered muscle man with your business card, the dramatic rescue attempt you're planning—we know everything."

His own transformation was the most disturbing to watch. Unlike the others, who seemed to be struggling with the change, Grayson appeared to be embracing it. His white dinner jacket hung in tatters as his chest and shoulders expanded, but his face showed no pain—only anticipation.

"You need to get out of there now," Vivian's voice was sharp with urgency. "I can see shapes moving through the brush toward your position. They're flanking you."

I started the Plymouth's engine, knowing stealth was finished. Around the garden, forty supernatural predators were completing their transformation into creatures that could outrun my car and tear through steel.

The woman by the fountain had completed her change. What stood there now was something between human and wolf—upright but wrong, familiar but alien. Her evening dress hung in shreds, but she showed no embarrassment. Instead, she lifted her head and tested the night air with senses no human possessed.

She was scenting for prey.

"In fact," Grayson continued, his words now carrying the growling undertone of something no longer human, "we've been counting on it. You see, a public hunt is exactly what we need to announce our new relationship with Los Angeles."

His transformation was nearly complete now. The distinguished businessman was gone, replaced by something that retained human intelligence but possessed the physical attributes of an apex predator. When he smiled, his teeth had become weapons.

The other founding members flanked him—Theodore Ashworth and Harrison Blackwood, both completing their own metamorphosis into creatures that Hollywood's monster makers couldn't have imagined. They moved with liquid grace, their formal wear hanging in tatters, their faces showing the satisfaction of predators preparing to hunt.

The detector was screaming now, needles buried in the red zone and vibrating with electromagnetic overload. Through the field glasses, I could see the full scope of what we were facing.

Forty werewolves stood in the garden, some still completing their transformation, others already moving with inhuman speed and coordination. They weren't the mindless beasts of folklore—I could see intelligence in their movements, strategy in their positioning.

They were surrounding me.

"They spotted me. Getting out of here."

"Negative," Vivian replied. "I count at least a dozen shapes moving through the canyon between you and the exit. They've cut off your primary escape route."

"Finch, status on the canyon mouth?"

"Three vehicles just passed my position heading up the road. No lights, moving fast. They're sealing the trap."

Through my mirrors, I could see eyes reflecting the moonlight from the brush beside the road. Yellow-green gleams that moved too fast and too coordinated to be anything natural.

The pack was converging.

Grayson raised his hands—which had become something between human and paw—and the murmur that passed through the crowd was no longer human speech. It was communication, but not in any language humans had ever spoken.

Pack coordination.

"My friends," he said, his voice now a controlled growl that somehow remained articulated, "tonight we demonstrate what this city truly is. Not a human settlement that tolerates our presence, but our territory that permits humans to exist within it."

They moved like soldiers. Some blocked the exits, others came for me. Fast and smart.

"Too long have we hidden our nature," Grayson continued. "Too long have we pretended to be bound by human law, human morality, human weakness. Tonight, we hunt openly. Tonight, we feed publicly. Tonight, Los

Angeles learns who really rules this basin."

The howling started. Low, terrible sound that echoed off the canyon walls. Came from everywhere.

Made my skin crawl. Something deep down knew that sound meant death.

"They're not just transforming. They're organizing. I can see them positioning around the entire canyon. This isn't a party—it's a military operation."

The howling stopped as suddenly as it had begun, leaving silence that felt more ominous than the sound had been.

"Eleanor Vance," Grayson called, his voice now carrying impossible distances. "You've seen what we are. You understand what we're capable of. But you've also given us exactly what we needed—a reason to stop hiding."

Movement in my peripheral vision made me turn. Three shapes were approaching through the brush, moving with the fluid coordination of born hunters. Even in the darkness, I could see their outlines—too large for humans, too intelligent for animals.

"Nice work, detective. Too bad it won't save you."

More shapes appeared in my mirrors. The road behind me was no longer an escape route—it was a kill zone with predators positioned at every turn.

"But circumstances are what they are. And circumstances dictate that you serve a different purpose tonight." His laugh carried notes that human throats couldn't produce. "You will be our announcement to Los Angeles that the age of human dominion is over."

The detector was screaming. Sparks shot from the case, then it died.

I threw the car into reverse and began backing down the canyon road, headlights off, trying to navigate by moonlight and memory. In my mirrors, I could see shapes flowing through the darkness like liquid shadow, moving faster than any car could travel on winding mountain roads.

"I count about twenty shapes moving toward your position from the north. Another fifteen coming from the south. They're boxing you in."

"Finch, I need that escape route clear!"

"Working on it. But Ellie—there are more of them than we planned for. A lot more."

Through the field glasses, which I was now using to navigate backwards down the twisting road, I could see the full scope of the gathering. What we'd thought was a monthly meeting of forty werewolves was something far more organized and extensive.

This was a military muster.

Vehicles that hadn't been there during my initial surveillance were now visible throughout the estate grounds. The service trucks I'd seen earlier had disgorged passengers—dozens of additional figures who had completed their own transformations and were now joining the hunt.

We hadn't stumbled onto a feeding gathering. We'd discovered the beginning of an invasion.

"My friends," Grayson's voice echoed across the canyon, "the hunt begins. Show Los Angeles what it means to be prey."

The howling started again, but this time it came from everywhere—the estate, the canyon walls, the brush around my fleeing car. Dozens of voices joined in supernatural chorus, announcing to anyone within miles that the apex predators were no longer hiding.

I reached the first switchback and spun the wheel, tires screaming on asphalt as the Plymouth slid through the turn. In my mirrors, eyes reflected the moonlight—not just from the brush beside the road, but from the road itself.

They were keeping pace.

Running alongside my car at thirty miles per hour as if it were a gentle jog.

But I didn't need instruments to know what was happening. I could feel it in my bones, taste it in the air, see it in the impossible coordination of predators that retained human intelligence while possessing supernatural capabilities.

The hunt had begun.

Canyon of Death

"**M**ove!" Vivian shouted as shapes poured from the hills. Dozens of them.

I gunned the Plymouth, tires shrieking as we shot down the narrow canyon road between Jack Rafferty's estate and Sunset Boulevard. In the mirror, werewolves poured over the estate's walls—forty monsters moving faster than anything had a right to.

"How many silver bullets do we have?" Vivian braced herself against the dashboard as I took the first switchback at sixty miles per hour.

"Six in my .38, maybe thirty or so more in the box." The Plymouth's back end slid sideways, tires fighting for grip. "You?"

"Full magazine in the rifle, plus two spare clips." She rolled down her window and leaned out, scanning the ridgeline above us. "They're not just chasing—they're herding. Look at the pattern."

She was right. Some followed behind us, others took the high ground. They were herding us into a trap.

"Ashworth!" Vivian pointed left. "Big bastard with the silver streak!"

A second werewolf appeared on our right, keeping pace despite the Plymouth's speed. Then a third, and a fourth. They moved like liquid shadow, covering ground with bounds that should have been impossible even for supernatural creatures.

I downshifted and floored it, engine roaring as we pulled ahead. Too many of them, too fast. And we were stuck on the road.

"Finch, you copy?" Vivian spoke into the radio handset while keeping her rifle trained on the canyon walls.

Static, then his voice: "Copy. I see your position. Multiple contacts moving on you from everywhere." "How many?"

"The whole damn pack. They're all coming."

Which meant this wasn't just a chase—it was an execution. The Crescent Club had decided Eleanor Vance and her allies were too dangerous to live.

"Left side!" Vivian's rifle cracked. Through my window, I saw a werewolf drop.

But two more took his place, and now they were close enough that I could see their eyes—human smarts in animal faces, calculating hunters who knew exactly what they were doing.

One of them—Harrison Blackwood, judging by his size—launched himself at our windshield. I yanked the wheel right, sending the Plymouth into a skid that threw him wide. He landed, rolled, came up running without missing a step.

"Damn smart bastards," Vivian muttered, working the bolt.

The next werewolf came from the passenger side, timing its leap to intersect our trajectory at the worst possible moment. Vivian put two rounds center mass as it flew through the air, dropping it into the road behind us where it became a speed bump for the pack members following on foot.

"Ammunition count?"

"Rifle's at seven rounds. You?"

"Haven't shot yet." I checked my .38 Special. "Saving them for close work."

"This isn't bad enough?"

Ashworth hit the hood, cracked the windshield. Claws on steel, yellow eyes staring at me.

"Hold on!" I hit the brakes hard, sending the Plymouth nose-diving. Should have launched Ashworth into the canyon. Instead, he flowed like water, claws finding new holds, getting ready to punch through the windshield.

Vivian's rifle spoke twice, bullets punching through the hood inches from Ashworth's torso. He snarled and swung at her through the passenger side window, claws raking across her cheek and drawing blood.

"Goddamn it!" She worked the bolt, ejected spent brass, chambered a new round. "Slippery bastard!"

I swerved, trying to shake him. He held on, getting ready to punch through the glass. Behind us, the rest of the pack had closed to thirty yards and was gaining fast.

"Duck!" I emptied my .38 through the windshield.

Glass exploded outward, and Ashworth's grip failed. He tumbled into the darkness, leaving claw marks in the hood and the stink of cordite and werewolf blood.

"Reload!" Vivian shouted, her own rifle speaking as fast as she could work the bolt. "Three more coming up the left side!"

I fumbled with the speed-loader, hands shaking from adrenaline and the Plymouth's shaking as we hit more switchbacks. The canyon was getting steeper, the road nastier, and our pursuers smarter every minute. "There!" Vivian pointed ahead where the road curved around granite. "Ambush. They've got werewolves in the rocks."

She was right. I could see shapes moving among the boulders—pack members who'd taken the high ground while we were dealing with the pursuit from behind. They were going to hit us from three directions at once, in a kill zone where the Plymouth's speed advantage would be meaningless.

"Hold on to something."

I yanked the wheel left and gunned it, sending the Plymouth off-road and down a steep slope. Vivian's rifle flew against the ceiling as we bounced over rocks and brush, the undercarriage screaming against granite.

"Are you insane?" she shouted over the noise.

"Probably!"

We hit the bottom of the embankment doing forty, all four wheels leaving the ground for a terrifying moment before slamming back down on what might generously be called a fire road. The Plymouth's suspension groaned, but held, and suddenly we were paralleling the main canyon road fifty feet below the werewolf ambush.

"That actually worked," Vivian said, checking her rifle for damage.

"Don't sound so surprised."

But our win was temporary. The pack was already adapting, some jumping down to our level while others kept the high ground. And ahead, where this fire road rejoined the main route, I could see more shapes setting up another ambush.

"How much farther to Sunset?" Vivian asked.

"Two miles, maybe three."

"At this rate, we'll never make it. Too many bodies, too much coordination." She ejected her magazine, checked what was left. "Four rounds, plus one spare clip." "Then we better not miss."

The fire road climbed again, switchbacking up the canyon wall toward what I hoped was Laurel Canyon Drive. But the werewolves had figured this out too—they flowed up the hillsides, cutting off every escape route with military precision.

"Jack Rafferty, two o'clock high," Vivian called out, tracking movement among the scrub oak.

Her rifle cracked, and Rafferty stumbled but kept moving. Even at this range, silver had found him, but not deep enough.

"Tough son of a bitch," she muttered, working the bolt.

"Save the ammo. We're going to need every shot."

Even as I said it, I could see we were boxed in on three sides, with only the steepest canyon drop-off left as an escape route. And that wasn't escape—it was a hundred-foot fall onto granite that would kill us as sure as werewolf claws.

"Vivian, there's something I need to tell you—"

"Save it for when we're not about to die."

"That's exactly when you're supposed to say it."

She looked at me, rifle braced against her shoulder, blood from Ashworth's claws drying on her cheek. "Then say it fast."

"Working with you on this case... it's been an honor. You're the kind of partner every detective dreams of having."

"Ellie—"

"And if we don't make it out of this canyon, I want you to know that Roger would be proud of how you've carried on his work."

She was quiet for a moment, still tracking targets through her rifle scope. "You're not planning to do something stupid, are you?"

"Define stupid."

Before she could answer, werewolves erupted from the hillside directly ahead—Marcus Grayson leading a charge of eight pack members, all in full transformation, moving with the coordinated precision of a military assault team.

There was nowhere left to run.

I stood on the brakes, bringing the Plymouth to a sliding stop in a cloud of dust and burning rubber. "Out! Get behind the car!"

We bailed out on opposite sides, Vivian rolling clear with her rifle while I grabbed the ammunition box from the back seat. The werewolves hit our position three seconds later, and suddenly the night exploded with gunfire and inhuman snarling.

"Silver bullets to the chest!" I shouted over the din, putting two rounds into the first werewolf through my .38.

"Don't waste shots on limbs!"

Vivian's rifle spoke methodically, each shot carefully aimed and devastatingly effective. But there were too many targets, closing from too many angles, and our ammunition was disappearing fast.

A werewolf landed on the Plymouth's roof with a crash that buckled the metal. I put him down with a shot through the engine block, silver bullet punching through steel to find flesh. But his weight had compromised the car's structure, and now we were fighting from behind cover that wouldn't stop a determined assault.

"Contact right!" Vivian's voice was steady despite the chaos. Her rifle cracked twice more, dropping werewolves who were trying to flank our position. "I'm down to the spare magazine!"

"Make every shot count!"

But even as we fought, more werewolves were arriving—pack members who'd taken the longer routes but were now converging on our position with fresh energy and tactical coordination. We'd accounted for maybe eight or nine of their number, but thirty-plus remained, and they were learning our firing patterns.

"Vivian, when I give the word, we move to those rocks." I pointed to a granite outcrop twenty yards away that would give us better cover and higher ground. "Sprint pattern, covering fire." "Got it."

"Three... two... one... go!"

We ran for the rocks. Vivian shot to cover me. Blackwood jumped me halfway there, still moving with silver in his chest.

"Silver don't last forever."

I put two in his chest. He dropped.

"Vivian!" I reached her position as she struggled to sit up, blood streaming from a gash on her forehead. "How bad?"

"Dizzy," she said, blood on her forehead.

The rifle was busted, ten feet away.

My .38 was down to three rounds, maybe four. The ammunition box held plenty more cartridges, but reloading would take time we didn't have.

Marcus Grayson stood at their center, human smarts burning in predator eyes.

"Eleanor Vance," his voice carried across the canyon. "You've caused us considerable trouble."

"That was the idea."

"Indeed. But it's finished now. You're trapped and low on ammunition." He gestured to the werewolves around him. "Give up and I'll make it fast."

I helped Vivian to her feet, keeping the .38 on Grayson. "Go to hell."

He laughed. "Kill them slow."

The pack closed in, forty werewolves moving with coordinated precision. We had maybe thirty seconds before they reached striking distance.

"Vivian, can you shoot a pistol?"

"Give me something to kill with."

I handed her my backup—a snub-nose .32 loaded with silver. Not much firepower, but better than rocks.

"When they charge," I said, "center mass and keep firing till they stop."

She nodded, blood still dripping from the head wound but her hands steady. "Ellie?" "Yeah?"

"It's been an honor."

The werewolves were twenty yards out when the night exploded with engine noise and gunfire from the canyon rim.

"What the hell—" Grayson spun toward the new sounds.

"Cavalry," Vivian said. "Finch called in backup."

Three cars roared down the fire road, headlights blazing and passengers firing silver from every window. The werewolf formation scattered as the vehicles plowed into them, breaking up Grayson's coordinated attack and giving us breathing room.

"Move!" I grabbed Vivian's arm and we scrambled higher, gaining elevation and better cover. Below us, the canyon became a war zone as Finch's reinforcements—whoever they were—engaged the pack in running firefights.

"Who are they?" Vivian asked, trying to track the action through her concussion-blurred vision.

"Right now, I don't care. They're shooting werewolves, which makes them friendlies."

Even with help, the fight was far from over. The pack still out-numbered the newcomers two to one, and werewolves learned fast. Already, some were flanking the cars.

"There!" I pointed to Marcus Grayson, directing pack movements from behind granite. "Drop their alpha, the rest might scatter."

"Long shot with a .32."

"Then we get closer."

We worked through the rocks, using the chaos as cover while we got into better position. Slow going—Vivian was still shaky from the head wound, and every few seconds we had to freeze as werewolves passed nearby.

Finally, we reached a ledge thirty yards above Grayson's position. I could see him clearly, coordinating his pack's counterattack with military precision.

"One shot," I whispered. "We get one before they spot us."

She nodded, bracing the .32 against rock. Below, Marcus Grayson raised his head to bark orders at werewolves flanking left.

The .32 spoke once.

Grayson staggered, silver finding his shoulder, spinning him around but not dropping him. He looked up, yellow eyes locking onto us with killing fury.

"Kill them!" he roared. "All of you! Now!"

But his wound was worse than he'd thought—silver poisoning already affecting his coordination. When he tried to direct another flanking move, his gestures were slow and uncertain.

The pack lost cohesion without clear leadership. Some kept attacking Finch's people, others broke off to hunt us, still others waited for orders that came confused and late.

"Now we run," I told Vivian. "While they're scattered."

We scrambled higher into the canyon walls, putting distance between us and the fighting. Behind us, silver bullets and werewolf howls echoed off granite as the battle raged on.

"How far to Sunset?" Vivian asked.

"Quarter mile, maybe less." I checked my .38—two rounds left. "Think you can make it?" "I'll have to."

We reached a ridge with our first clear view of Sunset Boulevard—streetlights and neon glowing like civilization after the supernatural violence of Laurel Canyon. Close now, but with a dangerous descent ahead. "How you holding up?" I asked.

Vivian touched the gash on her forehead, came away with fresh blood on her fingers. "Dizzy. Vision's getting fuzzy. But I can walk."

"Then we walk together."

Behind us, the sounds of fighting were dying down as Finch's reinforcements either won or got overwhelmed.

Either way, the canyon would soon crawl with werewolves hunting survivors.

"Come on," I said, helping her to her feet. "Let's get out of here before they regroup."

We began picking our way down the canyon wall toward the distant lights. The hunt wasn't over, but for now, we were both still alive.

A Dame Worth Dying For

Vivian's head wound was getting worse.

"You're weaving," I told her as she stumbled against an irrigation ditch for the third time in ten minutes.

"Just tired." Her voice was wrong, eyes unfocused. The cut had stopped bleeding, but something was bad wrong.

Behind us, howls echoed from three directions. They were coming, following our blood trail.

"How much farther?" Vivian asked.

"Mile, maybe two." I checked the .32 she'd given me—six silver rounds, plus two left in my .38. Against how many werewolves? Too many to count.

We pushed through Valencia oranges, sweet smell mixing with the copper stink of dried blood on our clothes.

Vivian leaned against trees to stay upright. The head wound was getting worse.

"Tell me about Roger." Needed her talking, needed to drown out the sounds behind us.

"What about him?"

"How'd you two meet?"

She managed a weak smile. "Bookstore. He was researching old LA, I wanted something to read." She almost smiled. "Funny how things work out."

Movement in the trees. Too big, too fast.

I grabbed Vivian's arm and pulled her behind an orange tree.

"Stay quiet," I whispered.

It stopped, sniffing the air. Yellow eyes. Looking for us.

I drew careful aim with the .38 and held my breath.

The creature turned and ran back toward the canyon. Fast as hell. Maybe lost our scent, maybe going for help.

"Gone?" Vivian asked.

"For now. But they know where we're heading."

Vivian was slowing down, each step careful, resting more. Getting worse.

"Ellie," she said after we'd crossed another ditch. "If something happens—"

"Nothing's going to happen."

"If something happens, tell Miller about Roger's stuff. All of it. The research, the weapons."

"You'll tell him yourself."

"Promise me."

Blood caked on her face from Ashworth's claws. We both knew she might not make it.

"I promise."

"Good. Now help me over this fence."

The barbed wire was rusty but solid, and getting Vivian over took time we didn't have. She nearly passed out halfway across, and I had to catch her before she fell onto the wire. When we made it to the other side, she was shaking and breathing hard.

"Just need a minute," she said, sitting down heavily against a fence post.

Howl came from straight ahead. Between us and Sunset Boulevard. They'd cut us off.

"Son of a bitch," Vivian muttered. She tried to stand, stumbled, tried again. "How many silver bullets do we have?"

"Eight bullets. You?"

"Just the .32. Six rounds."

Fourteen bullets. Should be enough if we were both healthy and had good cover. But Vivian was hurt, and we were trapped in the open.

Werewolf appeared thirty yards away. Massive, coming straight for us.

"Which one?"

"Too dark. Big as Blackwood though."

"Killed him already."

"Maybe his brother."

Close enough to see details now. Wolf head, human body, claws like knives. Yellow eyes, smart as a man.

Coming for us.

"When I shoot, run for those trees. Don't look back."

"Like hell."

"That's an order from your partner."

"Then give me a better order."

The werewolf was twenty yards away and closing. Time for philosophy was over.

I opened fire with the .38, two silver bullets center mass. The creature staggered but kept coming—silver had found flesh, but not vital organs. It roared, a sound like tearing metal, and launched itself at us.

Vivian's .32 spoke three times, fast and accurate. The werewolf landed hard, rolled, came up with silver burning in its chest and shoulder. Still moving, still dangerous, but slowed by pain and silver poisoning.

"Behind the tree!" I shouted.

We dove for cover as the werewolf charged. It hit the orange tree hard enough to shake fruit from the branches, claws raking bark in showers of wood chips. But the trunk held, giving us seconds to reposition.

"Two rounds left," I called.

"Three," Vivian replied. "But I can't see straight enough to aim."

The werewolf circled the tree, testing our defenses, looking for an opening. It was hurt—silver bullets had found their mark—but not critically wounded. And it was learning our patterns, adapting with the intelligence of a creature that had hunted humans for decades.

"It's trying to drive us into the open," Vivian said. "Classic predator behavior."

"Then we don't give it what it wants."

I waited for the werewolf to commit to an attack angle, then put my last two .38 rounds into its left shoulder.

The impact spun it around, and Vivian got a clean shot at its exposed flank.

The .32 cracked twice, silver bullets finding ribs and lung tissue. This time, the werewolf went down and stayed down, silver poisoning finally overwhelming its enhanced healing.

Silence returned to the orange grove, broken only by our heavy breathing and distant LA traffic.

"Is it dead?" Vivian asked.

I approached the body cautiously, .32 ready in case it was faking. But werewolves don't fake death—the silver had done its work, and what remained was fur and flesh and bone.

"Dead," I confirmed. "But that was probably just the advance scout. The main pack can't be far behind."

Vivian tried to stand and immediately sat back down. "Ellie, I don't think—"

"Just rest a minute. We'll figure something out."

But even as I said it, I could hear more howls in the distance. Multiple voices, closing in from several directions. The gunfire had given away our location, and now the entire hunting party was converging on us.

"Go," Vivian said quietly.

"What?"

"You know what I mean. Leave me here and run for Sunset. You might make it if you're not carrying dead weight."

"You're not dead weight."

"I can't walk straight, I can't shoot straight, and I'm slowing you down." She pulled the .32 from her jacket and pressed it into my hands. "Take this. You'll need every bullet."

"Vivian—"

"That's twice now I've given you that gun. Third time's the charm, right?"

The howls were getting closer. I could see shapes moving between the trees, still distant but closing fast. We had maybe five minutes before they reached us.

"Tell Miller I died fighting," she said. "Tell him the research was worth it. And tell him..." She paused. "Tell him Roger would be proud."

I wanted to argue, wanted to find some way to get us both out alive. But the math was simple and brutal: one person might reach Sunset

Boulevard before the pack arrived. Two people, with one injured, had no chance.

"I'll tell him," I said.

"Good. Now get going before I change my mind."

We looked at each other in the moonlight, both knowing this was goodbye. Then I leaned down and kissed her, deep and desperate, tasting blood and fear and something that might have been love if we'd had more time.

"Go," she whispered against my lips.

I began moving through the orange trees toward the distant glow of neon and streetlights. Behind me, Vivian Vanderbilt found a defensive position against the fence post and began checking her remaining ammunition.

The howls were getting closer, but I didn't look back. Couldn't look back. Some things you carry with you, and some things you have to leave behind to survive.

Sunset Boulevard got brighter with each step. Safety there. A chance to keep fighting. But Vivian was dead in an orange grove behind me, and that didn't feel like winning.

Behind me, a single gunshot echoed across the farmland. Then another. Then silence.

I kept walking toward the city lights. Tomorrow I'd have to tell Miller what happened. Tomorrow I'd have to explain why Vivian wasn't coming back.

This wasn't about finding missing people anymore. This was about staying alive. And staying alive meant leaving Vivian behind.

I kept walking.

Dawn was coming up when I reached Sunset Boulevard. The hunt was over for tonight. But somewhere in those hills, they were regrouping. Figuring out their next move. Deciding what to do about the detective who'd gotten away.

I found a phone booth outside an all-night diner and dialed Miller's number. He needed to know what was really hunting people in this city. And he needed to know Vivian was dead.

The missing persons case was over. Now it was something else.

Alliance of the Desperate

The phone booth outside the diner smelled like cigarettes and broken dreams. I fumbled with coins, hands still shaking from Laurel Canyon, and dialed Miller's number. Three rings, then his voice—groggy but alert the way cops learn to be.

"Miller."

"It's Ellie. We need to talk."

Silence on the other end while he processed my tone. "Where are you?"

"Sunset Boulevard. Near La Cienega." I looked through the glass at the diner's neon sign, pink letters spelling

"Mel's" in script. "Can you meet me?"

"Give me twenty minutes." The line went dead.

I bought coffee and found a corner booth where I could watch the street. Dawn was breaking over Los Angeles, painting the sky the color of dried blood. Early commuters were starting their drive downtown, ordinary people heading to ordinary jobs, unaware their city was a hunting ground for creatures that wore human faces during business hours.

Miller arrived in eighteen minutes, still wearing yesterday's shirt and the hollow-eyed look of a man who'd spent the night staring at case files that made no sense. He slid into the booth across from me and signaled the waitress for coffee.

"You look like hell," he said.

"Feel worse." I wrapped my hands around my coffee cup, using the warmth to stop the shaking. "Miller, I need to tell you some things. And you're not going to believe any of them."

"Try me."

So I told him everything. Roger Talbot's research into the Crescent Club, the founding families who'd arrived in 1891, forty years of systematic infiltration. Vivian Vanderbilt's intelligence gathering and weapons cache.

Alistair Finch and his father's investigation that had gotten Benjamin Finch killed in 1915.

Miller listened without interruption, his cop face giving away nothing. When I described the full moon gathering at Jack Rafferty's estate, the transformation sequence, the high-speed chase through Laurel Canyon, his eyes never left my face.

But when I got to Vivian's death in the orange grove, his expression changed.

"She stayed behind," I said quietly. "Head wound from the canyon fight. She couldn't walk straight, couldn't shoot straight. She knew if she tried coming with me, we'd both die." I stared into my coffee. "So she gave me her gun and told me to run."

"Jesus, Ellie."

"I heard the shots as I was walking away. Two, maybe three. Then nothing." I looked up at him. "She died buying me time to reach you. To tell you what we learned."

Miller was quiet for a long moment, processing what I'd told him. The waitress refilled our cups without being asked, then retreated to give us privacy.

"Werewolves," he said finally.

"Werewolves."

"Lycanthropes. Shapeshifters. Monsters in human form."

"That's right."

He pulled out his cigarettes, lit one with steady hands. "Ellie, I've been a cop for fifteen years. I've seen things that would make most people lose sleep. But what you're telling me..."

"I know how it sounds."

"It sounds insane." He took a long drag. "Which is why I believe you."

I blinked. "What?"

"You're not crazy, Ellie. Stubborn as hell, maybe too brave for your own good, but not crazy. And what you're describing fits patterns I've been seeing for months."

Miller reached into his jacket and pulled out a small leather note-book, the kind detectives carry to record witness statements and crime scene details. He flipped through pages of handwritten notes.

"Forty-three homicides in the last year," he said. "All during full moon periods. All with similar injury patterns—massive trauma to chest and throat, claw marks the coroner called animal attacks. But no wild animals in Los

Angeles could do that kind of damage."

"You've been tracking them."

"Tracking something. I just didn't know what until now." He closed the notebook. "There's something else,

Ellie. Something I haven't told anyone."

He stubbed out his cigarette and reached for his wallet. From behind his driver's license, he pulled out a small object wrapped in tissue paper. When he unwrapped it, I saw a silver bullet—but not like Finch's. This one was different, older, with strange markings etched into its surface.

"My father gave me this before he died," Miller said. "He was a beat cop in the twenties, walked the same downtown streets I work now. But he kept unofficial records, notes about cases that made no sense.

Disappearances during full moon periods. Animal attacks in neigh-borhoods with no animals. Bodies found with wounds that looked too organized, too deliberate for random attacks."

I leaned forward to get a better look at the bullet. The markings weren't decorative—they looked like symbols, maybe religious in nature.

"He spent twenty years documenting patterns," Miller continued. "Building a case file on something the department wouldn't officially acknowledge. When he retired in 1925, he told me Los Angeles was being hunted by creatures that weren't supposed to exist."

"Did you believe him?"

"I thought he was getting old, seeing monsters where there were just ordinary criminals. But he made me promise to keep the bullet, told me someday I'd understand why it was important." Miller's smile was grim. "Guess someday is today."

"What are those markings?"

"Religious symbols. Christian, Jewish, a few I don't recognize. Dad had the bullet blessed by every priest, minister, and rabbi who'd agree to do it. He figured if he was going up against supernatural creatures, he might as well cover all the bases."

I thought about Finch's silver bullets, effective but plain. This one felt different—heavier somehow, like it carried more than just physical weight.

"Father Rodriguez at Saint Vibiana's Cathedral was the last one to bless it," Miller said. "Old priest who'd heard enough confessions to believe in things that weren't supposed to exist. Dad told me Rodriguez spent an hour in Latin, blessing not just the bullet but the man who might someday need to use it."

"Have you ever fired it?"

"Never had reason to. Until now." He rewrapped the bullet carefully, placed it back in his wallet. "But I'm not sure one blessed bullet is enough to stop forty werewolves."

"Finch gave me six regular silver bullets. Between those and what Vivian had in her weapons cache, we might be able to arm a small army."

"What weapons cache?"

I told him about Vivian's garage, the rifles and ammunition Roger had acquired, the stockpile they'd been building for a war they knew was coming. Miller listened, calculating ammunition counts and tactical possibilities.

"It's not enough," he said finally. "Even if we could recruit help, we'd need special ammunition. Lots of it."

"I know a guy," I said. "Jeweler downtown, owes me a favor from when I helped his daughter with a blackmail problem. If we brought him enough raw material, he could probably cast fifty rounds in a day or two."

Miller's eyebrows went up. "How much would it cost?"

"More than either of us makes in a month. But if we're doing this, we're doing it right."

Miller stubbed out his smoke and reached for his wallet again. This time he pulled out a business card —"Goldstein & Sons Fine Jewelry, Est. 1923"—and wrote an address on the back.

"I've got some money saved," he said. "My retirement fund. Fifteen hundred dollars." "Miller, that's your future."

"What future? If we don't stop Grayson and his pack, there won't be a future. Not for us, not for anyone in this city." He slid the card across the table. "Meet me there at two. Bring whatever silver you got, we'll see about getting properly armed for werewolf hunting."

I picked up the card, studied the address. Hill Street, between a pawn shop and a haberdashery. The kind of neighborhood where you could do business quietly, without too many questions.

"What about help? We can't take on forty werewolves by ourselves."

"Finch is in. After what happened to his father, he's got skin in the game. And I've got a few contacts in the department—cops who've been asking the same questions I have, noticing the same patterns. They might not believe in werewolves yet, but they'll believe in taking down organized criminals who've been killing citizens." Miller stood and dropped money for coffee, then paused.

"Ellie, there's something else about that bullet." He nodded toward his wallet. "Dad didn't just have it made for protection. He had it made for justice. He said if the time ever came to use it, I'd know. And when I did, it would find the heart it was meant for."

"You think that's Grayson?"

"I think forty years of hunting and killing in this city has created a debt that needs to be paid. And maybe, with enough help and enough silver bullets, we can be the ones to collect it."

He pulled on his coat and headed for the door, then turned back.

"Consider it a gift," he said, patting his wallet. "For luck."

I sat in the empty booth ten more minutes, thinking about two generations of cops who'd tried protecting their city from monsters in human faces. About the woman who'd died in an orange grove so I could sit here planning the next move in a war that had been going on since before Los Angeles was a city.

The blessed bullet was Miller's inheritance, passed down from father to son along with the knowledge that some evils were too big for the official justice system. But with allies and silver ammunition, maybe we could finish what his father had started.

I pocketed Goldstein's business card and walked out into morning sunshine. Had a few hours to get ready for a fight that would decide who ran this city.

Vivian was dead. But her research and weapons were still good. Still useful.

Her death had to mean something.

Miller's blessed bullet carried forty years of preparation. Might not be enough against things that'd been hunting this long.

But it was something. And sometimes something was better than nothing.

PART THREE

THE SILVER BULLET

The Arsenal

Rain was coming down hard when I reached Goldstein & Sons on Hill Street. The shop sat between a pawn broker and a men's clothing store, narrow front with peeling paint. Gold lettering in Hebrew and English said "Est. 1923." The window showed more empty velvet than jewelry.

Miller was waiting under the awning, collar up against the drizzle. Stubbled jaw, tired eyes, hand near his service weapon. When he spotted me, he nodded. Ready.

"You bring everything?" he asked.

I hefted the canvas bag that had been Vivian's. Military surplus, practical. Inside, silver clinked against silver. "Hundred and twelve silver dollars from my safe, about eight pounds of sterling. Mother's tea service, plus a cigarette case I took off a dead German." The bag felt heavy. "You?"

Miller patted his briefcase. "Two hundred in silver certificates, wedding rings, grandmother's candlesticks. Plus fifteen hundred in cash. My retirement fund."

"Christ, Miller. You sure?"

"Yeah."

The shop smelled of metal polish and old wood. Mustiness. Jewelry cases held expensive merchandise, watch repair tools on a corner workbench. The man behind the counter looked up.

Abraham Goldstein looked up from a jeweler's loupe. Maybe seventy, liver spots on his hands. Slight shake to them, but his eyes were sharp when they fixed on Miller's badge.

"Detective Miller. Been wondering when you'd come collect on that favor."

"Hello, Mr. Goldstein. This is Eleanor Vance—she's working with me on something important."

Goldstein studied me. "Private investigator. Can tell from how you carry yourself. Army?"

"Nurse in the Army Medical Corps for three years. Spent my last few months in France."

"My nephew David fought in Italy. Came home with stories about field hospitals and the women who kept boys alive when the doctors gave up hope." He set down the loupe and leaned against the counter. "What kind of favor are we discussing, Detective?"

Miller opened his briefcase on the glass counter, revealing cash and silver that caught the overhead light like promises of violence. "We need bullets cast. Fifty rounds, .38 caliber. Pure silver."

The old jeweler went quiet for a long moment, studying the money and metal spread before him. Then he looked up with eyes that had seen enough of the world to understand what pure silver bullets meant. "So you're hunting something lead won't stop."

"Something like that."

"In my neighborhood, we have stories about such creatures. Things that wear human faces until the moon gets full. Beasts that feed on people like people feed on cattle." Goldstein's voice dropped to just above a whisper. "My father came here from Poland in 1892. Told me about villages where children vanished when the moon was right. Where men with too much money and too little conscience invited darkness into their homes— darkness that should have stayed in the deep woods where it belonged."

My pulse quickened. Vivian had mentioned similar stories during our tactical planning sessions, fragments of European folklore that had followed immigrant families across the ocean. "Your father knew about lycanthropes?"

"He knew about evil that walked on two legs and four legs both. Knew about bloodlines that went back centuries—families that weren't quite human but weren't entirely monsters either." Goldstein picked up one of my silver dollars, turning it in his palm like he was testing its weight and purity. "He also knew about silver.

Why it burns them. Why they fear it more than fire or flood or any earthly weapon man can make." Miller and I exchanged glances. This was more help than we'd dared hope for.

"Will you do it?"

"Casting silver bullets isn't like melting down jewelry for rings. Silver has to be pure—ninety-nine point nine percent or better. Has to be heated to exactly the right temperature, poured into molds designed for perfect balance and weight distribution." Goldstein paused, studying both our faces. "And it has to be blessed." "Blessed?"

"Bullets are just metal until they're given purpose. My father taught me the words—Hebrew prayers that turn silver into something more. Something that can touch creatures normal weapons can't harm."

The old man opened a drawer behind the counter and pulled out a worn leather journal. Pages fell open to reveal handwritten notes in Hebrew, but the technical drawings were clear enough—precise diagrams for creating ammunition that could kill things that shouldn't exist.

"How long?" Miller asked.

"Twenty-four hours. Maybe thirty if I want them done right." Goldstein closed the journal and looked at us with grandfather's eyes that had seen too much history. "You understand what you're asking me to make? These aren't bullets for target practice or hunting deer. These are for ending lives that shouldn't be walking around in the first place."

"We understand."

"And you understand that once I make them, once you use them, there's no going back? Creatures like this— they remember who kills their kind. They remember who helps. My shop, my family, we all become targets."

The weight of what we were asking hit me hard. This old man would become part of our war just by helping us.

His grandchildren would inherit enemies that moved through shadows and looked human during business hours.

But then I thought about Walt Henley torn apart in Griffith Park. About seventeen innocent people killed during the pack's rampage through the city. About Roger Talbot broken and captive somewhere in the Hollywood Hills.

About Vivian Vanderbilt dying in those orange groves because she'd chosen to fight instead of hiding.

About two million people living their lives unaware that predators controlled their government, their police, their newspapers.

"Mr. Goldstein, these things have been feeding on this city for forty years. They're not going to stop. They're not going to show mercy to folks who know their secret. The only choice is whether we fight them or wait around for them to come calling."

He studied my face for another long moment, then nodded slowly. "My father would have understood. In Poland, waiting for monsters to show mercy was how whole villages disappeared." He picked up Miller's grandmother's candlesticks, testing their weight with practiced hands. "These are good silver. Tiffany, from before the war. And your coins—Morgan dollars, they used real silver then, not the cheap alloy they use nowadays."

Goldstein began sorting our metal by quality, his movements showing decades of expertise. "I'll melt the pure stuff first—your tea service, Miller's rings, these Morgan dollars. Should give me enough silver for forty solid rounds. The rest will work for practice ammunition, maybe seventy-five percent silver."

"Will seventy-five percent work?"

"Against regular werewolves, yes. Against an alpha who's survived forty years..." He shrugged. "We save the pure silver for him, use the practice rounds on his pack."

Miller counted out bills from his briefcase. "What will this cover?"

"Labor, materials, keeping my mouth shut about who wanted silver bullets and why." Goldstein pocketed the money without counting it. "The blessing comes free. My father would have wanted it that way."

As we arranged to collect the ammunition tomorrow evening, I thought about Vivian's weapons cache back at her garage. Rifles, regular ammunition, surveillance equipment—resources that were still available if we needed them. She'd prepared for a long campaign against supernatural predators, understanding that this kind of war required more than just silver bullets.

"Detective Miller," Goldstein called out as we prepared to leave. "You mentioned collecting on a favor. What favor?"

Miller paused at the door. "Your son David. That burglary charge from last year—the one that got dropped because evidence mysteriously vanished from the property room."

"David was innocent of that charge."

"I know. But the prosecutor didn't. Neither did the judge or the jury pool." Miller's smile held no warmth.

"Sometimes the system works the way it should. Sometimes it needs a push."

Outside, the rain had turned into the kind of steady downpour that transformed Los Angeles streets into temporary rivers. Miller and I stood under the jewelry shop's awning, watching water cascade from gutters and pool around storm drains that couldn't handle the volume.

"What now?" I asked.

"Now we get more help. Fifty silver bullets might kill Grayson and a few of his pack, but there are still thirty werewolves out there. We need allies who understand what we're up against."

I thought about Alistair Finch and his father's forty years of research. About Bill Kowalski, the studio security guard who'd given me wolfsbane and warnings about creatures that wore human faces. About Detective Miller's father's records and photographs—evidence that supernatural predators had been hunting in Los Angeles since before most of its residents were born.

And I thought about Vivian, who'd understood the tactical realities better than any of us. Her military background had taught her that wars were won through intelligence, preparation, and coordinated action. Not through lone heroes with more courage than sense.

"Finch?"

"Finch. And anyone else we can trust who's willing to die fighting monsters instead of living under their rule."

Miller pulled his coat collar higher and stepped out into the rain. "Meet me at the bookstore tomorrow at eight.

By then we'll have an arsenal and, God willing, enough people to use it right."

I watched him disappear into the gray curtain of water and concrete—a lone cop walking into the night to build an army against creatures that had controlled his city since before he was born. In twenty-four hours, we'd have silver bullets blessed with prayers older than California statehood.

The question was whether we'd live long enough to use them.

I pulled my own coat tight and headed for my Plymouth, parked three blocks away in the thin hope that distance might provide some protection against werewolves who could track scents across miles of urban sprawl. The silver bullet Miller had given me sat heavy in my pocket—a single round that might mean the difference between success and becoming another victim whose death would be explained as an animal attack or mob violence.

But as I drove through rain-slicked streets toward my office and whatever tomorrow would bring, I felt something I hadn't experienced since the war ended. Hope. Not the naive optimism of someone who'd never faced real evil, but the grim satisfaction of a soldier who'd finally been given weapons that could kill the enemy.

Vivian had felt this same hope, I realized. During those final moments in the orange groves, even as werewolf claws opened her throat, she'd known we had a real chance of winning. Her sacrifice had bought us time and tactical advantage. Now it was up to Miller and me to make sure that advantage counted for something.

In twenty-four hours, we'd go after the Crescent Club.

And for the first time since this case started, we had a chance of winning.

Unlikely Allies

Spring Street at night was darker, meaner. Shadows between streetlights, neon signs throwing color across wet pavement. Finch's bookstore sat between a pawn shop and a diner, narrow storefront dark except for one light upstairs.

Miller pulled his unmarked sedan to the curb and killed the engine. We'd driven separate routes from the jewelry shop, checking mirrors for tails. War habits. Vivian would've done the same.

"Looks quiet," Miller said, but his hand stayed near his service weapon.

I studied the bookstore's darkened windows and the apartments above. "Too quiet. Finch knew we were coming."

We'd called from a payphone outside the jewelry shop, using the number Finch had given me when I'd first visited his store for information about lycanthropes. The conversation had been brief---Miller explaining we needed to discuss mutual problems with mutual solutions. Finch had agreed to meet us after hours, when the bookstore was closed and the streets belonged to creatures that preferred darkness.

The front door was locked, but a narrow alley ran between the bookstore and the pawn shop next door. Miller followed me into shadows that smelled of garbage and urban decay, our footsteps echoing off brick walls that had absorbed seventy years of Los Angeles history. A metal fire escape zigzagged up the building's rear wall, leading to a door that hung slightly open.

Light spilled from the gap---warm yellow bulb illumination that seemed to push back the October chill. I climbed first, Miller behind me, both of us moving quiet. Noise attracted trouble. Something Vivian had taught me.

Finch's apartment took up the entire second floor. Books every-where---every wall, floor to ceiling, stacked in towers. Maps hung between the bookcases. Detailed surveys showing property bound-aries, elevation, terrain.

Finch sat behind an old desk. He looked up as we entered, pale blue eyes sharp behind wire-rimmed glasses.

"Miss Vance. Detective Miller." His voice carried the crisp sound of someone who read books for a living.

"Wondered when you'd need more than just information."

Miller closed the door behind us and turned the deadbolt. "We need allies, Mr. Finch. People who understand what we're fighting and why it matters."

"Fighting." Finch set down his fountain pen and folded his hands. "Interesting choice of words. Most people would say 'investigating' or 'researching' or some other word that makes the reality easier to swallow."

"Most people haven't seen six werewolves torn apart by silver bullets," I said. "Most people don't know that

Marcus Grayson survived and is planning to hit back with thirty years of built-up rage."

Finch didn't change expression, but something shifted in his eyes. Recognition, maybe. The satisfaction of being right about something nobody else would believe.

"Sit," he said, gesturing to two chairs that faced his desk. "Tell me what you've learned, and I'll tell you what my father spent forty years documenting."

Miller and I settled into chairs that creaked with age and use. The detective pulled out his notebook and flipped to pages covered with careful handwriting---names, dates, locations, the methodical police work that turned chaos into cases that could be solved.

"The Crescent Club has been operating in Los Angeles since 1903," Miller began. "Three lycanthrope families--Grayson, Ash-worth, and Blackwood---came here in the 1890s when the city was still small enough for a handful of predators to control com-pletely. They've been feeding on the population ever since, using their wealth and supernatural abilities to build positions of power in government, law enforcement, and entertainment."

"Harrison Blackwood is dead," I added. "Killed two nights ago during a pack hunt in Laurel Canyon. Jack Rafferty too, along with four others. But Marcus Grayson is still alive, still alpha, and now he knows we can hurt him."

Finch listened without interruption, occasionally making notes with his fountain pen. When we finished, he stood and walked to a bookcase that held volumes in languages I couldn't read---German, Latin, what looked like Old Church Slavonic.

"My father arrived in Los Angeles in 1908," Finch said, pulling down a leather-bound journal thick as a phone book. "Benjamin Finch, immigrant from Yorkshire who'd seen too much of the old country's darkness to believe the New World would be any different. He came here chasing stories about men who weren't entirely men--families with bloodlines that went back to wolves instead of human ancestry."

He opened the journal to pages covered with careful handwriting and pasted-in photographs. Some showed buildings I recognized---the Crescent Club's meeting hall on Vine Street, Consolidated Pictures before it became the studio empire that employed half of Hollywood. Others were portraits of men in expensive suits, their eyes catching camera flash like animal pupils.

"Benjamin documented everything. Financial records showing how the families got their property and businesses. Newspaper articles about mysterious deaths and disappearances. Police reports that were filed and then quietly buried when the victims' cases became inconvenient."

Miller leaned forward to study a photograph of three men standing outside what looked like a bank. "Grayson, Ashworth, and Blackwood?"

"In 1915, when they were already powerful enough to own judges and police commissioners. My father tried to build a case against them---collected evidence, found witnesses, even located a prosecutor who was willing to listen."

"What happened?"

Finch's smile held no humor. "Benjamin Finch was found dead in Griffith Park on November 15th, 1915. Torn apart by what the newspapers called 'wild animals,' though the medical examiner's private notes described wounds that no known animal could have made."

The room went quiet except for the sound of rain against windows and the distant hum of street traffic. I thought about Walt Henley, killed in the same park for the same reason---knowing too much about creatures that preferred to remain hidden. About Vivian, who'd died knowing the same truth but choosing to fight instead of staying quiet.

"But your father's work didn't die with him," Miller said.

"No. He'd been careful---kept duplicate records, hid them in places the Club couldn't reach. When I inherited this building in 1935, I found everything in a safe behind false books. My father had spent seven years documenting the supernatural predators who'd built Los Angeles. I've spent thirty-three years continuing his work—forty years of research between us."

Finch walked to another bookcase and pressed something that made a clicking sound. A section of shelving swung open like a door, revealing a space behind the wall that looked like an arsenal designed by someone who'd studied both military tactics and medieval folklore.

Silver knives hung in neat rows, their blades polished to mirror brightness. A crossbow with silver-tipped bolts sat mounted on wooden brackets. In the center of the collection, a spear with a leaf-shaped silver point caught the desk lamp's light and threw it back like captured sunlight.

"Jesus Christ," Miller whispered.

"My father believed in being ready," Finch said. "He had these made by a silversmith in San Francisco---a man who'd fled Prague in 1895 after his entire family was killed by creatures that called themselves nobility but hunted peasants for sport."

I stood and walked to the hidden armory, running my fingers along knife handles wrapped in leather that had darkened with age. The weapons felt balanced and deadly, crafted by someone who understood that silver was more than just precious metal---it was salvation made tangible.

It reminded me of Vivian's weapons cache, though hers had been more practical---rifles and ammunition rather than medieval implements. But the purpose was the same: tools for killing things that conventional weapons couldn't touch. She would have appreciated Finch's collection.

"There's more," Finch said. He pulled down a rolled map and spread it across his desk. "Property surveys showing every building the Crescent Club owns or controls. Not just their meeting hall on Vine Street, but safe houses in the Hollywood Hills, warehouses near the docks, even a ranch in Malibu County where they take victims who need to disappear slowly."

The map covered Los Angeles County from ocean to desert, marked with symbols drawn in red ink. Circles showed known Crescent Club properties. Triangles marked locations where suspicious deaths had occurred.

Squares indicated the homes and businesses of confirmed werewolves.

"How did you get this information?" I asked.

"Carefully, and over many years. But I haven't been working alone."

Finch walked to a telephone that sat on a smaller desk near the window. He dialed a number from memory and waited while it rang.

"Bill? It's Alistair. They're here." A pause. "Yes, both of them. Can you come up?" Another pause. "Good. Use the fire escape."

Miller and I exchanged glances. "Bill Kowalski," I said. "The security guard from Consolidated Pictures."

"Among other things," Finch replied. "He's been feeding me information about Club activities for three years.

Ever since his brother disappeared after asking too many questions about Jack Rafferty's private parties."

Footsteps echoed on the metal fire escape outside. Finch opened the door to admit a stocky man in his fifties, wearing work clothes and a suspicious expression that softened when he recognized me.

"Miss Vance. Didn't expect to see you again after what happened at the studio." Bill Kowalski stepped inside and shook hands with

Miller. "Detective. Bill Kowalski---we met briefly when you were investigating those 'animal attacks' in Griffith Park."

Miller nodded. "You're the one who's been tracking Club movements through studio security reports."

"Among other methods. Amazing what you can learn when nobody thinks the night watchman is paying attention." Kowalski walked to Finch's map and pointed to several triangular markers. "These three locations--the warehouse on Terminal Island, the house in Laurel Canyon, that ranch in Malibu---they've all seen increased activity since you killed Rafferty and the others."

"What kind of activity?"

"Vehicles coming and going at odd hours. Deliveries that don't match any shipping manifests. Lights in buildings that are supposed to be empty." Kowalski pulled out a small notebook and flipped through pages of handwritten observations. "My guess is they're consolidating resources, bringing werewolves from other cities to replace the ones they lost."

Finch returned to his hidden armory and began taking down weapons. "Which means we have a window of opportunity---maybe a week or two before their strength is back to full capacity." "Opportunity for what?" Miller asked.

"To hit them before they can hit us. The Crescent Club has survived forty years by staying hidden, by making their enemies disappear quietly and completely. But you changed the rules when you killed six of them in one night. Now they can't afford to let you live, and they can't afford to let this become public knowledge."

I studied the map again, noting defensive positions and escape routes that would be available if we tried to go after any of the marked locations. "You're talking about open warfare against creatures that are stronger, faster, and better organized than we are."

"I'm talking about survival," Finch replied. He handed me a silver knife with a nine-inch blade and a grip designed for close combat. "Because whether we go after them or try to hide, Marcus Grayson will come for all of us. The only question is whether we face him on ground we choose or ground he controls."

The weapon felt good in my hand---balanced, deadly, purposeful. Vivian would have approved of its craftsmanship.

Kowalski nodded agreement. "They've already started moving against people who helped you. Eddie Kowalski, my nephew at Consolidated Pictures---he was found dead in his apartment yesterday. 'Gas leak,' according to the official report, but Eddie was too smart to leave a stove on all night."

The weight of another death settled over the room like smoke from a house fire. Eddie Kowalski had probably never heard of werewolves. He'd answered my questions about Roger Talbot, and that was enough to get him killed.

"How many more?" I asked. "How many more people die because we started this?"

"All of them," Miller said quietly. "If we don't finish it. Grayson isn't just consolidating resources to come after us---he's preparing for the endgame. Forty years of careful infiltration and control, and now they're ready to stop pretending to be human."

Finch returned to his desk and pulled out another journal, this one bound in black leather that looked as old as the city itself. "My father's final entries, written in the weeks before his death. He'd learned something about the Club's ultimate goals---not just control of Los Angeles, but something much bigger."

He opened the journal to pages covered with increasingly frantic handwriting. Diagrams showed population growth charts and migration patterns. Notes mentioned "breeding programs" and "sustainable harvest rates" and other phrases that made my stomach clench with recognition.

"The Crescent Club isn't just a collection of supernatural predators," Finch read from his father's notes. "'They're the advance force for a complete change in the relationship between predator and prey. Los Angeles is a test case---can lycanthrope families successfully rule a major American city without detection or resistance? If the experiment succeeds here, it will be replicated in Chicago, New York, San Francisco, and eventually every population center in the country.'"

The scope hit me. We weren't just fighting for Los Angeles. We were fighting to keep this from spreading across the country.

"Jesus," Miller breathed. "They're not just trying to control one city. They're trying to conquer the entire country."

"And they're winning," Kowalski added. "Three years ago, my contacts in other cities started reporting similar patterns---wealthy families with unusual appetites, mysterious disappearances during full moon periods, police and government officials who seemed to protect certain suspects no matter how overwhelming the evidence."

I picked up the silver-pointed spear. Heavy, well-balanced. Could punch through a ribcage and pin the heart.

Vivian had carried something similar in those orange groves.

"So it's four of us," I said. "Silver weapons and forty years of research, against an organization that's been running things since before we were born."

"Four people who know the truth," Finch said. "Four who'll fight instead of hide. My father didn't have that."

Miller stood and walked to the window, looking out at Spring Street and the neon darkness toward downtown.

Rain streaked the glass.

"What do we need?"

"Intelligence on their current locations and strength," Finch replied. "Silver ammunition---enough to arm a small army. And most importantly, we need to rescue Roger Talbot."

"Roger's still alive?"

Kowalski nodded grimly. "Being held at their original stronghold in the Hollywood Hills. The Grayson family estate---Marcus bought the property in 1895, back when Hollywood was just orange groves and ambitious real estate developers. They're using Roger as an example, showing other potential defectors what happens to humans who try to expose lycanthrope society."

"He's also bait," I realized. "They know we'll come for him, and they're counting on it. Rescue mission turns into a trap that elimi-nates the resistance before it can become a real threat."

"Probably," Finch agreed. "But we can't leave him there. Roger Talbot knows more about current Club operations than anyone outside the inner circle. If we can get him out alive and coherent, he becomes our best weapon against them."

Miller turned from the window. "When?"

"Tomorrow night. Full moon is in three days---they'll want to complete whatever they're doing to Roger before then, use the lunar influence to break his mind completely. After that, he won't be worth rescuing."

I thought about the silver bullets Goldstein was casting, about forty rounds of pure silver ammunition that would be ready in eighteen hours. About the weapons hidden behind Finch's bookcase and Vivian's cache waiting in her garage---tools for killing things that shouldn't exist. About maps showing every building the Crescent Club owned or controlled.

The memory of Vivian's final kiss lingered like smoke in my mouth. She'd known this moment would come--when we'd have to choose between safety and doing what was right. She'd made her choice in those orange groves near Sunset Boulevard, buying time for the rest of us to continue the fight.

"We'll need more than four people to get him out."

"I have contacts," Kowalski said. "Security guards, night watch-men, a few beat cops who've seen things they can't explain through normal channels. Men who'd fight if they knew what they were fighting against."

"And I have my father's network," Finch added. "Researchers, historians, a few clergy who still believe in supernatural evil. People who've been waiting forty years for someone to start shooting back."

Miller checked his watch. "Twenty-two hours until we have am-munition. Forty-eight hours until we hit the

Grayson estate. Anyone wants out, say so now."

Nobody spoke. Rain kept falling. Somewhere distant, a police siren wailed.

But we weren't hunting human criminals. We were hunting things that'd been feeding on people since before this city existed. Things that saw two million people as livestock.

I slipped the silver knife into my coat pocket. Vivian had died believing we could win. I owed her that much.

"All right," I said. "Let's go get Roger Talbot."

In two days, we'd either be dead or this would be over. Either way, the hiding was done.

Roger's Fate

The photograph was grainy, shot from distance, but clear enough. Roger Talbot chained to a chair in a basement cell, face gaunt from weeks of torture. Bruises covered his arms and chest in patterns—deliberate damage from someone who knew what they were doing.

"When was this taken?" I asked.

Bill Kowalski checked his notebook. "Yesterday afternoon. My contact at the phone company monitors service calls to properties in the Hollywood Hills. Repair truck needed access to lines near the Grayson estate—driver got curious about the soundproofing work in the basement."

We were back in Finch's apartment, the four of us studying reports that painted a picture uglier than a morgue photograph. The Crescent Club wasn't just holding Roger prisoner—they were breaking his mind, using methods they'd spent decades perfecting on humans who knew too much about lycanthrope activities.

Miller studied the photograph through a magnifying glass, his cop's eyes cataloging details that might prove useful later. "Concrete walls, no windows. Single door with reinforced frame. They're keeping him in a cell built for long-term confinement."

"Not confinement," Finch corrected, pulling down another journal. "Reeducation. My father documented their methods—techniques for breaking people down to nothing, turning them into something barely human."

The journal fell open to pages that made my war-hardened stomach clench with recognition. Detailed drawings showed restraint systems and isolation chambers. Clinical notes described the progression of mental deterioration in subjects who'd been exposed to what the author called "lycanthrope psychological conditioning."

Vivian had seen similar techniques during the war. Nazi methods for breaking resistance fighters. She'd told me about it once. The werewolves had learned the same lessons.

"Christ," Miller breathed. "They've been perfecting mind control for decades."

"Longer than that," Kowalski said. "The methods came from Europe—old families who kept their people in line through fear and pain. When the world started changing, when governments began limiting their power, some of those families came to America."

I thought about Edward Whitmore and his pale eyes. The way he'd spoken in my office—not threats, just certainty. Like I was livestock.

"How long does the process take?" I asked.

Finch turned pages covered with increasingly desperate handwriting. "My father's sources suggest about six weeks for adult males, four weeks for women and children. But Roger has been in their custody for..." He consulted a calendar hanging above his desk. "Eighteen days."

"So we still have time to save his mind."

"Maybe. The process isn't uniform—some subjects break quickly, others hold out for months before their resistance collapses." Finch closed the journal and looked at each of us in turn. "But every day we wait reduces the chances of recovering the man Roger Talbot used to be."

Miller stood and walked to the map spread across Finch's desk, studying the symbols that marked Crescent Club properties throughout Los Angeles County. His finger traced routes between the Grayson estate and other locations—escape routes, probably, or supply lines that connected their operations.

"The estate is here," he said, pointing to a red circle in the Hollywood Hills. "Fifteen acres, purchased in 1895 when the area was still orange groves and horse ranches. Main house dates to 1897, but they've done extensive renovation work over the years."

"What kind of renovation work?" I asked.

Kowalski pulled out a manila folder thick with photocopied documents. "Basement excavation in 1923—listed as 'wine cellar construction.' Underground tunnels added in 1931, called 'storm drainage.' Soundproofing in 1945, described as 'music room improvements.'"

We studied the permits and building plans. The Grayson estate wasn't just a mansion—it was a fortress.

Underground rooms where screams wouldn't carry. Escape tunnels. Cells for prisoners.

Vivian would've seen it immediately. Read the modifications, understood what they meant. She'd studied places like this during the war.

"How many people does the estate normally hold?" Miller asked.

"Hard to say," Finch replied, consulting his father's property surveys. "The main house has twelve bedrooms, but the real capacity is underground. Benjamin estimated the basement complex could house up to thirty individuals—either as prisoners or as long-term residents who preferred to avoid sunlight."

I did the math. Thirty werewolves in a reinforced position with underground escape routes, holding a human hostage in soundproof chambers. Even with silver bullets and the element of surprise, a direct assault would be suicide.

"We need inside intelligence," I said. "Floor plans, security procedures, information about guard rotations and weak points."

Kowalski nodded. "I might be able to help with that. The estate uses Consolidated Pictures security services for their grounds maintenance—guards who patrol the perimeter, check locks and alarms. Most think they're just protecting some eccentric rich family that values privacy."

"Most of them?"

"A few have asked questions about the basement renovation work, about why certain areas are off-limits even to security personnel. Management always transfers those guards to other assignments, but not before they've seen things that don't add up."

Miller leaned forward. "What kind of things?"

"Deliveries at odd hours—medical equipment, restraint systems, soundproofing materials. Vehicles arriving during full moon periods and leaving empty. And sounds."

"Sounds?"

Kowalski's voice dropped to barely above a whisper. "Howling. Like animals, but not quite right. Guards hear it coming from the basement levels during certain nights of the month. Management explains it as plumbing problems or construction work, but the guards know better."

The room went quiet except for rain pattering against windows and the distant hum of Spring Street traffic. We were discussing the calculated torture of a human being by creatures that saw us as nothing more than prey animals with delusions of equality.

"There's something else," Finch said, pulling out a folder I hadn't seen before. "Information that arrived this afternoon through channels my father established decades ago."

He opened the folder to reveal photographs that looked like they'd been taken with a hidden camera—grainy shots of men in expensive suits entering and leaving the Grayson estate. Some faces I recognized from newspapers and business journals: city councilmen, federal judges, police commissioners.

"The conditioning process isn't just about breaking Roger's mind," Finch explained. "It's about demonstrating the Club's power to their human collaborators. These men—politicians and law enforcement officials who've been taking Crescent Club money for years—they're brought in to witness the process. To see what happens to people who threaten the arrangement."

The scope of it hit me. Roger wasn't just a prisoner—he was a demonstration. An object lesson for the corrupt officials who kept the Club in power.

"How many?" Miller asked.

"At least a dozen confirmed collaborators in city government, probably twice that many in law enforcement agencies." Finch spread the photographs across his desk. "Men who've been bought, blackmailed, or convinced that cooperation with supernatural predators is preferable to resistance."

I studied the faces, matching them to names from newspapers. City councilmen. Judges. Police brass. Men who'd watch torture to keep their positions.

"We can't trust anyone official," I said. "No police backup. No feds. Anyone we approach might be theirs."

"Or tip them off," Miller added. "Then they'll move Roger." Pause. "Or kill him."

Kowalski checked his watch. "There's a viewing scheduled for tomorrow night. My source in the security company says they've been told to expect 'important visitors' at the estate—men who'll need privacy for 'sensitive business discussions.'" "Another torture session."

"The final one, probably. The full moon was last night, but the lunar influence remains strong for several days. They'll want to use tomorrow night's residual power to cement Roger's psychological transformation and conduct their ceremony."

Finch walked to his armory and started pulling down weapons. Silver knives, crossbow bolts, the spear with its leaf-shaped point. "Tomorrow night's our only shot. Wait longer, there won't be anyone to rescue."

Miller studied the architectural plans spread across the desk. "How do we get inside?"

"Service entrance here," Kowalski said, pointing to a spot on the estate's southern boundary. "Kitchen staff use it for deliveries, maintenance crews for equipment access. Security is lighter there because it's considered lowrisk—just servants and tradesmen, nobody important enough to pose a threat."

"What about the basement levels where they're holding Roger?"

"Harder. Access is through the main house, down a staircase that's guarded around the clock. But there's also this..." He pointed to architectural plans that showed the tunnel system added in 1931. "Emergency exits from the basement chambers lead to a drainage tunnel that runs underneath the estate's north wall. Empties out near Laurel Canyon Boulevard."

The plan began forming in my mind. Not a frontal assault, but infiltration—get inside through the service entrance, navigate to the basement levels, locate Roger's cell, and extract him through the tunnel system before the guards knew he was missing.

Vivian would've approved. Stealth over force. Get in quiet, get the job done, get out. That's how she'd operated. "How many guards?"

"During normal operations, maybe six or eight. But tomorrow night, with important visitors attending the session..." Kowalski shrugged. "Could be twice that many."

"Armed?"

"Handguns mostly, maybe a few shotguns. But remember—they're not expecting trouble from anyone with silver ammunition. Lead bullets are just annoyances to creatures with enhanced healing capabilities."

Finch closed his father's journal and looked at each of us with eyes that had spent decades preparing for this moment. "Forty years ago, my father tried legal channels. Built evidence, found witnesses, found prosecutors.

They killed him and buried it."

He picked up the spear, tested its balance. "This time, no courts. No judges. Just silver bullets and us."

Miller checked his service revolver and the spare ammunition clips in his jacket pockets. "What about backup?

If something goes wrong, if we get cornered inside the estate?"

"Then we die fighting," I said, thinking about Vivian's final moments in those orange groves. She'd known the odds were against her, known she probably wouldn't survive the night. But she'd chosen to fight anyway, buying time for the rest of us to continue the mission. "Because the alternative is letting Grayson and his pack turn two million people into cattle."

What we were planning was suicide. Four people with silver bullets against creatures in a fortress. But we were doing it anyway.

"Equipment check," Miller said, falling back on police procedure to impose order on chaos. "Finch, what can you provide?"

"Silver weapons for all of us—knives, crossbow bolts, that spear for whoever wants to carry it. Maps of the estate and surrounding area. Emergency medical supplies in case someone gets hurt but not killed." "Kowalski?"

"Access to the service entrance, guard schedules, intelligence about visitor arrivals. My security company credentials should get us through the outer perimeter without raising alarms."

"I've got the silver bullets," I added, patting the pocket where Goldstein's ammunition would rest tomorrow evening. "Pure silver rounds that will drop a werewolf permanently. Plus backup weapons from Vivian's cache if we need them."

Miller nodded. "I've got backup plans if this goes sideways. Safe houses where we can regroup, contacts in other cities if we need to disappear. And I've got eighteen years of police experience dealing with situations that were supposed to be impossible."

We spent the next hour reviewing architectural plans and developing contingency strategies. Escape routes if the rescue went bad. Rally points if we got separated. Emergency protocols if someone was captured or killed.

But underneath the tactical planning, we all understood the real truth. Tomorrow night, we were walking into the domain of creatures that had been perfecting the art of killing humans for longer than Los Angeles had been a city. Whether we succeeded or failed, whether Roger Talbot survived or not, things were about to escalate beyond anything either side had seen before.

The only question was who would be left standing when the silver bullets stopped flying.

"Twenty-four hours," Miller said as we prepared to leave. "See you all tomorrow night."

We separated into the Los Angeles evening, each of us carrying the weight of what tomorrow would bring.

Tomorrow night, we'd either save Roger Talbot or die trying.

Either way, the age of hiding was ending.

The Trap Tightens

The first sign of trouble came at four-thirty in the morning, when Officer Danny Reeves climbed Finch's fire escape looking like death served cold. Reeves had worked downtown beats for eight years, long enough to know when something didn't belong in any police manual ever written.

Miller and I were drinking coffee in Finch's apartment, going over plans for tonight's rescue, when Reeves knocked on the back door like a man running from the devil himself.

"Detective Miller? Christ, I've been looking for you all night." Reeves stepped inside, uniform torn and bloody, service revolver shaking in his hand. "They said you'd know what to do about what I saw."

Miller guided the younger cop to a chair and took the gun from his trembling fingers. "Easy, Danny. Start from the beginning. What happened?"

"Warehouse District. About two this morning, we got a call about suspicious activity near Terminal Island— vehicles moving around in areas that should've been empty. Captain assigned me and Martinez to check it out, said it was probably just smugglers or black market operators."

Reeves took coffee from Finch and held the cup with both hands like a man trying to keep warm in a blizzard. "We found the vehicles. Maybe twenty cars and trucks, all expensive models, parked around this warehouse that's supposed to be empty. Lights on inside, voices, construction noise."

"What kind of construction work?" I asked, though what I'd learned from Roger's research had already given me a dozen bad possibilities. Vivian had described similar setups from her time on military bases during the war— facilities being modified for activities their original architects never intended.

"That's what we went to find out. Martinez figured we'd take a look, write up a report, maybe catch some bootleggers or fence operators in the act." Reeves took a sip of coffee and regretted it immediately, his stomach too shaky to handle anything stronger than water.

"The warehouse had been modified. Loading dock sealed up, new ventilation system installed, what looked like stadium lighting hanging from the ceiling. And cages."

Miller and I exchanged glances. Nothing good ever came from finding cages where people conducted business after midnight.

"What kind of cages?"

"Big ones. Eight feet square, steel bars thick as your thumb. Twenty or thirty cages arranged in rows like livestock pens." Reeves set down his cup, hands still shaking. "Most were empty, but not all."

Finch had gone very still. "What was in the occupied cages?"

"People." Barely audible. "Men and women, maybe fifteen or twenty total. Some I recognized from missing persons reports. Others looked like they'd been there longer—thin, dirty, eyes like they'd given up hope."

The implications hit like a sledgehammer to the chest. The Club wasn't just gathering werewolf reinforcements —they were stockpiling human prisoners for whatever they'd planned. Vivian had warned me about this during our tactical discussions, drawing on intelligence reports from the European theater. When predators start collecting large numbers of prey animals, she'd said, it means they're planning something that requires scale.

"What happened to Martinez?" Miller asked.

Reeves closed his eyes. "We tried to get closer, see if we could identify more of the prisoners, maybe figure out how to call for backup without alerting whoever was running the operation. That's when we heard voices coming from the office area—men discussing schedules and quotas and other business details."

"You recognize any of the voices?"

"One of them. City councilman Robert Fleming—I'd heard him speak at police ceremonies. He was talking about 'harvest schedules' and 'demonstration requirements' and something called 'the downtown operation.'"

Ice ran through my veins. Whatever the Crescent Club had planned, it was bigger than just eliminating a few troublesome investigators.

"What downtown operation?"

"That's what Martinez wanted to know. He got too close to the office windows, tried to hear more details about timing and targets." Reeves opened his eyes and looked at each of us with the expression of a man who'd seen hell with the lid off. "They caught him."

"Jesus."

"Not they. It. The thing that grabbed Martinez..." Reeves shook his head. "It looked like a businessman in an expensive suit when it walked out of the office, but when it smelled police on him, when it realized we were cops..."

"It transformed," Finch said quietly.

"In maybe thirty seconds, this businessman turned into something with claws and teeth and yellow eyes that caught the warehouse lights like mirrors. It grabbed Martinez before he could draw. Lifted him off the ground easy."

Miller poured whiskey into Reeves' coffee. "What did you do?"

" I ran. Christ help me, I abandoned my partner and ran like a coward. But as I was getting out of there, I heard Fleming giving orders---something about accelerating the timeline, moving up the demonstration to tomorrow night, while the moon's still waxing. "

The room went quiet except for the sound of rain against windows and Reeves' ragged breathing. We'd been planning to rescue Roger Talbot from the Grayson estate, but it sounded like the Crescent Club had something much larger in mind.

Vivian would've seen it. Warehouse modifications, prisoners, accelerated timeline. All building toward something big.

"Did you report this to your captain?" Miller asked.

"I tried. Called it in from a payphone, requested backup and ambulance services for an officer down. You know what I was told?" Reeves' laugh held no humor. "Captain said there was no record of

Martinez and me being assigned to investigate Terminal Island. Said I must be confused about the location, probably saw smugglers in some other warehouse district."

"They're covering it up."

"Or they're part of it. Captain Bradley, Sergeant Walsh, maybe half downtown. On the Club's payroll for years."

Kowalski stood up from the corner where he'd been listening. "It's worse than money. Some of them have seen what happens to cops who ask too many questions about certain families or certain areas of the city. They keep quiet because the alternative is ending up like Martinez."

Miller walked to Finch's map and studied the warehouse district near Terminal Island. "How many prisoners did you say were in those cages?"

"Maybe twenty. But Fleming was talking about numbers that sounded much higher—hundreds of subjects, enough for what he called 'a city-wide demonstration of power.'"

I thought about the missing persons reports that had been piling up in police stations across Los Angeles County. Transients and runaways, prostitutes and small-time criminals—people whose disappearances wouldn't generate much public attention. The perfect victims for creatures that needed to feed regularly but couldn't afford to attract law enforcement scrutiny.

"They're not planning to kill us," I said. "They're going public. Announcing themselves to the whole city."

Finch pulled down one of his father's journals and flipped to pages covered with increasingly desperate handwriting. "Benjamin wrote about this—the endgame scenario that lycanthrope families had been working toward for decades. Not just control through infiltration and corruption, but open rule backed by demonstrated supernatural power."

"What kind of demonstration?" Miller asked.

"Mass killings in public venues. Coordinated attacks on government buildings, police stations, newspapers— anyplace that might organize resistance. The idea was to kill enough people in sufficiently horrible ways that the surviving population would accept werewolf rule as preferable to continued warfare."

Kowalski checked his watch. "Tomorrow night. If they're planning something for then, we've got maybe eighteen hours to figure out their targets and stop them."

"Or rescue Roger and get out of Los Angeles before the killing starts," Reeves suggested. "Take whatever evidence we've got to federal authorities, let them handle creatures that are beyond local law enforcement capabilities."

Miller's expression made it clear what he thought of that idea. "Federal authorities who might be just as corrupted as city officials? FBI agents who'll dismiss our reports as the ravings of cops who've been working too many night shifts?"

"Besides," I added, thinking about Vivian's final words in those orange groves, "running away just means the slaughter happens without anyone fighting back. Two million people turned into prey animals because we decided saving our own necks was more important than protecting them."

The weight of responsibility settled over the room like smoke from a house fire. We'd started this by killing six werewolves in self-defense. Now it looked like the Crescent Club was preparing to escalate beyond anything the city had ever seen.

Vivian had understood this moment would come. During our tactical planning sessions, she'd emphasized the importance of commitment—the difference between people who fight until things get difficult and people who fight until the job is done. She'd made her choice in those orange groves, buying time for the rest of us to see this through to the end.

"What are their most likely targets?" I asked, studying the map of Los Angeles County.

Finch traced routes between the warehouse district and downtown. "City Hall, police headquarters, newspaper offices—places that represent organized human authority. But also targets that would generate maximum terror: movie theaters, department stores, anywhere large numbers of civilians gather."

"The Hollywood Bowl," Kowalski suggested. "There's a symphony performance tomorrow night, maybe three thousand people in attendance. Perfect target for a mass killing that would make headlines from coast to coast." Miller nodded grimly. "Union Station.

The main post office. Maybe even some of the movie studio lots—kill enough actors and directors, and you cripple the entertainment industry that made Los Angeles famous worldwide."

I thought about the logistics of coordinated attacks across a metropolitan area covering hundreds of square miles. "How many werewolves would they need for something like that?"

"More than they have left," Finch replied. "Which is why they've been importing reinforcements from other cities. Sacramento, San Francisco, maybe even from out of state—lycanthrope families who've been waiting decades for the signal to abandon human disguises."

Reeves looked up from his coffee cup with eyes that had seen too much. "When I was hiding in the warehouse, waiting for a chance to escape, I heard Fleming talking about numbers. Fifty werewolves for the initial attacks, another hundred for cleanup operations. They're planning to kill thousands of people tomorrow night."

The scope of it hit like a physical blow. This wasn't just about Roger Talbot or even about Los Angeles. The Crescent Club was preparing to launch a supernatural coup that would transform American civilization into a feeding ground for creatures that saw humans as nothing more than livestock.

"We have to warn people," Miller said. "Get word to anyone who'll listen, try to prevent the attacks before they start."

"Warn them how?" I asked. "Walk into police stations controlled by corrupt cops and announce that werewolves are planning mass murder? Call newspaper editors who've been taking Club money for years? Even if we found honest officials willing to listen, what proof do we have that would convince anyone?"

Finch closed his father's journal. "The proof is in those cages at Terminal Island. Twenty prisoners who can testify about being kidnapped by creatures that aren't entirely human. Physical evidence of a conspiracy that goes beyond normal criminal activity."

"If they're still alive by tomorrow night," Kowalski pointed out. "And if we can reach them before the Club decides to eliminate witnesses."

Miller stood and walked to the window, looking out at Spring Street and the gray dawn light that was beginning to penetrate the

October clouds. "So we have two missions now. Rescue Roger Talbot from the Grayson estate, and somehow prevent mass slaughter in downtown Los Angeles." "With four people and fifty silver bullets," I said.

"Four people who know the truth," Finch corrected. "Four people who've seen what the Club really is and decided to fight instead of hiding. That's four more than Los Angeles had yesterday."

Reeves set down his coffee cup and straightened up with something that looked like determination. "Make it five. I've got eighteen years with the department, contacts throughout the city, access to police communications and equipment. And after what I saw happen to Martinez, I've got personal reasons to see these things dead."

The alliance was growing, but so was the scope of what we were fighting. The Crescent Club wasn't just planning to eliminate a few troublesome investigators—they were preparing for the conquest of an entire American city.

"We need to split our forces," Miller said. "Two teams, two missions. Finch and Kowalski take the rescue operation—get Roger out of the Grayson estate and extract whatever intelligence he can provide about Club operations. Ellie, Reeves, and I hit the warehouse district, try to document evidence and free as many prisoners as possible before the mass attacks begin."

"And then what?" I asked. "Even if we succeed, even if we rescue Roger and expose their plans, we're still talking about fighting a hundred werewolves with conventional weapons."

Finch returned to his hidden armory and pulled out weapons we hadn't seen before—silver-tipped arrows, blessed crucifixes, even what looked like a silver net designed for capturing creatures that could tear through normal restraints.

"Then we make every shot count," he said simply. "We use everything my father learned, everything I've discovered, every piece of silver we can get our hands on. And we make the bastards pay for forty years of feeding on innocent people."

The plan was insane. Split our tiny force to fight on multiple fronts against enemies that had been preparing for this moment since before any of us were born. The odds were so bad that any rational person would have surrendered or fled the city.

But rationality was a luxury we'd abandoned the moment we chose to fight instead of becoming complicit in mass murder. Vivian had understood that choice, had made it herself when she chose to stay behind in those orange groves rather than let the pack reach Sunset Boulevard.

"Equipment distribution in six hours," Miller said, falling back on police procedure to impose order on chaos.

"Final briefing at sunset. Operations commence after dark."

As we prepared to leave Finch's apartment, Officer Reeves called out. "Detective Miller. There's something else you should know about what I heard at the warehouse."

"What?"

"Fleming mentioned a name—someone called 'the Alpha' who was personally overseeing the downtown operations. Said this Alpha had special plans for anyone who'd killed Club members, wanted to make examples of them during the public demonstrations."

The ice water in my veins turned to liquid nitrogen. Marcus Grayson wasn't just planning mass murder—he was planning revenge. Personal, methodical, designed to send a message about what happened to humans who dared fight back against supernatural predators.

"So we're not just trying to prevent attacks," I realized. "We're walking into traps that have been designed to capture us alive."

Miller nodded grimly. "Which means we'd better make sure we don't get taken alive."

Outside, Los Angeles was waking up to what might be its last normal day. Traffic beginning to move through rain-soaked streets, people hurrying to jobs and appointments that suddenly seemed trivial, families starting routines that might end in unimaginable horror before another sunrise.

In eighteen hours, either the city would be free of the supernatural parasites that had controlled it for forty years, or two million people would discover that the creatures in their nightmares were real and had been living among them all along.

The Pack's Gambit

They hit us at sunset, when Los Angeles was changing shifts and nobody was paying attention. I was in my office loading silver bullets when the first explosion rattled windows three blocks away.

The sound came from downtown—a deep boom that seemed to last forever, followed by sirens and the distant crackle of fire. I went to my window and saw black smoke rising from the direction of police headquarters, thick and oily against the dying light.

My phone rang.

"Ellie, it's Miller." His voice was tight as piano wire. "They hit Central Division. Car bomb in the parking garage—took out half the building, killed maybe twenty cops."

"Christ."

"It gets worse. They're not hiding anymore. Witnesses say they saw things—creatures that looked human until they started tearing people apart. The attack isn't just about the building—it's about making sure survivors know what they saw."

I checked my watch. Six-fifteen, and the sun was already disappearing behind the downtown skyline. The moon was rising, still bright from last night's peak, which meant any werewolves still in human form wouldn't stay that way much longer.

"Where are you?"

"Safe house near MacArthur Park. But Ellie, that's not the only target. I'm getting reports of attacks across the city—buildings on fire, vehicles blown up, people torn apart in ways that don't look like any normal violence."

The implications hit like a sledgehammer. This wasn't random terror—it was coordinated warfare, demonstrating that nowhere in Los Angeles was safe from creatures that could strike anywhere.

Vivian had warned me about this during our tactical discussions. When predators decide to abandon stealth, she'd said, it means they're confident enough in their strength to risk open confrontation. That's when they become most dangerous, but also most vulnerable.

"They're coming for us," I realized. "Grayson knows where we live, where we work, where we've been meeting.

This is personal."

"Get out of your office. Now. Head for the bookstore and warn Finch, then meet me at the safe house. We'll regroup and figure out how to respond to this."

The line went dead.

I grabbed my coat and the canvas bag containing spare ammunition, then headed for the door. The building's hallway was already filling with tenants who'd heard the explosion and were debating whether to evacuate or wait for more information. Their voices carried the edge of fear that came from knowing something was wrong but not understanding what.

Mrs. Patterson from the insurance office caught my arm as I passed. "Miss Vance, do you know what's happening? The radio is saying there's been some kind of attack downtown, but the details keep changing." "Gas main explosion," I lied smoothly. "Nothing to worry about. Just stay inside until the all-clear."

She nodded and returned to her office, but I could see the doubt in her eyes. Mrs. Patterson had lived through two wars and the Great Depression—she knew the difference between official explanations and truth.

Spring Street looked normal in the dying light, but something felt wrong. People walked faster, looked over their shoulders, stayed close to buildings like open spaces had turned dangerous. The kind of fear that spreads when predators are hunting.

I walked quickly toward Finch's bookstore, watching for cars that moved too slow or people who seemed to be following me. The silver bullets felt heavier with each step.

Two blocks from the bookstore, I started smelling smoke.

Not the distant smoke from downtown, but something closer. The sharp smell of burning books and paper, mixed with electrical fire and melting plastic.

I broke into a run.

Finch's bookstore was burning. Not the slow, creeping fire of an electrical accident, but the intense blaze that came from professional arson. Flames poured from the second-story windows where his apartment had been, casting dancing shadows across Spring Street and turning the evening air into a furnace.

A crowd had already gathered—neighbors and shopkeepers drawn by the spectacle of destruction, fire department personnel trying to establish a perimeter around the building. But something was wrong with the scene. The firemen weren't trying to fight the blaze—they were just containing it, as if they'd been ordered to let the building burn.

I pushed through the crowd, looking for any sign that Finch had escaped before the fire started. The bookstore's front door hung open, revealing an interior consumed by flames. Smoke poured from the opening like blood from a wound.

The sight hurt more than I expected. Another ally dead. Another person who knew the truth, killed for knowing.

Like Vivian.

"Excuse me, miss." A hand fell on my shoulder. "You need to stay back from the building."

I turned to face a man in a fire department uniform who didn't look like any fireman I'd ever seen. Too well dressed, too calm about the destruction, teeth that seemed just slightly too sharp for normal human dentistry. "I'm looking for the man who lived here," I said. "Alistair Finch. Was he inside when the fire started?"

The fireman smiled. Eyes stayed cold. "No survivors, miss. Tragic accident. Gas leak, probably. Old building." His hand stayed on my shoulder. Too strong. Not human. Could crush bone easily.

"You're Eleanor Vance," he continued conversationally. "The private investigator who's been asking uncomfortable questions about certain prominent families. Marcus Grayson has been looking forward to meeting you."

I reached for the .38 in my coat pocket, but the fireman was faster. His other hand clamped around my wrist with force that sent lightning up my arm, and suddenly I was being pulled toward a black sedan parked at the edge of the crowd.

"Miss Vance needs help," the fireman announced. "Smoke inhalation. Taking her to the hospital."

Two more men in fire department uniforms appeared beside the sedan—both with the same too-sharp teeth and too-calm demeanor. The crowd parted to let them through, either fooled by the official uniforms or too frightened to interfere with what looked like emergency response procedures.

I was twenty feet from the sedan when the real fire department arrived.

Three trucks came screaming down Spring Street with sirens wailing and emergency lights flashing, followed by police cars and an ambulance. Real firemen began spilling from the vehicles—men who looked concerned about the blaze and immediately began deploying hoses and equipment.

In the confusion of arrival and deployment, the fake fireman's grip on my shoulder loosened just enough. I twisted away from him and ran toward the genuine emergency personnel, shouting about suspicious individuals in stolen uniforms.

The fake firemen didn't pursue me. They melted back into the crowd and disappeared, probably unwilling to risk exposure by fighting real city employees in full view of dozens of witnesses.

But the damage was done. Finch's bookstore was a total loss, forty years of research going up in smoke and flames. And somewhere in that inferno was Alistair Finch himself—the man who'd inherited his father's war against supernatural predators and had been carrying it forward in patient isolation.

Another death. Another fighter killed by creatures who preferred murder to inconvenience. The grief came hard, mixing with memories of Vivian's blood in those orange groves.

A real fire captain approached me as the blaze finally began to come under control. "Miss, you mentioned suspicious individuals? Can you describe them?"

"Three men in fire department uniforms who weren't trying to fight the fire. They said there were no survivors, but they seemed more interested in keeping people away from the building than in rescue operations."

The captain frowned. "All our personnel are accounted for, and we didn't have any units on scene before our arrival. You're saying someone was impersonating fire department officers?"

"I'm saying someone wanted to make sure this building burned down, and they were willing to wear your uniforms to do it."

He took down my information and promised to report the incident to proper authorities, but I could see in his eyes that he considered it just another symptom of the panic and confusion that seemed to be spreading across Los Angeles. People seeing conspiracies and deception where there were probably just communication failures and bureaucratic screw-ups.

By the time the fire was extinguished, there wasn't much left of the bookstore or the apartment above it. Smoke-blackened brick walls stood like tombstones around a basement full of ash and debris. The fire captain confirmed what the fake fireman had already told me—no survivors found, though it would be days before the rubble cooled enough for thorough investigation.

I was preparing to leave the scene when I heard my name being called.

"Miss Vance. Over here."

The voice came from the alley behind the burned building, barely audible over the sounds of emergency vehicles and cleanup operations. I looked around to make sure none of the fake firemen had returned, then followed the voice into shadows that smelled of smoke and death.

Bill Kowalski stepped out from behind a delivery truck, his work clothes singed and his face streaked with soot.

In his hands he carried a canvas bag that looked heavy enough to contain books or papers, and beside him—

Alistair Finch lay propped against the alley wall, his scholar's face gray with pain and smoke damage, blood soaking through his shirt from wounds that looked like they'd been made by claws. He was still breathing, but barely.

"Bill? Jesus—" I dropped to my knees beside Finch. "We need to get him to a hospital."

"No hospitals," Finch whispered, his voice barely audible. "They... own the hospitals." He coughed, bringing up blood. "Bill... got me out through the basement. But the smoke..."

"I was down there collecting materials from his storage area when the attack started," Kowalski explained, his voice hoarse. "Heard them breaking into the apartment above, heard Finch fighting them off. By the time I got upstairs, they'd already—" He stopped, unable to finish.

Finch's hand reached out, grabbed my wrist with surprising strength. "They tortured me. Wanted... wanted to know where Father's research was hidden. Who else knew the truth." His breathing was getting shallower. "I didn't... didn't tell them anything."

"Save your strength," I said, though we both knew it was pointless. The wounds were too deep, the smoke damage too severe. Finch was dying, and there was nothing I could do to stop it.

"The journal," he said, eyes focusing on the canvas bag Kowalski held. "Everything... everything you need is in there. Father's research. The Club's weakness. How to..." Another coughing fit, more blood. "How to stop Grayson."

Kowalski opened the bag to show me—journals, photographs, maps. The core of Benjamin Finch's forty-year investigation into the Crescent Club, saved from destruction by his son's foresight and courage.

"There's one more thing you need to know," Finch continued, each word costing him visible effort. "About the conversion ceremony. The alpha's role. Kill Grayson during the ritual, and..." He coughed again. "And the bloodline renewal fails. All of it."

His grip on my wrist weakened. "Vivian... tell Vivian she was right. About everything. About fighting back."

I didn't have the heart to tell him Vivian was already dead. "I will."

"Miss Vance..." His eyes were starting to lose focus. "Eleanor. Finish this. For Father. For everyone they've killed." One last breath, rattling and wet. "Promise me."

"I promise."

Alistair Finch died in that alley with his father's journal clutched in Kowalski's hands, another casualty in a war that had been going on since before Los Angeles became a city. Another scholar who'd chosen to fight monsters rather than pretend they didn't exist.

The image of another friend dying made my stomach clench. Finch, like Vivian, had chosen to endure pain rather than betray the people counting on him. Both had died protecting secrets that might mean the difference between victory and defeat.

Kowalski opened the canvas bag fully to show me journals, photographs, and maps. "He made me promise to get these to you if anything happened. Said you'd know what to do with them."

"But there's something else," he continued. "Something Finch discovered just before the attack. Information about the Club's greatest weakness—something his father learned in 1915 but never had a chance to act on." "What kind of weakness?"

Kowalski pulled out a leather journal that looked older than the others, its pages yellow with age and brittle from decades of handling. "The lycanthrope bloodlines aren't self-sustaining. They require regular infusions of fresh genetic material to prevent degradation and sterility."

"What does that mean?"

"It means they've been kidnapping and converting new members for decades—not just to increase their numbers, but to prevent their existing bloodlines from dying out. But there's a catch. The conversion process only works during certain lunar phases, and only on subjects who meet specific genetic requirements."

I thought about the prisoners in the warehouse cages, about the careful selection criteria that would determine who lived and who died during the Club's feeding operations.

"They're not just planning mass murder tomorrow night," I realized. "They're planning a conversion ceremony.

Turn dozens of carefully selected humans into new werewolves to strengthen their bloodlines."

"Right. But here's the crucial part—the conversion process requires the continued presence of the alpha who initiated it. Kill the alpha during the ceremony, and all partially converted subjects die. The bloodline renewal fails."

The implications hit like lightning. Marcus Grayson wouldn't just be leading tomorrow night's attacks—he'd be personally overseeing the conversion ceremony that was supposed to secure the Club's genetic future. Kill him at the right moment, and we could eliminate not just the current threat but their ability to rebuild.

"Where?" I asked.

Kowalski flipped through pages of the old journal until he found a hand-drawn map of Los Angeles from the 1890s. "The original Crescent Club meeting hall—the building where they held their first ceremonies after arriving in California. It's been abandoned for decades, but according to Benjamin's notes, it still contains the ritual chambers where lycanthrope conversions take place."

The map showed a location near downtown, in an area that had since been developed into warehouses and light industry. A building that would be isolated enough for supernatural activities but close enough to the city center for importance.

"How do we get there?"

"Carefully, and with more weapons than we have." Kowalski closed the journal and shouldered the canvas bag.

"The Club has spent all day demonstrating their power—police stations bombed, government buildings attacked, anyone who might organize resistance eliminated or scattered. By tomorrow night, they'll be confident that no one can threaten their ceremony."

"Which makes it the perfect time to prove them wrong."

We walked back toward Spring Street, where emergency vehicles were beginning to clear the scene. The bookstore fire was officially being treated as a gas leak accident, and the suspicious individuals were dismissed as panic-induced hallucinations. Los Angeles was getting its first taste of the official cover-up that would follow supernatural attacks—truth buried under bureaucratic explanations and witness intimidation.

But the real war was just beginning. The Crescent Club had played their opening gambit, demonstrating that they could strike anywhere in the city with impunity. Tomorrow night, they would attempt to crown their forty-year campaign with a ritual that would ensure their dominance for generations to come.

All we had to stop them was a handful of silver bullets and the desperate courage of people who'd chosen to fight rather than submit to predators wearing human faces.

As we reached the street, Kowalski grabbed my arm. "There's one more thing Finch wanted you to know.

Something about the Club's plans for you."

"What?"

"They're not just trying to kill you—they want to convert you. Grayson believes that turning their most dangerous enemy into one of them would be the ultimate demonstration of werewolf superiority. He's reserved a place for you in tomorrow night's ceremony."

Ice ran through my veins. Not just death, but transformation into the very thing I'd been fighting. Forced to spend eternity as a creature that fed on innocent people, my own skills and determination turned to serve the predators I'd tried to destroy.

I thought about Vivian's final kiss, about the taste of blood and fear and something that might have been love if we'd had more time. She'd died human, died fighting, died with her soul intact. Whatever happened tomorrow night, I'd make the same choice she had.

"Then I guess I'd better make sure I die fighting instead of getting taken alive."

Kowalski nodded grimly. "Finch said you'd say that. He also said to tell you that silver works both ways—what kills them can also prevent conversion, if you time it right."

We parted company at the corner of Spring and Fifth, Kowalski heading toward whatever safe house Miller had established, me returning to my office to collect the rest of my weapons and prepare for what was looking like the last night of my life.

But as I walked through streets that seemed different now—more dangerous, filled with shadows that might hide creatures waiting to strike—I felt something that surprised me.

Relief.

The hiding was over. The uncertainty was finished. Tomorrow night would settle it. Either Los Angeles stayed human or it didn't.

I'd rather go down fighting than live on my knees.

Vivian had understood. Made that choice in the orange groves. Her kiss had been a promise.

The moon hung over Los Angeles, still bright enough to cast shadows. The city didn't know what was coming.
But I did.

The Silver Bullet Plan

Miller's safe house was a two-bedroom apartment above a Chinese laundry on Temple Street. People minded their business there. The smell of soap and starch drifted up through the floors, mixing with cigarette smoke.

I found Miller, Kowalski, and Reeves around a kitchen table covered with maps, photographs, and what looked like building plans copied from city offices. The silver bullets from Goldstein sat in neat rows beside coffee cups—fifty rounds that represented our entire arsenal against creatures that had spent decades perfecting murder.

"Ellie." Miller looked up as I entered, his face showing the strain of a man who'd spent the evening watching his city burn. "Kowalski told us about Finch. I'm sorry."

"He died fighting," I said simply, settling into an empty chair. "Same as we're going to do if this plan doesn't work."

The words came out harder than I meant. But Vivian had understood it. Sometimes you did the job even if it killed you.

Reeves spread out a hand-drawn map that showed downtown Los Angeles as it had looked in the 1890s. "This is the original Crescent Club meeting hall—built in 1895, abandoned when they moved operations to more fashionable locations in the 1920s. According to the records Kowalski saved, it's where they've held their most important ceremonies for over fifty years."

The building sat in what was now a warehouse district near the Los Angeles River, surrounded by light industrial properties that would be largely empty during nighttime hours. Perfect location for activities that needed to remain hidden from normal city life.

"Current status?" I asked.

Kowalski consulted notes written in Finch's careful handwriting. "Officially abandoned since 1923, but utility records show intermittent electrical and water usage during full moon periods. Building permits filed in 1940 for 'structural renovation,' though no details about what kind of work was done."

Miller traced routes between the meeting hall and other Club properties. "How many werewolves are we talking about?"

"Hard to say, but Benjamin Finch's estimates suggest anywhere from fifty to eighty individuals will be present for a major ceremony. That includes the core membership, imported reinforcements from other cities, and human collaborators who help with security and logistics."

The numbers were bad. Four people, fifty silver bullets, eighty enemies. Half of them werewolves.

But sanity had stopped mattering when we chose to fight instead of becoming food.

"What about the prisoners?" I asked. "The people they're planning to convert?"

Kowalski opened one of the salvaged journals to pages covered with diagrams and clinical notes. "According to Benjamin's research, lycanthrope conversion requires subjects to be in a specific psychological and physiological state—weakened by captivity but not broken, their natural resistance reduced but their survival instincts still intact."

"How long does the process take?"

"Several hours for the ceremony, but the actual change happens over three days after the ritual. Kill the alpha who started the conversion before it's complete, and all the half-converted subjects die instead of becoming werewolves."

Reeves looked up from photographs that showed the interior of the meeting hall during its active years. "So we need to get inside during the ceremony, locate Marcus Grayson, and kill him before he can finish the conversions."

"While fighting our way through fifty other werewolves who'll be trying to stop us," Miller added grimly.

I studied the architectural blueprints, noting details about the building's layout and potential access points. The meeting hall was larger than it appeared from street level—three stories above ground with basement facilities that had been excavated during the original construction.

"Main ceremony chamber is here," Kowalski said, pointing to a large room in the center of the building's ground floor. "Designed to accommodate up to a hundred participants, with raised platforms for ritual activities and observation galleries for witnesses."

"Security?"

"Multiple entry points, but all of them will be guarded. Front entrance through the main lobby, service doors on the east and west sides, emergency exits that connect to the basement levels."

Miller traced evacuation routes with his finger. "What about getting out after we kill Grayson?"

"That's the problem," Reeves said quietly. "Even if we succeed in disrupting the ceremony, we'll still be trapped inside a building full of enraged werewolves. The chances of anyone surviving long enough to escape are..."

"Minimal," I finished. "So we make sure the mission succeeds even if we don't."

Vivian would have understood that calculation. During the war, she'd seen plenty of operations where success mattered more than survival, where the objective was worth more than the lives of the people assigned to accomplish it. She'd made that choice herself in the orange groves, buying time for the rest of us to continue the fight.

Kowalski opened another journal to pages that showed detailed drawings of ritual chambers and ceremonial equipment. "There's something else we need to consider. The conversion ceremony isn't just about creating new werewolves—it's about demonstrating the Club's power to their human collaborators and potential new converts."

"Meaning?"

"Meaning there will be witnesses. City officials, police commissioners, business leaders who've been taking Club money for years. Men who need to see the ceremony succeed in order to maintain their loyalty and cooperation."

The implications were clear. Kill Grayson during the ceremony, and we'd also be eliminating dozens of corrupt officials who helped maintain the Club's control over Los Angeles government and law enforcement.

"How do we identify Grayson among all the other werewolves?" I asked.

Miller consulted police files that contained photographs and physical descriptions of known Club members. "He's distinctive—six feet tall, silver hair, the kind of aristocratic bearing that comes from generations of believing you're genetically superior to everyone around you. During ceremonies, he wears ceremonial robes that mark him as the alpha."

"And he'll be personally overseeing each conversion," Kowalski added. "Benjamin's notes indicate that the alpha must maintain physical contact with subjects during the critical transformation phases—something about lycanthrope genetic material requiring direct transmission through skin contact."

I divided the silver bullets into four roughly equal piles. "Twelve rounds each, plus whatever regular ammunition we're carrying for backup. Not much margin for error."

"Every shot has to count," Reeves agreed. "Miss a vital target, and we're dealing with wounded werewolves that can heal from most injuries within minutes."

We spent the next hour reviewing entry strategies and timing considerations. The ceremony would begin shortly after sunset, when the full moon's influence was strongest but before darkness made tactical movement impossible. We'd need to breach the building, locate the main ceremony chamber, identify Grayson among dozens of participants, and eliminate him before he could finish the conversion process.

"Equipment check," Miller said, falling back on police procedure to impose order on what was a suicide mission. "What does everyone have?"

I inventoried my gear. ".38 revolver with twelve silver bullets, backup .32 automatic with regular ammunition, silver knife from Finch's collection, lock picks, emergency medical supplies." I paused, thinking about resources we hadn't used. "Plus there's Vivian's weapons cache if we need it. Rifles, regular ammunition, surveillance equipment—it's all still there."

Thinking about her brought back that final kiss. Blood and fear. She'd prepared for a long fight, knowing silver bullets alone wouldn't be enough.

"Service revolver, twelve silver rounds, police flashlight, handcuffs in case we need to restrain anyone," Miller replied.

Kowalski showed us a canvas bag filled with items salvaged from the bookstore fire. "Silver-tipped arrows, crossbow, maps of the building interior, and this." He held up what looked like a silver crucifix attached to a long chain. "Benjamin called it a lycanthrope detector—pure silver blessed by clergy who understood what they were blessing it for."

"How does it work?"

"Proximity to werewolves causes the silver to become hot enough to burn human skin. The closer you get to lycanthrope blood, the more intense the burning sensation becomes."

Reeves contributed items borrowed from police equipment rooms. "Tear gas canisters, emergency flares, radio equipment for communication if we get separated inside the building."

The plan stayed simple. We couldn't get fancy with these odds. Surprise and the alpha kill—that was all we had.

"Entry through the east service door," Miller decided. "Kowalski has keys copied from building maintenance records, so we should be able to get inside without alerting perimeter guards."

"Move through basement levels to avoid main floor security," I added. "Use building plans to locate the ceremony chamber from below, then breach upward through service corridors."

"Identify Grayson using the silver detector," Reeves continued. "Concentrate all fire on the alpha—ignore other targets unless they're directly preventing us from completing the primary mission." "And if we succeed in killing Grayson?" Kowalski asked.

Miller's expression made it clear he considered that outcome unlikely but not impossible. "Then we try to get out alive. But the mission succeeds whether we survive or not—prevent the conversions, eliminate the alpha, disrupt their plans for supernatural conquest of Los Angeles."

The weight of what we were planning hit the room hard. Four people with improvised weapons, preparing to assault a fortress held by creatures that could tear humans apart with their bare hands. The odds were so bad that any sane person would have run.

But sanity was a luxury we'd surrendered when we chose to fight predators rather than becoming their prey. Vivian had understood that choice. She'd made it when she stayed behind in those orange groves, choosing death with honor over survival through submission.

"Letters," Miller said quietly. "Anyone who wants to write final messages, now's the time. I'll make sure they get delivered if..."

"If we don't come back," I finished.

I thought about my empty office on Spring Street, about clients whose cases would never be solved and debts that would never be repaid. About my father's grave at Forest Lawn—the man who'd built this PI business from nothing and died of a heart attack before he could see what I'd become. Would he be proud that I was using his skills to fight monsters, or horrified that his daughter would die in a warehouse fighting creatures that shouldn't exist?

And I thought about my mother in San Diego. A schoolteacher who hadn't spoken to me in three years, who'd told me to sell the detective agency and find respectable work. She'd never know if I died tonight. Would never know that her estranged daughter had chosen to stand between two million people and the things that wanted to feed on them.

But mostly I thought about Vivian, lying somewhere in the Los Angeles County morgue with identification tags that would never tell the real story. She'd died believing we could win this fight. The least I could do was make sure her faith hadn't been misplaced.

"Nothing to write," I said.

Miller nodded. "Same here. Lost my family to normal human violence years ago—cancer, car accident, the usual tragedies that kill people in a world where werewolves aren't the biggest threat."

Kowalski and Reeves also declined to write letters. Men who'd chosen dangerous professions and dangerous allies, who'd made peace with mortality long before tonight's mission became necessary.

We synchronized watches and established final meeting times. Six hours until sunset, when the ceremony would begin. Five hours until we entered the building. Four hours until we either succeeded in preventing supernatural conquest of Los Angeles or died trying.

"Anyone wants to change their mind, now's the last chance," Miller said. "Walk away, leave the city, try to build a life somewhere werewolves don't control local government."

Nobody moved.

"All right then," I said, pocketing my silver bullets and checking the action on my .38. "Let's go save Los

Angeles from creatures that think humans exist for their entertainment."

We left the safe house separately, taking different routes through a city that looked normal in the afternoon sunlight but felt different now that we knew what was hiding beneath its surface. People going about their daily routines, unaware that tonight would determine whether they continued living as free citizens or became livestock managed by supernatural predators.

I walked back toward my office to collect the rest of my gear, watching shadows that might hide werewolves and evaluating everyone I passed for signs of inhuman features. The silver knife in my pocket felt warm against my hip, as if it could sense enemies nearby.

But underneath the fear and tactical planning, I felt something unexpected.

Peace.

The uncertainty was over. The hiding had ended. Tonight, either Los Angeles would be free of the creatures that had controlled it for forty years, or those creatures would rule openly instead of from the shadows.

Either way, the long war between human and lycanthrope would finally reach its conclusion.

Vivian had felt this same peace, I realized. During those final moments in the orange groves, even as werewolf claws opened her throat, she'd known we had a real chance of winning. Her sacrifice had bought us time and tactical advantage. Her love had given us something worth fighting for.

And I'd rather die fighting than live as prey.

The sun was beginning its descent toward the western horizon, and somewhere across the city, Marcus Grayson was preparing for a ceremony that would secure werewolf dominance for generations to come.

But he hadn't counted on four people with fifty silver bullets and the desperate courage of those who'd chosen death over submission.

The moon was rising over Los Angeles, bright enough to cast shadows even before darkness fell.

And we were ready.

Into the Wolf's Den

The Grayson estate squatted in the Hollywood Hills like something that had been eating the neighborhood from the inside. Spanish Colonial walls, sure, but twisted by decades of modifications that had nothing to do with normal folks living normal lives.

Some architect back in the twenties had built this place for pool parties and Sunday brunches. Now it looked like a fortress. Iron spikes jutted from walls that blocked out the stars, and the windows were too dark, too still.

The gardens had grown into something you wouldn't want to walk through sober.

We approached through the ravine that ran along the property's northern boundary, using the same route Kowalski had scouted during his years of surveillance work. The October air carried smells that didn't belong in Los Angeles—pine needles and wet earth, animal musk, and underneath it all something that made my gut clench with recognition.

Vivian would've spotted the wrongness right off. She had a nose for trouble—comes from growing up knowing there are things that hunt people for sport. The air here carried something that made my stomach clench, animal musk mixed with something else. Something that didn't belong in any civilized place.

"Service entrance is fifty yards ahead," Kowalski whispered, checking a rough sketch he'd put together from memory and papers he'd lifted from city hall. "Staff door's usually locked," he whispered, "but they don't watch it close. They figure anybody stupid enough to break in deserves what they get."

Miller checked his service revolver and the twelve silver bullets that represented his entire contribution to our assault on creatures that had been killing humans since before Los Angeles was a city. "What about alarms?"

"Old building, old wiring. They trust their noses more than electronic gadgets. But once we're inside, we've got maybe ten minutes before they smell us."

I felt for the silver knife in my coat pocket, drawing comfort from its weight and the blessed metal's promise of effectiveness against enemies that conventional weapons couldn't touch. The .38 revolver held six rounds of pure silver ammunition, with six more in the spare cylinder I'd prepared. Not much firepower for what we were attempting, but every shot would count.

"Remember the objective," I said quietly. "We're here for Roger Talbot, not to fight a war we can't win. Get in, locate him, extract him through the tunnel system before they can organize a response."

"And if we run into Grayson?"

"We kill him if we can, but Roger comes first. He's the only witness who can testify about what they've been doing, the only evidence that might convince the feds to take action."

The bushes grabbed at us like they had it in for strangers. Kowalski knew the way, but even he stumbled twice on roots that seemed to reach up just when you weren't expecting them. I kept thinking I heard something breathing behind us, but every time I turned around, there was nothing but darkness.

The service door stood slightly ajar, as if someone had been expecting our arrival. Warm light spilled from the gap, along with sounds that didn't belong in any normal household—low voices speaking in languages that predated English, the scrape of metal against stone, and underneath it all a rhythmic chanting that seemed to pulse in time with our heartbeats.

"Too easy," Miller muttered, but he followed Kowalski through the opening into a kitchen that looked like it had been designed for feeding an army rather than a family.

This kitchen could've fed an army. Huge stoves, cutting tables marked up like they'd seen some serious butcher work. The pots

hanging overhead caught our flashlight beams and threw crazy shadows on the walls.

But it was the smell that told us we were in the right place. Under
the kitchen odors of grease and spices was something else—blood,
animal musk, and the staleness that came from places where normal
life had been replaced by something darker.

"Basement access should be through here," Kowalski said, pointing
toward a door marked with symbols that might have been decorative
carvings or might have been warnings in a language none of us
recognized.

Stone steps led down into nothing. Our flashlights didn't seem to
reach far enough, and the air tasted like old meat and fear. Every step
down felt like we were walking into something's stomach.

Twenty steps down, we reached a landing where corridors
branched in three directions. The chanting was louder here, echoing
through passages that carried sound in ways that suggested tunnel
systems beneath the estate. Then I heard crying. Human crying,
mixed with the rattle of chains and voices begging for things I didn't
want to think about.

Vivian had taught me to listen for the sounds that mattered—where
people moved, how many, when they felt safe enough to make noise.
Right now, the sounds were coming from below.

"Which way?" Miller asked.

Kowalski consulted building plans that had been drawn from
memory and forty years of intelligence gathering. "Holding cells
should be to the east, main ceremony chamber straight ahead. If
they're keeping Roger separate from the conversion candidates, he'll
be in the high-security area."

"Where's that?"

"Deeper. Another level down, behind steel doors and reinforced
walls. The kind of place they keep prisoners who need special attention."

We moved east through corridors that belonged in medieval dun-
geons rather than twentieth-century California. Stone walls wept
condensation, electric lights flickered with unreliable power, and
every twenty feet we passed doors marked with symbols that suggested their contents were better left undisturbed.

Behind one door, something large moved against restraints that sounded like anchor chains. Behind another, voices whispered in languages that made our skin crawl with instinctive revulsion. A third door showed scratches in the wood that looked like they'd been made by claws trying to get out rather than in.

"Jesus," Miller breathed. "How long has this been going on?"

"Since 1895," I replied. "Sixty years to perfect whatever they do down here."

We reached another staircase, this one descending into darkness so thick our flashlights seemed to make no impression. The air grew colder as we went down, carrying scents that belonged in morgues and charnel houses rather than residential properties.

The second basement level looked different—more recent construction, with reinforced concrete walls and steel doors that had been designed by someone who understood both security and soundproofing. Electric lights were brighter here, powered by a generator system that hummed with mechanical reliability.

"This is it," Kowalski said, consulting his mental map of the property. "High-security detention area. If Roger's still alive, he'll be behind one of these doors."

There were six cells along the corridor, each marked with plaques that bore names and dates going back decades. Some of the dates were recent—within the past year or two. Others went back to the 1920s and 1930s, suggesting long-term prisoners who'd been held for reasons we could only imagine.

"Check them all," Miller said. "But quickly. We've been inside too long already."

The first cell held a man who might once have been a banker or lawyer, judging from his expensive clothes and soft hands. But weeks or months of captivity had reduced him to something that barely looked human—hollow eyes, matted hair, the kind of thousand-yard stare that came from seeing too much horror.

The second cell was empty except for chains and stains that suggested its previous occupant hadn't left voluntarily.

The third cell contained someone who'd been dead for days, though the body showed wounds that no normal animal could have made.

"Here," Kowalski called softly. "Fourth cell. It's him."

Roger Talbot sat chained to a chair that had been bolted to the concrete floor, his once-handsome face gaunt and hollow-eyed from weeks of calculated torture. But he was alive, and when our flashlight beam hit his face, something that might have been recognition flickered in eyes that had seen too much but hadn't yet given up hope.

"Roger," I whispered, pulling out lock picks to work on the cell door. "Roger, it's Eleanor Vance. We're here to get you out."

He looked at me with the expression of someone who'd long ago stopped believing in rescue, but when he spoke, his voice was stronger than I'd expected.

"Miss Vance? Christ, you're real. I thought... I thought maybe they'd killed you already."

Miller kept watch while I worked on the lock, his service revolver ready and silver bullets chambered. "How many guards between here and the surface?"

"Varies," Roger replied, testing his voice and finding it still functional despite weeks of abuse. "Sometimes just Whitmore, sometimes others. They don't expect rescue attempts—most people who learn about this place don't live long enough to tell anyone."

The lock clicked open. Kowalski moved to work on Roger's restraints while I helped him stand on legs that hadn't supported his weight in days.

"Can you walk?"

"I can try. But there's something you need to know—about what they're planning, about why they kept me alive this long."

"Tell us while we move," Miller said. "We need to get out of here before—" The lights went out.

Emergency lighting flickered on a moment later, bathing the corridor in hellish red illumination that made everything look like scenes from Dante's nightmares. And in that crimson glow, we saw Edward Whitmore standing at the end of the corridor, his pale blue eyes reflecting the light like mirrors.

"Miss Vance," he said in his cultured accent. "How good of you to join us. Marcus will be delighted to see you again."

Miller's gun was up and aimed before Whitmore finished speaking, but the werewolf was already moving. Not the awkward transformation we'd seen from others, but a fluid shift from human to something that combined the worst aspects of man and wolf—intelligence maintained, predatory instincts unleashed, supernatural strength focused through cunning that had been refined over decades of hunting humans.

The first silver bullet took Whitmore in the shoulder, spinning him around but not dropping him. Enhanced healing meant wounds that would kill normal men were just inconveniences to creatures with lycanthrope blood.

Miller's second shot missed as Whitmore leaped across the corridor in a movement that defied human reflexes. Claws raked across Miller's chest, tearing through fabric and flesh with surgical precision.

But Miller was a twenty-year police veteran who'd survived knife fights and shootouts with criminals who had nothing supernatural about their lethality. As Whitmore's claws opened his chest, Miller pressed his service revolver against the werewolf's ribs and pulled the trigger three times in rapid succession.

Silver bullets punched through enhanced bone and muscle, disrupting the supernatural healing that had kept Whitmore alive through decades of violence. The werewolf staggered backward, human features reasserting themselves as silver poisoning began shutting down his lycanthrope abilities.

"Go," Miller gasped, pressing his hand against wounds that were bleeding too much and too fast. "Get Roger out. I'll hold them off."

"Frank—"

"Go! That's an order from a superior officer!"

The command hit me like a physical blow. Another ally dying to buy time for the mission, another person choosing sacrifice over survival. Just like Vivian in those orange groves, making the hard choice so the rest of us could continue fighting.

Kowalski grabbed Roger's arm and pulled him toward the staircase we'd used to reach the detention level. I hesitated for a moment, torn between helping Miller and finishing the mission that had brought us here.

"Miss Vance," Roger said, his voice carrying strength I wouldn't have expected from someone who'd endured weeks of torture. "There's something else. Something they made me tell them about the other investigators, about people who might continue the fight even if you were eliminated."

"What did you tell them?"

"Everything. Names, addresses, contacts—they have ways of making you talk, ways that don't leave marks but break you down until you'll say anything to make it stop."

The implications hit like ice water. If Roger had been forced to reveal information about other people investigating lycanthrope activities, the Crescent Club would be moving to eliminate them even as we attempted our rescue.

"How many names?"

"Maybe a dozen. Private investigators, police officers, reporters who'd been asking awkward questions. They're all targets now because of what I told them."

We reached the first basement level, where the chanting had grown louder and more urgent. Through gaps in the stone walls, we could see lights moving in the main ceremony chamber—not electric illumination, but the dancing glow of torches and candles that suggested ritual activities were approaching their climax.

"The tunnel exit," Kowalski said, pointing toward a corridor that led away from the ceremony chamber. "We can be out of the building in five minutes."

But as we moved toward escape, Roger grabbed my arm with surprising strength.

"You can't just leave," he said. "Not when you know what they're planning. The conversion ceremony—it's not just about creating new werewolves. It's about demonstrating their power to government officials who've been wavering in their loyalty."

"We'll come back with reinforcements—"

"There won't be time. The ceremony ends at midnight, and after that, they'll have fifty new lycanthropes plus confirmed loyalty from every corrupt official in Los Angeles County. By tomorrow morning, they'll control the city."

I looked back toward the corridor where Miller was fighting for his life against creatures that had been perfecting the art of killing humans since before California was a state. Looked ahead toward the tunnel that would take us to safety and eventual federal assistance that might or might not arrive in time to prevent supernatural conquest of Los Angeles.

Behind us, Miller's service revolver fired its last silver bullets. The sounds that followed suggested he was no longer winning his fight.

Vivian had faced this same choice in the orange groves. Safety versus duty, survival versus mission completion. She'd chosen to stay behind, to buy time for the rest of us to continue the war against creatures that saw humans as nothing more than prey animals.

Her final kiss had tasted like goodbye, but also like a promise. A promise that some things were worth dying for, that some fights mattered more than the people fighting them.

"The choice is yours, Miss Vance," Roger said quietly. "Save me and hope someone else stops them, or finish what you started and make sure they can't hurt anyone else."

I checked my .38 revolver. Six silver bullets remained, plus the blessed round Miller's father had prepared twenty years ago. Not much ammunition for what I was contemplating, but every shot would count.

"Get Roger to the tunnel exit," I told Kowalski. "If I'm not there in fifteen minutes, get him out of the city and to federal authorities who might listen."

"Where are you going?"

"To finish what Miller started. To make sure Marcus Grayson doesn't live to see another full moon."

I headed back toward the ceremony chamber, toward the sounds of chanting and torchlight and human voices raised in fear. Behind me, Kowalski and Roger made their way toward escape and possible salvation.

Ahead lay the final confrontation with creatures that had controlled Los Angeles for sixty years, creatures that saw two million human beings as nothing more than livestock to be managed and harvested at will.

The silver bullets felt warm in my hand as I approached the chamber where the war between human and lycanthrope would finally reach its bloody conclusion.

Either Marcus Grayson would die tonight, or Los Angeles would belong to predators who wore human faces during business hours.

Vivian had made her choice in those orange groves. Miller had made his choice in the basement corridors. Now it was my turn to choose between safety and duty, between survival and the mission that mattered more than any of our individual lives.

The choice was mine to make, and I was ready to make it.

The Alpha's Challenge

The main ceremony chamber was a testament to sixty years of predators pretending to be civilized. What had once been a simple meeting room had been transformed into something from hell—stone walls carved with symbols that hurt to look at directly, a ceiling that swallowed light, and a raised platform where creatures wearing human faces conducted rituals older than California.

I moved through service corridors that Miller had died defending, staying quiet and low. Behind me, the fighting had faded to occasional gunshots and the wet sounds that came when things fed. Miller's sacrifice had bought Kowalski and Roger time to reach the tunnel exit, but it had also announced our presence to every lycanthrope in the building.

The chamber's main doors stood open, spilling torchlight and the sound of chanting into corridors that reeked of blood and fear. Through the opening, I could see what the Crescent Club had been building toward for decades —a conversion ceremony designed to create dozens of new werewolves while demonstrating their power to the corrupt officials who helped maintain their control over Los Angeles.

Twenty human prisoners knelt in a circle around the platform, hands bound, faces showing the hopelessness that came from knowing they were about to die badly. Some I knew from missing persons reports—small-time crooks, prostitutes, transients, people whose disappearances wouldn't make headlines or generate public outrage.

Around the prisoners stood men in expensive suits who should have been protecting Los Angeles instead of watching citizens fed to monsters. City councilmen, police commissioners, federal judges—the corrupt bastards who'd been taking werewolf money for years, finally seeing the creatures they'd been serving in their full supernatural glory.

But it was the figures on the raised platform that made my blood freeze.

Marcus Grayson stood at the center of the ceremony, his silver hair gleaming in torchlight, his aristocratic features carrying the casual arrogance of someone who'd spent decades believing himself genetically superior to everyone around him. He wore ceremonial robes that looked like they'd been cut from shadow and starlight, marked with symbols that seemed to shift and writhe when viewed directly.

Beside him stood a man I recognized from Finch's photographs—Theodore Ashworth, the last surviving founding member of the families that had brought lycanthrope bloodlines to California in the 1890s. He was smaller than Grayson but carried himself with the confident bearing of someone who'd been killing humans since before Los Angeles was a city.

Between them lay an altar carved from black stone, its surface stained with substances that looked like blood but seemed to move with their own life. Ceremonial knives and chalices sat arranged in patterns that suggested rituals older than Christianity, older than most of recorded human history.

Vivian would have understood this scene immediately. Her reconnaissance work had taught her to read operational setups, to understand how spaces were organized for maximum psychological impact. Ritual chambers are designed to break resistance, she'd explained during our tactical discussions. The architecture itself becomes a weapon.

"Brothers and sisters," Grayson's voice carried easily through the chamber, pitched to reach every corrupt official and terrified prisoner. "Tonight we abandon the pretenses that have limited our activities for sixty years.

Tonight we demonstrate our true nature to those who would serve us and those who would feed us."

A murmur of approval rose from the suited officials who ringed the prisoners. Men who'd spent years pretending werewolves were just another criminal organization they could control through bribery and intimidation, finally seeing the creatures they'd been serving without their human masks.

"The old ways are ending," Grayson continued, his pale eyes reflecting torchlight like mirrors. "No more hiding behind human facades. No more limiting our feeding to acceptable levels. Los Angeles belongs to us now, and after tonight, its population will understand their proper place in the natural order."

Ashworth stepped forward, his voice carrying a slight accent that suggested origins in places where peasants still disappeared during full moon periods. "The conversion candidates have been prepared according to the ancient methods. Their resistance has been broken, their survival instincts enhanced, their bodies ready to accept the gift of lycanthrope blood."

Seven shots. Maybe fifteen enemies. The math wasn't working in my favor, but sometimes you don't get to pick your odds.

But sometimes the mission mattered more than survival. Vivian had understood that in the orange groves. Miller had understood that in the basement corridors. Now it was my turn to make the same choice.

I stepped through the main doors and into torchlight that turned everything the color of fresh blood.

"Marcus Grayson," I called out, my voice echoing off stone walls carved with symbols that seemed to writhe in the flickering illumination. "Eleanor Vance, private investigator. I believe you've been looking for me."

The chanting stopped. Conversations died. Twenty prisoners looked up with eyes that held the first spark of hope they'd felt in weeks, while their captors reached for weapons with movements that were just slightly too fast for normal human reflexes.

But Grayson himself seemed genuinely pleased to see me.

"Eleanor Vance," he said, like he was welcoming me to a dinner party. "The little nurse who's been such a pain in my ass. So glad you could make it to the festivities."

"Wouldn't miss it for the world. Though I have to say, the guest list leaves something to be desired."

Grayson's laugh was genuinely amused. "Always the smart mouth, even when you're about to die. I like that in prey—makes the hunt more entertaining."

"I'm not prey, Grayson. I'm the hunter who's been killing your pack one silver bullet at a time."

"Indeed you are. Six of my oldest associates dead, several promising young recruits eliminated, years of careful planning disrupted by one stubborn human who refused to accept the natural order." His pale eyes studied my face with the expression of a scientist examining an interesting specimen. "Tell me, Miss Vance—what drives someone to fight battles she cannot possibly win?"

"Professional pride. I was hired to find Roger Talbot, and I don't like leaving cases unfinished."

"Ah yes, Mr. Talbot. I trust you found him in acceptable condition?"

"He'll live. Which is more than I can say for the bastards who've been torturing him."

I could still taste Vivian's last kiss—blood and desperation and something that might've been goodbye. She'd known it would come down to this.

Ashworth stepped forward, his older face showing the kind of cruel amusement that came from decades of watching humans die in creative ways. "You speak boldly for someone who walked into a room containing two dozen creatures that could tear you apart without working up a sweat."

"I speak honestly. Something you bloodsuckers wouldn't recognize if it bit you on the ass."

The guards began moving into positions that would prevent my escape, but Grayson raised a hand to stop them.

"Wait. I have a proposal for Miss Vance."

"I'm listening."

"Join us." His voice carried the sincere tone of someone making a genuine offer. "Accept the gift of lycanthrope blood. Become something more than human, more than prey. Help us guide Los Angeles into the new age that begins tonight."

I felt the weight of the .38 in my hand, the silver bullets warm against my palm. Around the chamber, corrupt officials watched the exchange with expressions that ranged from curiosity to barely concealed hunger. On the platform, twenty prisoners waited to learn whether they'd be rescued or fed to creatures that wore human faces during business hours.

"What makes you think I'd want to become a monster?"

"Because you've seen what we're capable of," Grayson replied. "You understand that humans are prey animals pretending to be predators. You know that individual courage means nothing against superior force backed by supernatural abilities."

He gestured toward the kneeling prisoners. "These people represent the future of human-lycanthrope relations. They'll be fed upon, converted, or eliminated based on their usefulness to our larger goals. But you—you could be different. You could work with us, you know. Better than ending up like your girlfriend."

I thought about Walt Henley torn apart in Griffith Park. About seventeen innocent people killed during the pack's rampage through Los Angeles. About Roger Talbot broken and chained in a basement cell designed for psychological torture. About Vivian dying in those orange groves because she'd chosen to fight instead of submitting to creatures that saw her as nothing more than meat.

About Miller bleeding out in basement corridors, using his last silver bullets to buy time for a mission that mattered more than any of our individual lives.

About two million people who had no idea their city was controlled by predators that saw them as livestock to be managed and harvested at will.

"Counter-proposal," I said, raising my .38 and aiming at Grayson's chest. "How about you all go to hell?"

The first silver bullet hit him square in the chest, ripping through those fancy robes and into whatever passed for his heart. He stumbled but didn't go down—tough bastard was harder to kill than his pack.

But silver disrupted those healing abilities, and pure silver ammunition did more than just disrupt—it actively poisoned lycanthrope blood, turning their supernatural advantages against them.

Fast change this time—not like the others I'd seen fumbling through it. Ashworth had been doing this since before my grandmother was born. One moment he was an elderly man in expensive clothes, the next he was something with claws and fangs and yellow eyes that reflected torchlight like mirrors.

My second bullet caught him mid-change, silver disrupting the transformation and leaving him stuck between human and wolf—something with the worst parts of both and none of the advantages of either.

But there were still guards moving to surround me, still corrupt officials reaching for weapons, still a dozen threats that I couldn't handle with the five silver bullets that remained in my cylinder.

That's when the prisoners decided they'd rather die fighting than kneeling.

Twenty people who'd spent weeks in cages, who'd been starved and beaten and told they were nothing more than food for superior creatures, suddenly discovered they still had enough humanity left to choose how they wanted to die. Bound hands became weapons, desperate men and women threw themselves at guards who'd been treating them like cattle marked for slaughter.

The chamber erupted into chaos.

Gunshots echoed off stone walls as guards tried to maintain control over prisoners who'd decided death in battle was preferable to conversion into monsters. Corrupt officials scattered toward exits, their loyalty to the werewolf cause evaporating when faced with actual violence. Torches were knocked over, sending shadows dancing across walls carved with symbols that seemed to move in the flickering light.

But through it all, Marcus Grayson remained standing.

Grayson came at me fast and wrong—eight feet of something that had forgotten how to be human. All claws and teeth and yellow eyes, moving like death in a dinner jacket.

"You can't win this, Eleanor Vance," Grayson's voice came out wrong now, more growl than words. "Silver or no silver, you're still just meat that's gotten ideas above its station."

"Maybe," I replied, checking my remaining ammunition. Two silver bullets left. Plus Miller's special round— the one his father had blessed back when hope seemed like enough. Not much to work with, but it would have to do. "But you won't live to see it."

Theodore Ashworth had completed his transformation despite the silver bullet lodged in his chest, becoming something that looked like it had crawled out of mankind's oldest nightmares. Scars covered his massive frame —evidence of decades spent fighting humans who'd discovered the truth about lycanthrope activities.

"She's mine," he growled, his voice barely recognizable as human speech. "I want to taste the blood of the woman who killed Jack Rafferty."

But Grayson raised a clawed hand to stop his lieutenant. "No. This one is special. She's earned the right to face the alpha personally."

Around us, the battle continued to rage. Prisoners fought guards with bare hands and desperate courage, while corrupt officials fled toward exits that might or might not be guarded by more werewolves. Bodies fell on both sides—humans torn apart by claws, guards dropped by improvised weapons and the few silver bullets I'd managed to distribute before entering the chamber.

But the real fight was just beginning.

Everything I knew about fighting went out the window the second I saw what Marcus Grayson really was. Claws, not fists. Speed that made my eyes water just tracking it. Silver bullets were supposed to work—if I could hit something that moved like it was cheating at physics.

Marcus Grayson, alpha of the Los Angeles werewolf pack, direct descendant of the lycanthrope families that had been feeding on humans since before California was a state. A creature that combined supernatural strength with sixty years of experience killing anyone who threatened his species' dominance.

Against Eleanor Vance, private investigator and former Army Medical Corps sergeant. A woman with five silver bullets and the desperate courage of someone who'd rather die fighting than live as prey.

The outcome should have been predetermined.

But sometimes, David managed to kill Goliath.

Sometimes, the monster lost.

And sometimes, love and sacrifice and the memory of people worth dying for could give ordinary humans the strength to do extraordinary things.

"Come on then," I said, raising my .38 toward the creature that had been terrorizing Los Angeles since before I was born. "Let's finish this."

Both shots hit him square in the chest. Should've dropped him like a sack of flour, but he kept coming. The bastard was tougher than the others, bleeding black but not slowing down near enough.

Vivian's voice in my head: "Can't outrun them, can't outfight them. Make them come to you where you want them." Easy for her to say from memory.

He roared like nothing I'd ever heard—part animal, part something worse. The bullet had found something important; I could tell from how his left arm hung wrong.

The alpha werewolf smiled, showing teeth that could tear through human bone like paper. Around us, the chaos of battle provided a soundtrack of gunshots and screams and the wet sounds of predators feeding.

But in the space between Marcus Grayson and myself, there was only silence.

The kind of silence that came just before someone died.

The only question was which one of us it would be.

The Final Hunt

Everything I knew about fighting went out the window the second I saw what Marcus Grayson really was. Claws, not fists. Speed that made my eyes water just tracking it. Silver bullets were supposed to work—if I could hit something that moved like it was cheating at physics.

Grayson came at me fast and wrong—eight feet of something that had forgotten how to be human. All claws and teeth and yellow eyes, moving like death in a dinner jacket. His claws caught torchlight as he moved, fourinch razors that could open a man from throat to groin in a single swipe.

I put two silver bullets in his chest before he covered half the distance between us.

Both shots hit him square in the chest. Should've dropped him like a sack of flour, but he kept coming. The bastard was tougher than the others, bleeding black but not slowing down near enough.

The silver was working—I could see it in the way he moved less smoothly, in the dark blood that flowed from wounds that should have been closing. But working wasn't winning, and I had three bullets left against something that could take damage that would kill a dozen men.

Vivian's voice in my head: "Can't outrun them, can't outfight them. Make them come to you where you want them." Easy for her to say from memory.

His first swipe missed my throat by inches, claws whistling through air where my head had been a moment before. I rolled left, came up firing, put my third silver bullet in his shoulder as he spun to follow my movement.

He roared like nothing I'd ever heard—part animal, part something worse. The bullet had found something important; I could tell from how his left arm hung wrong.

But it also made him angry.

The wounded shoulder didn't slow him down much. If anything, pain seemed to focus his predatory instincts, stripping away the civilized veneer that had allowed him to pass for human during sixty years of feeding on Los Angeles citizens.

His second attack came faster than the first, a blur of claws and fangs that forced me to dive behind the black stone altar where ceremonial knives glittered in torchlight. Stone chips exploded as his claws raked across surfaces that had been carved by craftsmen who understood they were building furniture for monsters.

"You can't win this, Eleanor Vance," Grayson's voice came out wrong now, more growl than words. "Silver or no silver, you're still just meat that's gotten ideas above its station."

I checked my .38. Two silver bullets left. Plus Miller's special round—the one his father had blessed back when hope seemed like enough. Not much to work with, but it would have to do.

"Tell me something, Grayson," I called out, staying low behind the altar while I tried to figure out angles and timing. "What happens to your pack when their alpha dies? Do they scatter like cowards, or do they stick around long enough for federal agents to hunt them down one by one?"

His laugh was genuinely amused, though it came out as more of a growl now. "Federal agents? Miss Vance, surely you understand by now that government authority extends only as far as we allow it to extend. Every agency, every department, every level of law enforcement—they all have our people in positions of influence."

"Maybe. But dead lycanthropes can't collect paychecks or intimidate witnesses."

"Which is why you will die tonight, along with anyone else who threatens the natural order we've worked so hard to establish."

Around us, the battle between prisoners and guards was winding down. Most of the humans were dead or dying, their desperate courage no match for creatures with superhuman strength and reflexes. But they'd bought me time and space, and more importantly, they'd proven that people would fight back when they understood what they were really facing.

Theodore Ashworth had found his footing again, the silver bullet in his chest slowing him down but not stopping him. He moved with the careful precision of someone managing serious injury, but his yellow eyes tracked my movements with predatory focus that promised violence.

"Let me have her, Marcus," he growled. "This woman killed Jack, killed Harrison. She deserves to die slowly."

But Grayson raised a clawed hand to stop his lieutenant. "No. The alpha claims this kill. She's earned the right to face me personally."

I used their conversation to change position, moving from behind the altar to a spot near the chamber's eastern wall where shadows provided better concealment. The .38 felt heavy in my hand—not from the weight of metal and ammunition, but from the knowledge that everything depended on making these last shots count.

I could still taste Vivian's last kiss—blood and desperation and something that might've been goodbye. She'd known it would come down to this.

"Question for you, Grayson," I called out, trying to draw him away from the altar and the ceremonial knives that could serve as backup weapons. "How many innocent people have you killed over the years? How many families destroyed because you needed to feed?"

"Innocent?" His voice carried genuine puzzlement. "Miss Vance, you speak as if prey animals have some inherent right to life independent of their usefulness to predator species. Cattle do not question the farmer who feeds them before slaughter. Why should humans question the lycanthropes who manage their population for sustainable harvest?"

"Because we're not cattle, you bastard. We're people with families and dreams and lives that matter."

"Lives that matter to whom? To other humans who will themselves be harvested in due time? To a god who has clearly favored predator over prey in the grand design of natural selection?"

He was moving as he talked, circling the chamber with fluid grace that made my skin crawl. Even wounded, even slowed by silver poisoning, he moved like liquid death looking for a place to happen.

"Your species had its chance to evolve beyond prey status," he continued. "You developed tools, agriculture, civilization—all impressive achievements for creatures that began as nothing more than potential food sources.

But you never transcended your nature. You remained prey animals pretending to be predators."

I tracked his movement through my gun sights, waiting for a clear shot at center mass. But he was too smart for that, staying in motion, using shadows and torchlight to break up his silhouette.

"We gave you opportunities," Grayson said. "We allowed you to build cities and governments and all the other structures that made you feel important. We even let some of you prosper, let you believe you were in control of your own destinies. But it was always conditional—always dependent on your usefulness to creatures who saw the larger picture."

"What larger picture?"

"The natural order, Miss Vance. Predator and prey, hunter and hunted, the strong feeding on the weak according to laws that predate human civilization by millions of years."

He was getting closer now, moving in a spiral that would put him within striking distance of whatever cover I was using. The smart play would be to break and run, try to reach one of the chamber exits before he could intercept me.

But running wouldn't save Los Angeles. Running wouldn't prevent the conversion ceremony that would create dozens of new werewolves. Running wouldn't stop Marcus Grayson from spending the next sixty years feeding on innocent people who had no idea they were being hunted.

Sometimes you had to make a stand, even when the odds were impossible. Vivian had understood that. Miller had understood that. Now it was my turn to choose between survival and the mission that mattered more than any of our individual lives.

I stepped out from behind my cover and put my fourth silver bullet in Grayson's chest, aiming for the heart that pumped lycanthrope poison through veins that had been carrying death for sixty years.

The bullet hit true, punching through enhanced bone and muscle to find vital organs that even werewolf healing couldn't easily repair.

Grayson staggered, dark blood flowing from wounds that should have been fatal to any normal creature.

But alphas weren't normal creatures. They were apex predators that had survived by being tougher, faster, and more ruthless than anything else on the evolutionary ladder.

He kept coming.

His claws caught me across the ribs as I tried to dodge, tearing through fabric and flesh with surgical precision.

Pain exploded through my chest, but I rolled with the impact, came up bleeding but still functional.

One silver bullet left, plus Miller's blessed round.

Grayson was slowing down now, the accumulated damage from four silver bullets beginning to overwhelm even lycanthrope healing abilities. His movements were less fluid, his breathing labored, dark blood flowing from multiple wounds that refused to close.

But he was still eight feet of muscle and fury, still armed with claws that could open a human throat in a single swipe, still carrying sixty years of experience killing anyone who threatened his species' dominance over Los Angeles.

"You're dying, Grayson," I said, backing toward the chamber's main entrance while keeping my gun trained on his chest. "Silver poisoning, blood loss, shock. Even werewolves have limits."

"Perhaps," he agreed, his voice weaker now but still carrying aristocratic arrogance. "But I will live long enough to kill you. And after that, Theodore will finish the conversion ceremony. Your sacrifice will have accomplished nothing."

"Maybe. But at least I'll die knowing I fought back instead of kneeling like sheep in a slaughterhouse."

Miller's face flashed through my mind—the way he'd looked when he pressed his service revolver against Whitmore's ribs and emptied his remaining silver bullets into the werewolf's chest. He'd known he was dying, known he wouldn't see another sunrise, but he'd chosen to buy time for the mission rather than trying to save himself.

Just like Vivian in those orange groves. Just like everyone who'd chosen to fight instead of submit to creatures that saw humans as nothing more than livestock.

His final charge came without warning—a desperate lunge that covered fifteen feet faster than human eyes could track. But desperation made him sloppy, pain and blood loss affecting his judgment in ways that sixty years of easy kills hadn't prepared him for.

I put my last silver bullet in his throat as he reached for me.

The shot took him in the throat, punched right through into his spine. He went down like a felled tree.

We hit the ground hard, eight feet of dead werewolf crushing the breath out of me. Felt like being hit by a truck full of knives.

His claws scraped weakly at my chest, but there was no strength left in them.

"You... cannot... win..." he gasped, his voice barely audible through a throat filling with blood. "Even... if you... kill me... there are... others..."

"Maybe," I said, pressing Miller's blessed silver bullet against his chest, right over the heart that had been pumping lycanthrope poison through Los Angeles for sixty years. "But you won't live to see it."

Miller's special bullet—the one his father had blessed twenty years ago, carried by two generations of cops who knew monsters were real. Now it was my turn.

I pulled the trigger.

The blessed silver bullet punched through Grayson's ribs and into his heart with the authority of twenty years' worth of preparation and prayer. But this wasn't just metal shaped for killing—this was silver that had been consecrated by people who understood they were creating tools for war against evil itself.

The effect was immediate and final.

Marcus Grayson, alpha of the Los Angeles werewolf pack, direct descendant of the lycanthrope families that had been feeding on humans since the 1890s, died with his pale eyes reflecting torchlight one last time before going dark forever.

The quiet after Grayson died felt wrong—too complete, like when a thunderstorm suddenly stops and you're waiting for the next lightning strike.

I shoved Grayson's body off my chest and struggled to my feet. Everything hurt—ribs screaming, chest torn up, bruises I'd be feeling for weeks. But I was breathing, which was more than I'd expected five minutes ago.

Eight feet of dead werewolf, silver bullets in the chest and throat. Hard to believe something that looked like roadkill had been running Los Angeles for sixty years.

The suits who'd been watching the show were gone—city councilmen, cops, judges. The kind of people who take money to look the other way when bodies turn up with claw marks.

The torches kept burning, throwing shadows around the room. The altar with all its knives and goblets looked like junk now—the kind of theatrical props you'd find in some amateur magic show.

Around the room, the other prisoners were picking themselves up—bloody, beaten, but still breathing. Still human.

One of them was a woman I recognized from missing persons reports—Sarah Chen, reporter for the Los Angeles Times who'd been asking uncomfortable questions about patterns in disappearances. She stared at Grayson's body like she was already writing the story in her head. Reporter instincts die hard, even after weeks in a cage.

"Is it over?" she asked, her voice hoarse from screaming or chanting or whatever the hell they'd put her through.

I reloaded my .38 with regular bullets while I thought about how much of this story anyone would believe. "It's over. For Los Angeles, anyway."

Theodore Ashworth was changing back, the silver in his chest doing its work. Without Grayson, he was just another wounded animal facing someone who'd already killed his kind.

"It's over," I said, getting to my feet on ribs that felt like broken glass. "Your boss is dead, your pack's scattered, and the feds will be here soon enough."

Ashworth's transformation was already reversing, supernatural strength fading as the silver bullet in his chest continued its work of poisoning lycanthrope blood. Without the alpha's presence to maintain pack cohesion, he was just another wounded predator facing someone who'd proven capable of killing his kind.

"Doesn't... matter," he wheezed, blood on his lips. "We're... everywhere. Chicago... New York..."

"Then they'll have to manage without Los Angeles. And without the example you were supposed to set tonight."

I walked to where my .38 lay on the stone floor, reloading with conventional ammunition that would have to serve against any remaining threats. Around the chamber, the survivors of the prisoner rebellion were beginning to stir—men and women who'd chosen to fight rather than accept conversion into monsters.

But Theodore Ashworth was already moving toward one of the side exits, his retreat covered by shadows and the confusion of aftermath. The last surviving founding member of the families that had brought lycanthrope bloodlines to California, fleeing into the Los Angeles night with a silver bullet in his chest and the knowledge that sixty years of dominance had ended in a single evening.

I could've stopped Ashworth. Put bullets in his back as he ran. But sometimes you need one rat to survive, to carry the story back to the other rats.

Theodore Ashworth would survive long enough to tell other werewolf packs what had happened in Los

Angeles. Would describe how a private investigator with silver bullets had killed the alpha and broken sixty years of supernatural control over a major American city.

And maybe—just maybe—that story would make other predators think twice before deciding that humans were easy prey.

The war between human and lycanthrope wasn't over. There were other cities, other packs, other creatures that wore human faces while feeding on innocent people.

But Los Angeles was free.

And sometimes, that was enough to justify all the blood and bullets and desperate courage it had taken to win a single battle in a war that would probably last forever.

I walked out of that place and into the night, leaving behind the bodies of things that had been running Los Angeles since before I was born. The moon was setting, and the city was ours again.

Vivian died buying us time. Miller died getting us inside. Their courage gave me the guts to pull the trigger when it counted.

Dawn was coming, and with it, the work of explaining to two million people that the monsters in their nightmares had been real all along.

But that was a problem for tomorrow.

Tonight, the hunt was over.

Silver Moon's End

After Grayson died, there was nothing more. No more snarling, no more fighting—just torches crackling and my own breathing.

The torches kept burning, throwing shadows around the room. The altar with all its knives and goblets looked like junk now—the kind of theatrical props you'd find in some amateur magic show.

I shoved Grayson's body off my chest and struggled to my feet. Everything hurt—ribs screaming, chest torn up, bruises I'd be feeling for weeks. But I was breathing, which was more than I'd expected five minutes ago.

The survivors were stirring around the chamber—maybe half a dozen people who'd chosen to fight rather than become monsters. Their faces showed the hollow exhaustion of long captivity, but something else too. Hope, maybe, or just the satisfaction of knowing they'd helped bring down the things that had been feeding on their city.

"Is he dead?" asked a woman whose torn blouse and dirt-streaked face couldn't hide the sharp intelligence in her eyes. "The big one—is he really dead?"

I nudged Grayson's body with my foot. Eight feet of dead werewolf, silver bullets in the chest and throat. Hard to believe something that looked like roadkill had been running Los Angeles for nearly sixty years. "He's dead.

They're all dead or running."

"What about the others? The men in suits who were watching?"

The suits who'd been watching the show were gone—city councilmen, cops, judges. The kind of people who take money to look the other way when bodies turn up with claw marks.

"Gone," I said. "Probably halfway to Mexico by now, or San Francisco, or wherever corrupt bastards go when their supernatural benefactors get themselves killed."

The woman nodded, then sat down heavily on the stone floor as if the simple act of standing had exhausted what little strength she had left. "My name is Irene Stout. Reporter for the Los Angeles Times. I was investigating missing persons cases when they grabbed me."

"How long have you been here?"

"Three weeks, maybe a month. Hard to keep track of time in those cages." She stared at Grayson's body like she was already writing the story in her head. Reporter instincts die hard, even after weeks in a cage. "Will you tell me what happened here? The real story, not whatever official version the authorities will put out?"

I reloaded my .38 with regular bullets while I thought about how much of this story anyone would believe.

"What do you think happened here?"

"I think creatures that weren't entirely human had been controlling Los Angeles for decades, feeding on its population while maintaining the illusion of normal government and law enforcement. I think they were planning some kind of public demonstration tonight that would have announced their existence to the entire city. And I think you stopped them."

Smart woman. Vivian would have liked her—another person willing to dig for truth even when it led to dangerous places. During our tactical discussions, Vivian had emphasized the importance of finding allies who understood the real nature of the war we were fighting.

"That's about the size of it."

"Can you prove it?"

I gestured around the chamber—at the ritual altar, at the symbols carved into stone walls, at Grayson's body that was already beginning to revert to human form as lycanthrope blood cooled in his veins. "Look around, Mrs.

Stout. The proof is everywhere."

"But will anyone believe it? Will editors print stories about werewolves controlling city government? Will prosecutors file charges against creatures that don't officially exist?"

She was asking the right questions, the ones that would determine whether tonight's victory meant anything in the long term. Killing Marcus Grayson had broken the werewolf pack's leadership and prevented their planned conversion ceremony, but it hadn't eliminated the network of corruption that had allowed them to operate for nearly sixty years.

"Some will believe," I said. "The ones who've seen things they couldn't explain, who've been asking questions about certain families and parts of the city. They'll understand what happened here." "And the others?"

"Will explain it as a gas explosion, or a mob shootout, or some other story that lets them sleep at night without worrying about monsters under the bed."

Irene Stout pulled a small notebook from her dress pocket—reporter's instincts surviving even weeks of captivity and torture. "Then it's up to people like us to make sure the real story gets told, isn't it?"

Before I could answer, footsteps echoed from the corridor that led to the basement detention levels. I raised my .38, ready for whatever werewolves might have survived the night's carnage, but the figure that appeared in the doorway was human.

Bill Kowalski looked like he'd been through a war—which, in a sense, he had. His work clothes were torn and bloody, his face streaked with soot from the fires that had been set throughout the building, but he was alive and moving under his own power.

"Eleanor? Christ, you're alive." He stepped into the chamber and looked around at the bodies and destruction.

"Where's Miller?"

The question hit like a punch to the stomach. In the chaos of fighting Grayson, I'd almost managed to forget about Frank Miller's sacrifice in the basement corridors, about the sounds of gunfire that had faded to silence while I was preparing for the final confrontation.

"Frank's dead," I said simply. "Died fighting Edward Whitmore so we could get Roger out of the detention cells."

Kowalski closed his eyes for a moment, processing the loss of a man who'd been willing to risk everything to fight creatures most people wouldn't believe existed. "He was a good cop. One of the few honest ones left in this city."

Miller's face flashed through my memory—the way he'd looked when he pressed his service revolver against Whitmore's ribs and emptied his silver bullets into the werewolf's chest. Just like Vivian in those orange groves, choosing mission success over personal survival. Both of them understanding that some fights were bigger than the people fighting them.

"What about Roger?"

"Safe. Got him out through the tunnel system, handed him over to federal agents who'd been waiting for my signal. He's in protective custody now, probably being debriefed by men who still think werewolves are just folklore."

That was something, at least. Roger Talbot would survive to testify about what the Crescent Club had been doing, assuming federal authorities could be convinced to listen to testimony about supernatural predators infiltrating American government and law enforcement.

"What's the situation outside?" I asked.

"Chaos, mostly. Fire department, police, ambulances—half the city's emergency services converging on a building that's been officially abandoned for twenty-five years. And bodies. Lots of bodies, though most of them are human now that the lycanthrope transformations have reversed."

"What's the official story?"

Kowalski pulled out a police radio that crackled with reports from units positioned around the building. "Gas explosion followed by structural collapse. Some kind of illegal gathering that went wrong—maybe bootleggers or black market operators who were using the old meeting hall for storage."

It was exactly the kind of explanation Irene Stout had predicted—a story that covered the basic facts while ignoring the supernatural elements that would have challenged everything most people believed about the world they lived in.

"Anyone asking awkward questions?"

"A few. But most of the responding officers are more concerned with body count and fire suppression than with figuring out why some of the victims have wounds that don't look like they came from any normal weapon."

I helped Irene Stout to her feet and began leading the surviving prisoners toward the exit Kowalski had used. Whatever official investigation followed, it would be easier to control the narrative if civilian witnesses were already in federal custody rather than giving statements to local police who might or might not be compromised.

As we moved through corridors that still reeked of smoke and violence, Kowalski fell into step beside me.

"There's something else you need to know. About the other packs, the lycanthrope families in other cities." "What about them?"

"Word's already spreading. Theodore Ashworth made it out of the building alive—wounded, but functional enough to make phone calls. By dawn, every werewolf pack on the West Coast will know that Los Angeles has fallen."

The implications were sobering. We'd won a single battle, but the war between human and lycanthrope was far from over. If anything, Grayson's death might galvanize other packs, convince them that humans were becoming too dangerous to be managed through corruption and intimidation alone.

Vivian had understood this possibility. During our tactical discussions, she'd emphasized the importance of long-term thinking, of preparing for campaigns rather than just individual battles. Her weapons cache was still there, waiting. Her research notes were still valuable. Her sacrifice had bought time not just for tonight's victory, but for whatever fights lay ahead.

"What do you think they'll do?"

"Depends on how smart they are. The smart ones will go deeper underground, be more careful about their feeding patterns, avoid the kind of public displays that brought attention to the Los Angeles pack. The stupid ones will try to retaliate, maybe launch attacks on other cities to demonstrate that killing an alpha has consequences."

"And us?"

Kowalski's smile held no humor. "We've painted targets on our backs, Eleanor. Every lycanthrope in America now knows that Los

Angeles fell because a private investigator and a handful of allies were willing to fight back with silver bullets and desperate courage. They won't make the mistake of underestimating human resistance again."

We reached the building's main exit, where emergency vehicles had established a perimeter around what was being treated as a gas explosion site. Paramedics took custody of the surviving prisoners, while fire department personnel continued their efforts to contain blazes that had been started during the night's fighting.

But it was the federal agents who interested me most—men in expensive suits who moved with the careful precision of people who'd been briefed on situations that didn't officially exist. They approached Irene Stout and the other survivors with the kind of practiced calm that suggested they'd dealt with similar incidents before.

"Miss Vance?" One of the agents approached me with credentials that identified him as FBI, though his knowing expression suggested he was part of a more specialized organization. "Agent Reynolds. We need to talk about tonight... Let's just say some people in Washington have been expecting a call like this." So the feds knew about werewolves. Good to know someone in Washington was paying attention.

"What happens now?"

"Los Angeles is your beat now, Miss Vance. Keep it that way."

The federal agents began herding survivors toward unmarked vehicles that would take them to facilities where their statements would be recorded and their memories might or might not survive the debriefing process intact.

Irene Stout caught my eye as she was being led away, then broke away from her handler for a moment.

"Miss Vance," she said, approaching me with the same professional directness she'd shown in the chamber. "I'd like to interview you properly for the Times. About your work, your methods—the human interest angle.

Perhaps over dinner sometime this week?"

I studied her face, noting the way her eyes held mine just a moment longer than strictly necessary for professional courtesy. We both knew no newspaper would print the real story of what had happened tonight, just as we both knew this wasn't really about journalism.

Vivian would have understood the attraction immediately. Another woman willing to fight for truth, willing to risk everything to expose corruption and protect innocent people. Someone who'd seen the worst humanity had to offer and chosen to keep fighting anyway.

"I'd like that," I said, surprised by how much I meant it. "It's been a long time since I had dinner with someone who understands that monsters are real."

Something that might have been relief flickered across her features. "I'll call your office once they finish with me. We can discuss... details."

The federal agent cleared his throat impatiently, and Irene allowed herself to be led toward the waiting vehicles. But she glanced back once, and the look she gave me carried warmth that had nothing to do with newspaper interviews or professional obligations.

Bill Kowalski approached me as the scene began to wind down, declining federal escort in favor of remaining in Los Angeles to monitor whatever supernatural activity might try to take root in the power vacuum we'd created.

"Someone has to keep watch," he explained. "Make sure they don't try to rebuild, make sure any new packs know this city isn't safe for things that feed on humans."

"Dangerous work."

"So was everything we did tonight. At least now we know it's possible to win."

Agent Reynolds handed me a business card. No agency seal, no office address—just a Washington D.C. phone number with an extension. "You'll be hearing from us, Miss Vance. There are other cities with similar problems, other situations where someone with your particular skills might prove useful."

"I'll be here," I said, looking back at the building where Marcus Grayson's body was cooling on floors carved with symbols that hurt to look at directly. "Los Angeles is my city. Someone needs to make sure it stays human."

Dawn was coming up over the hills, and after the night I'd had, regular sunlight looked pretty damn good.

The moon was setting behind the mountains, its waning light giving way to dawn as natural light returned to a city that had been freed from nearly sixty years of supernatural tyranny.

We'd paid a hell of a price. Miller dead in those basement corridors. Finch's bookstore burned to nothing. Roger safe but broken. And Vivian dead in those orange groves, her death already being explained away as another Hollywood tragedy. The woman who'd taught me how to fight back, who'd given me something worth fighting for.

Her sacrifice in those orange groves had bought time for this victory. What she'd taught me about determination and preparation had kept me alive through nights of horror. Her love had given me something worth fighting for when the odds seemed impossible.

And somewhere in the California darkness, Ashworth would tell the other packs what happened here. How a private detective with silver bullets killed their big boss and sent them packing.

The fight wasn't over. Other cities, other packs, other monsters wearing human faces. But Los Angeles was free.

For the first time in nearly sixty years, the city wouldn't be controlled by predators who wore human faces during business hours. Two million people would wake up this morning in a world where the monsters under their beds were no longer calling the shots from city hall and police headquarters.

Some would know. Reporters like Irene Stout who'd seen the truth firsthand. Federal agents who'd been dealing with lycanthrope infiltration since the 1920s. Police officers like Miller who'd inherited their fathers' knowledge about the supernatural predators that hunted in America's cities.

I'd make sure it stayed that way. Vivian's weapons were still in her garage. Her research notes were still good.

And what we'd had together for a brief moment was still real, even if she wasn't here anymore.

The courage she'd shown in those orange groves would inspire me when the next pack tried to establish territory in my city.

Tonight, we'd won.

And in my line of work, you take the wins where you can get them.

"Ellie" Vance will return

in

A HUNGER GROWS IN HOLLYWOOD